"What do you expect from me?"

Riley asked.

Hannah placed her hands on her smooth stomach as though she longed to protect the child. His gaze dropped there. A child grew there. His child.

"I—I'm not sure what I want from you," she finally answered. "As I tried to tell you before, I feel terrible about dragging you into this mess."

"It takes two. You didn't create that child on your own."

She smiled shyly. "Yes, I know, it's just that I never meant to involve you . . . afterwards."

"So you intended to run off and have my child without telling me?" he demanded.

"I didn't know if you'd want me to contact you." She stared at him. "You . . . can't be seriously considering going through with this wedding."

"I've never been more serious in my life."

Dear Reader,

Welcome to **Silhouette Special Edition** . . . welcome to romance. Each month, **Silhouette Special Edition** publishes six novels with you in mind—stories of love and life, tales that you can identify with—romance with that little "something special" added in.

This month, **Silhouette Special Edition** has some wonderful stories on their way to you. A "delivery" you may want to keep an eye out for is *Navy Baby,* by Debbie Macomber. It's full steam ahead for a delightful story that shouldn't be missed!

Rounding out October are winning tales by more of your favorite authors: Tracy Sinclair, Natalie Bishop, Mary Curtis, Christine Rimmer and Diana Whitney. A good time will be had by all!

In each **Silhouette Special Edition** novel, we're dedicated to bringing you the romances that you dream about—the type of stories that delight as well as bring a tear to the eye. And that's what **Silhouette Special Edition** is all about—special books by special authors for special readers!

I hope you enjoy this book and all of the stories to come.

Sincerely,

Tara Gavin
Senior Editor

DEBBIE MACOMBER
Navy Baby

Silhouette Special Edition

Published by Silhouette Books New York

America's Publisher of Contemporary Romance

To my uncle, A. D. Adler.
How special you are to me.
I love you!

SILHOUETTE BOOKS
300 East 42nd St., New York, N.Y. 10017

NAVY BABY

ISBN: 0-373-09697-6

First Silhouette Books printing October 1991

Books by Debbie Macomber

Silhouette Romance

That Wintry Feeling #316
Promise Me Forever #341
Adam's Image #349
The Trouble with Caasi #379
A Friend or Two #392
Christmas Masquerade #405
Shadow Chasing #415
Yesterday's Hero #426
Laughter in the Rain #437
Jury of His Peers #449
Yesterday Once More #461
Friends—And Then Some #474
Sugar and Spice #494
No Competition #512
Love 'n' Marriage #522
Mail Order Bride #539
Cindy and the Prince #555
Some Kind of Wonderful #567
Almost Paradise #579
Any Sunday #603
Almost an Angel #629
The Way to a Man's Heart #671

Silhouette Special Edition

Starlight #128
Borrowed Dreams #241
Reflections of Yesterday #284
White Lace and Promises #322
All Things Considered #392
The Playboy and the Widow #482
°*Navy Wife* #494
°*Navy Blues* #518
For All My Tomorrows #530
Denim and Diamonds #570
Fallen Angel #577
The Courtship of Carol Sommars #606
+ *The Cowboy's Lady* #626
+ *The Sheriff Takes a Wife* #637
°*Navy Brat* #662
°*Navy Woman* #683
°*Navy Baby* #697

Silhouette Books

Silhouette Christmas Stories 1986
"Let It Snow"

*Legendary Lovers Trilogy
+ Taylor Family Series
°Navy Series

DEBBIE MACOMBER

hails from the state of Washington. As a busy wife and
mother of four, she strives to keep her family healthy
and happy. As the prolific author of dozens of best-
selling romance novels, she strives to keep her readers
happy with each new book she writes.

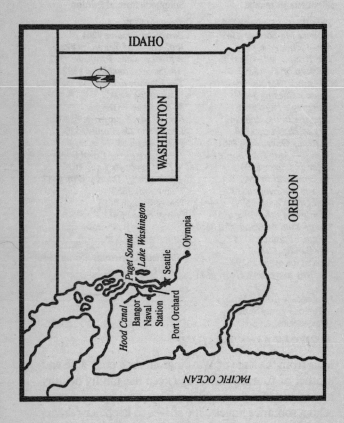

Chapter One

On her knees on the bathroom floor, Hannah Raymond viewed parts of the toilet that were never meant to be seen at such short range. Her stomach rolled and heaved like a tiny canoe being swept down a raging river. The tile felt icy against her knees, yet beads of perspiration moistened her brow. Closing her eyes in an effort to hold back the waves of nausea, Hannah drew in several deep, even breaths. That seemed to help a little, but not enough.

"Oh, God," she prayed silently, "please, oh, please, don't let me be pregnant." No sooner had the words crossed her lips when she lost what little breakfast she'd managed to down that morning.

Her monthly period was late. Over two months late. But that could be attributed to the stress she'd been under these past several weeks. The stress and the grief. It had been nearly four months since Jerry's death. She ached to the bottom of her soul for him, and would, she was convinced, until the end of her life. She'd loved Jerry for six years, had planned her entire life around him. They were to have married soon after the first of the year.

Now there would be no wedding because there was no Jerry. Grief caught her once more in a stranglehold of pain and she squeezed her eyes closed, battling the tears, as well as the nausea. Adding to her torment was the knowledge that if she was pregnant, the child she carried wouldn't be Jerry's.

The face of the sailor had imprinted itself onto her mind, bold as could be. He was tall, powerfully built and strong featured. With a sense of dismay she pushed his image away, refusing to think about that July night or dwell on her folly.

Once again her stomach heaved, and Hannah brushed the thick folds of shiny brown hair away from her face and leaned over the porcelain toilet.

"Hannah?" Her father knocked politely against the bathroom door. "Honey, you'd best hurry or you'll be late for Sunday school."

"I . . . I'm not feeling very well this morning, Dad." Her words were immediately followed by another bout of vomiting.

"It sounds like you've got the flu."

Bless his heart for offering her an excuse. "Yes, I think I must." She prayed with everything in her being that this was some intestinal virus. If living a good life, following the Golden Rule and being the best preacher's kid she knew how to be were ever to work on her behalf, the time was now.

"Go back to bed and if you feel up to it later, come over for the service. I'm preaching from the Epistle to the Romans this morning and I'd like your opinion."

"Sure, Dad." But from the way she was feeling now, she wouldn't be out of bed any time within the next week.

"You'll be all right here by yourself?" Her father's voice echoed with concern.

"I'll be fine. Don't worry." Once again she felt her stomach pitch. She gripped the sides of the toilet and her head fell forward, the effort of holding it up too much for her.

Her father hesitated. "You're sure?"

"I'll be all right in a little bit," she managed in a reed-thin voice.

"If you need me," George Raymond insisted, "just call the church."

"Dad, please, don't worry about me. I'll be much better soon. I'm sure of it."

Her father's retreating footsteps echoed in the hallway, and Hannah sighed with relief. She didn't know what she was going to do if she was pregnant. Briefly she toyed with the idea of disappearing until after the baby was born. Going into hiding was preferable to facing her father with the truth.

George Raymond had dedicated his life to serving God and others, and having to confess what she'd done didn't bear contemplating. Hannah loved her father deeply, and the thought of disgracing him, the thought of hurting him, brought a pain so strong and so sharp that tears instantly pooled in her eyes.

"Please God," she prayed once more, "don't let me be pregnant." Slowly rising from the floor, she swayed and placed her hand against the wall as an attack of dizziness sent the room spinning.

She staggered into her bedroom and fell on top of the mattress. Kicking off her shoes, she sat up long enough to reach for the afghan neatly folded at the foot of the bed. Spreading it over her shivering shoulders, she gratefully closed her eyes.

Sleep came over her in swells as though the ocean tide had shifted, lapping warm, assuring waves over her distraught soul. She welcomed each one, eager for something, anything that would help her escape the reality of her situation.

It had happened in mid-July, only three short weeks after the tragic accident that had claimed her fiancé's life. Her father had been out of town, officiating at a wedding in Yakima. He was staying over and wasn't scheduled to arrive back in Seattle until late Saturday afternoon. Hannah had been invited, too, but she couldn't have borne sitting through the happy event when her own life was filled with such anguish. How grateful she'd been that her father hadn't asked her to travel with him, although she knew he would have welcomed her company.

Before he left, George Raymond had asked if she'd take a load of boxes to the Mission House in downtown Seattle. He'd done it, Hannah knew, in an effort to draw her out of the lethargy that had claimed her in the weeks following Jerry's funeral.

She waited until late in the afternoon, putting off the errand as long as she could, then loaded up the back of her father's old Ford station wagon without much enthusiasm.

Hannah had driven into the city, surprised by the heavy flow of traffic. It wasn't until she'd found a parking spot in the alley in back of the Mission House that she remembered that Seafair, the Seattle summertime festival celebrating ethnic heritages and community, was being held that weekend. The whole town was festive. Enthusiasm and good cheer rang through the streets like bells from a church steeple. Several Navy ships were docked in Elliott Bay and the famed torchlight parade was scheduled for that evening. The city sidewalks and streets were crammed.

None of the excitement rubbed off on Hannah, however. The sooner she delivered the goods, the faster she could return to the safe haven of home. She'd been on her way out the door when she was waylaid by the mission director. Reverend Parker seemed genuinely concerned about how she was doing and insisted she sit and have a cup of coffee with him. Hannah had chatted politely, trying not to be impatient, and when he pressed her, she adamantly claimed she was doing well. It was a lie, but a small one. She didn't want to talk about how angry she was. How bitterly disillusioned. Others had borne even greater losses. In time she'd heal. In time she'd forget. But not for a while; the pain was too fresh, too sharp.

Hannah knew her friends were worried about her, but she'd managed to put on a facade that fooled most everyone. Everyone, that was, except her father, who knew her so well.

"God works in mysterious ways," Reverend Parker had told her on her way out the door. He'd paused and gently patted her back in a gesture of love.

Until Jerry's death, Hannah had never questioned her role in life. When others grieved, she'd sat at their sides, comforted them with the knowledge that whatever had befallen them was part of God's will. The words came back to haunt her now, slapping a cold hand of reality across her face. Several had issued the trite platitude to her, and Hannah had quickly grown to hate such meaningless clichés.

God's will. Hannah had given up believing all the religious jargon she'd been raised to embrace. If God was so loving and so good, then why had He allowed Jerry to die? It made no sense to her. Jerry was a rare man, good and godly. They'd been so much in love and even though they were engaged to marry, they'd never gone beyond kissing and a little petting. They'd hungered for each other the way all couples deeply in love do, and yet Jerry had always managed to keep them from succumbing to temptation. Now, with everything in her, Hannah wished that once, just once, she could have lain in his arms. She'd give everything she would ever have in this life to have known his touch, to have surrendered her virginity to him.

But it was never meant to be.

Stirring, Hannah woke, rolled over and stared blankly at the wall. Her hands rested on her stomach, which seemed to have quieted. A glance at her watch told her that even if she rushed and dressed she'd still be late for the church service. She didn't feel like listening to her father's sermon. It wouldn't do her any good now. Huge tears brimmed in her eyes and slipped unheeded down her cheeks, soaking into her pillow.

Sleep beckoned her once more, and she closed her eyes. Once again the sailor's face returned, his dark eyes glaring down on her as they had the night he'd taken her to the hotel room. She'd never forget his shocked, distressed look when he'd realized she was a virgin. The torment she'd read in his gaze would haunt her all the way to the grave. His eyes had rounded with incredulity and disbelief. For one wild second Hannah had feared he would push himself away from her, but she'd reached up and brushed his mouth with her own and then . . .

She groaned and with a determined effort banished him from her mind once more. She didn't want to think about Riley Murdock. Didn't want to remember anything about him. Certainly not the gentle way he'd comforted her afterward or the stark questions in his eyes as he'd pulled her close and held her until she'd slept.

Go away, she cried silently. *Leave me in peace.* Her strength was depleted, and without effort she drifted into a restless slumber.

Riley was there waiting for her.

Following her conversation with Reverend Parker, Hannah had gone out to the alley where she'd parked the station wagon. To her dismay she discovered that while she'd been inside the Mission House, several cars had blocked her way out of the alley. By all rights, she should have contacted the police and had the vehicles towed away at the owners' expense, but it would have been uncharacteristically mean.

Since the parade was scheduled to begin within the next hour, Hannah decided to stay in the downtown area and view it herself. There wasn't any reason to hurry home.

The waterfront was teeming with tourists. Sailors were everywhere, their white uniforms standing out in the crowd, their bucket hats bobbing up and down in the multitude.

Sea gulls lazily circled overhead, casting giant shadows along the piers. The fresh scent of the sea, carried on the warm wind off Elliott Bay, mingled with the aroma of fried fish and simmering pots of clam chowder. The smell of food reminded Hannah that she hadn't eaten since early that morning. Buying a cup of chowder was tempting, but the lines were long and it was simply too much bother.

Life was too much of a bother. How different all this would be if only Jerry were at her side. She recalled the many good times they'd spent with each other. A year earlier, Jerry had run in the Seafair race and they'd stayed for the parade, laughing and joking, their arms wrapped around each other. What a difference a year could make.

The climb up the steep flight of steps that led from the waterfront to the Pike Place Market exhausted Hannah. Soon, however, she found herself standing along the parade route, where people were crowded against the curbs. Several had brought lawn chairs and blankets, and it looked as if they'd been camped there a good long while.

Vendors strolled the street, selling their wares to children who danced in and out of the waiting crowd like court jesters.

Hannah was amused by their antics when little managed to cheer her those days. She was so caught up in the activities going on around her that she wasn't watching where she was walking. Before she realized what she was doing, she stumbled headlong into a solid male chest. For an instant she assumed she'd blundered into a brick wall. The pair of strong hands that caught her shoulders convinced her otherwise. His grip tightened to keep her from stumbling backward.

"I'm sorry," she mumbled, once she'd found her voice. He was a sailor. One tall and muscular sailor. As nonsensical as it seemed, he had the look of a pirate about him—bold and daring. His hair was as dark as his eyes. He wasn't strikingly handsome; his features were too sharp, too craggy for that. Then his finely shaped mouth curved into a faint smile, flashing white, even teeth.

"I'm...sorry," she stammered again, staring up at him, embarrassed at the way she'd been openly appraising him. She couldn't help being curious. He seemed so aloof, so withdrawn that she felt forced to embellish. "I wasn't watching where I was going." She offered him a feeble smile, and when he dropped his hands, she blushed and looked away.

"You weren't hurt?"

"No...no, I'm fine. What about you?"

"No problem." His gaze swept over her, and he moved on without saying another word.

Following the brief encounter, Hannah decided it would be best if she stood in one place. She selected a vantage point that offered her a good view of the parade, which was just beginning.

With mild interest she viewed the mayor and several other public officials as they rode by, sitting atop polished convertibles. She lost count of the number of bands and performing drill teams that passed. A fire-flashing baton twirler was followed by a variety of enchanting floats.

Enthralled almost against her will, Hannah stayed until the very end, when it was well past dark. The crowds had started to disperse, and hoping the station wagon was no longer blocked, she headed down the steep hills toward the Mission House. Since there were

still people about, she didn't think there'd be a problem of being alone in a bad section of town. But as she
neared the Mission House, she discovered there were
only a few cars left parked in the area. Soon there was
no one else in sight.

When she first noticed the twin shadows following
her she was pleased, naively thinking there was safety
in numbers. But when she turned and noted the way the
two were closing in on her, with menacing looks and
walks, she knew she was in trouble.

As she approached the street on which the Mission
House was located, she noted that the pair was still ad-
vancing. Quickening her pace, she clenched her purse
to her side. An eerie sensation ran up and down her
spine, and the taste of dread mingled with a growing
sense of alarm filled her mouth.

Although she was moving as fast as she could without breaking into a run, the pair was gaining. She'd
been a fool to separate herself from the crowds. She
hadn't been thinking right. Again and again her father
had warned her about such foolishness. Maybe she had
a death wish. But if that were the case, then why was she
so terribly afraid? She trembled, her heart was pounding like a storm trooper's.

The instant she saw the lights of a waterfront bar,
Hannah breathed a little easier. She rushed forward and
slipped inside grimacing as she walked straight into a
thick wall of cigarette smoke.

Men lined the bar, and it seemed that every one of
them had turned to stare at her. Beer bottles were
clenched in their hands, some raised halfway to their
mouths, frozen in motion. A pool table at the back of
the room captured her attention, as did the handful of
men dressed in black leather who stood around it hold-

ing on to cue sticks. One glance told Hannah they were probably members of a motorcycle gang.

Wonderful. She'd leaped out of the frying pan directly into the roaring flames. Hannah sucked in her breath and tried to behave naturally, as though she often wandered into waterfront bars. It seemed, however, that she'd become the center of attention.

It was then that she saw him—the sailor she'd bumped into earlier that evening. He was sitting at a table, nursing a drink, his gaze centered on the glass. He seemed to be the only one in the room unaware of her.

Where she found the courage to approach him, Hannah never questioned. Squaring her shoulders, she moved across the room and placed her hand on the chair opposite him. "Is this seat taken?"

He looked up, and his eyes lit with surprise before a frown darkened his piratical features. The only thing that made him less threatening than the others in the room was the fact he wore a sailor's uniform.

Not waiting for his reply, Hannah pulled out the chair and promptly sat down. Her knees were shaking so badly she didn't know if she could stand upright much longer.

"Two men were following me," she explained. Her hands continued to tremble, and she pushed the hair away from her face. "I don't mean to be rude, but it made sense to scoot in here." She hesitated and looked around her, noting once again the menacing-looking men at the bar. "At least it did at the time."

"Why'd you choose to sit with me?" He seemed to find the fact somewhat amusing. The corner of his mouth lifted in a half smile, but she wasn't sure it was one of welcome.

Why had she chosen him? "You were the only one not wearing leather and spikes," she said, but in retrospect she'd wondered what it was that had caused her to approach him. The fact she recognized him from earlier in the evening was part of the answer, she was convinced of that. Yet there was something more. He was so intense, so compelling, and she'd sensed integrity in him.

A half grin had widened into a full one at her comment about him being the only one there not wearing leather and chains.

He raised his hand, and the waitress appeared. "Two of the same."

"I don't know if that would be a good idea," Hannah said. She intended to stay only long enough to discourage the pair waiting for her outside.

"You're shaking like a leaf."

Hannah didn't argue with him. It would do little good, and he was right. She continued to tremble, but she wasn't completely convinced fear was the reason. Even then, something deep inside her had known. Not consciously, of course. It was as though some deep inner part of herself had reached out to this stranger. Intuitively she'd known he would never harm her. The waitress delivered two amber-colored drinks. Hannah didn't have a clue what she was tasting. All she did know was that a small sip of it was potent enough to burn all the way down her throat and settle in her stomach like a ball of fire. The taste wasn't unpleasant, just potent.

"Do you have a name?" the sailor asked her.

"Hannah. What about you?"

"Riley Murdock."

She grinned, intrigued by the name. "Riley Murdock," she repeated slowly. She watched as he raised the glass to his lips and was struck by how sensuous his mouth was. With some folks, Hannah had noted over the years, the eyes were the most expressive feature. One look at her father's eyes and she could easily read his mood. Riley was different. His eyes were blank. Impersonal. But his mouth competently telegraphed his thoughts. He was intrigued with her, amused. The way the corners turned up just slightly told her as much.

"Are you here for Seafair?" she asked, making polite conversation. A second sip burned a path down the back of her throat.

He nodded. "We're only in port for the next few days."

"So, how do you like Seattle?" She was beginning to grow warm. It was a good feeling that radiated out from the pit of her stomach, and it had the most peculiar effect on her. It relaxed Hannah. The tension eased from between her shoulder blades and the stiffness left her arms. She was a little dizzy, but that wasn't entirely unpleasant, either.

"Seattle's all right." Murdock sounded like a man who'd been in too many ports to appreciate one over another. He finished the last of the his drink and, not wanting him to think she was unappreciative, Hannah sipped from her own. Actually, once she grew accustomed to the flavor, the taste was mellow and smooth. It still burned, but the fire was warm and gentle. Welcome.

"Finish your drink and I'll walk you to your car," Murdock offered.

Hannah was grateful. It took her several minutes to down the potent liquor, but he was patient. He didn't seem to be the talkative sort and that suited her. She wasn't interested in conversation any more than he was.

If the two men who'd followed her were waiting for her outside, Hannah didn't see them. She was glad. A confrontation was something she wanted to avoid, although she was surprised by how formidable Riley Murdock looked when he stood. He was easily six feet if not an inch or two taller. And rock solid. His arms weren't bulging with muscles, but there was a strength in him that Hannah had sensed from the moment she'd first seen him. A physical strength, yes, but a substantial emotional fortitude, as well. Although she wasn't good at judging ages, she guessed him to be somewhere in his early thirties. Light-years beyond her twenty-three.

Moonlight cascaded over the street as they started walking. The sky was filled with stars as though someone had scattered diamond dust across endless yards of black satin. Riley rested his hand on her shoulder in a protective, possessive gesture that Hannah found comforting. If she were to shut her eyes, she could almost pretend it was Jerry at her side and not some sailor she barely knew. He was so near, so strong, and being with him, standing this close, blocked out the sharp edges of the pain that had dominated her life these past few weeks.

For the first time since her father had come to break the news to her about Jerry, the dull ache was gone. It felt so good not to hurt, so pleasant that she didn't want this time to end. Not so soon. Not yet.

An unexplainable comfort radiated from her shoulder where Riley had placed his hand. His touch was light, gentle, nonthreatening. Hannah had to force herself to lean into him and absorb his strength. It felt so good to have him at her side, so strong and reassuring.

They paused at a street corner and Hannah glanced up at him; her gaze slid warmly into his. She smiled briefly, feeling a little shy and awkward, yet at the same time more bold than she could ever remember being. It was the drink, she told herself, that had lent her the courage to behave the way she had.

From the corner of her eye she noticed the light change, but neither moved. He was openly studying her, reading her. Hannah boldly met his gaze. Gently his hand slid up the side of her neck. She closed her eyes and slowly, seductively, rubbed her chin across the tops of his fingers in a catlike motion. Warm sensations enveloped her and she smiled contentedly. This was what she'd had before and lost. Heaven help her, she needed something to hold on to through the years, something that could never be taken away from her the way Jerry had been. If she were to be damned for seizing the moment, then so be it. Without thinking, without calculating her actions, she turned and placed her arms around Riley's neck, stood on the tips of her toes and kissed him. She knew from his reaction that she'd taken him by surprise. Hannah had never done anything more brazen in her life. She guessed there were subtler ways of letting him know what she wanted, but she was a novice at this and was reacting to impulse and not reason.

Kissing a stranger was completely out of character for Hannah. Everything had taken on an unreal quality. At least when she was in Riley's arms she was feeling again. And it was so good to experience something other than pain, something more than the agony that stampeded her heart and soul.

Riley slipped his hands over her hips and held on to her waist as if he weren't sure what he wanted. His gaze pierced hers, and Hannah smiled shyly back. He plunged his fingers through her hair and stared down on her for several breath-stopping moments before he kissed her. Sighing, Hannah leaned toward him. Together they made warm, moist kisses, each one increasing in intensity. His tongue edged apart the seam of her lips and then traced the roundness of her mouth.

When they reluctantly parted, neither spoke. Hannah could feel him assessing her, but what conclusions he drew, she could only speculate. She didn't want him to ponder her boldness too much, because then she'd be forced into thinking herself, and that was the last thing she wanted to do. Leaning her weight against him, she stroked her long fingers against his nape, sliding them into his hair. Soon she was directing his mouth back to hers.

If there had been a sensible thought left in her head, Hannah banished it as she sought his kiss. He didn't disappoint her, displaying an eagerness, a willingness that made her stomach warm. Gradually the sensation plummeted to the lower half of her body. The delicious, delightful excitement seemed to increase with each sweet foray of his tongue and mouth. Wanting to squeeze out every inch of feeling, she started to rotate her hips, pressing against him where she ached the most.

He caught her by the waist, forcing her to still.

"Hannah—" he breathed her name in a soft sexy way that sent chills scooting down her spine "—do you know what you're asking for?"

She bit into her lower lip and nodded.

"Then let's get a hotel room. A decent one."

She should have stopped him, called a halt at that very moment. She might have if he hadn't kissed her again. It should be Jerry she was loving; but he was gone and Riley was very much alive, and she needed him. The havoc his touch created within her was too powerful to resist. It was as if she were wading in floodwaters, struggling to remain upright against a raging storm of need. Sensation abounded, so full, so abundant, her inhibitions toppled over one another like tumbling dominos.

Hannah remembered little of anything else until they were inside the rented room. She recalled that Riley had stopped every now and again on the moonlit sidewalk to kiss her as if he feared she might change her mind.

The fact they didn't have any luggage wasn't a concern to the clerk who handed them the key and pointed the way toward the elevator. The minute they were inside the antique contraption, Riley pulled her back into his arms.

Hannah was convinced that if the room had been on the tenth floor instead of the third, he would have made love to her then and there.

He unlocked the door but didn't bother to turn on the light switch. The drapes were open, and the moonlight spilled softly across the bed. With his arm around her waist, he guided her inside and closed the door, leaning her against it.

His hands, pressed on either side of her face, imprisoned her against the hard door. His eyes found hers, as if he needed some form of reassurance.

Hannah smiled and, raising her fingertips to his mouth, unhurriedly traced his lower lip. His mouth was warm and moist, soft to the touch. Enticing. Leaning forward, she kissed him, shyly using her tongue as he'd done with her.

Riley moaned, and catching the back of her head, deepened the kiss until they were both breathless with need. Even in the dark, Hannah could see how intense his eyes were, filled with a desire so powerful that just looking at him caused her skin to tingle.

Then slowly, purposefully, he unfastened the buttons of her blouse—one by one, starting at the bottom and working his way up. It was as though he expected her to stop him, and he seemed mildly surprised when she didn't. He removed her shirt and then her bra, dropping both to the floor. Once she was bare, he seemed to let an inordinate amount of time pass before he removed his own shirt.

Gently, as though he sensed he was frightening her, he caught the lush fullness of her breasts in his palms, lifting them. "You're very beautiful."

She blinked, not knowing what to say. "So-o are you."

He smiled as if she'd amused him and, leaning down, caught her nipple in his mouth, closing over the fullness of her soft, feminine mound before lavishing it with greedy attention. His tongue laved the tightening hardness and then he sucked fiercely. Hannah whimpered at the startling wave of pleasure it gave her. Gradually she grew accustomed to his attentions and relaxed, closing her eyes as she delved her fingers into his hair. He repeated the process with her other breast, and Hannah felt a stirring sense of wonder at each powerful tug of his mouth. The warm, heavy feeling she'd experienced earlier in the lower half of her body returned a hundredfold, and she moved instinctively against the hard bulge in his loins.

"That's right, baby," he murmured as his hand found the snap on her jeans.

Once they were both free of their clothes, Riley picked her up in his arms and effortlessly carried her to the bed.

He was eager then; too eager to go slowly. He mounted her, settling himself between her open thighs. Not sure how much pain to expect, Hannah tensed, gritted her teeth and turned her head to the side. He caught her by the chin, however, and kissed her deeply, causing the heat to rise to the exploding point. Not knowing how else to ask for him to make love to her, Hannah raised her hips.

It seemed to be what he was waiting for as he settled between her legs, his heated shaft nudging apart the creamy folds of her womanhood. Once again Hannah tightened her jaw as he relentlessly entered her, pausing only when he met the restrictive barrier of her virginity.

He stopped then, frozen. Hannah's gaze found his, and she read his confusion. He pulled back his head, gritting his teeth, his look tense and confused.

"It's all right," she whispered softly. Fearing he might leave her, she looped her arms around his neck and drew his mouth to her own. The kiss was wild, tempestuous, a battle of wills.

Hannah wasn't sure who won. In the end it didn't matter. Slowly, determined to bring her whatever pleasure he could, Riley continued forward, tiny increment by tiny increment until he was buried so deep inside her, she was convinced he could go no deeper.

She was panting with pain, panting with pleasure. He gave her a moment to adjust to him, to allow her senses to recover. She felt his heat, his strength, his hardness envelop her, and she felt as though her heart reached out to him, bonding them in ways she never expected. Twinges of pleasure gradually overcame those that had brought her pain.

Slowly he began to move within her, in long easy strokes that lingered and then opulently replenished the pleasure.

Heat encompassed her, and when it became too much, she moaned and bit into her lip, breathlessly searching, striving for what she didn't know. In the end, release came, making her senses explode in shattering waves so strong they lifted the upper portion of her body off the bed.

He held her for a long time afterward; he kissed the crown of her head gently, then rolled onto his side, taking her with him. His arms continued to hold her as he brushed the hair from her face with gentle fingers and wiped the moisture from her eyes. He was full of questions—Hannah sensed them as profoundly as if they were spoken—yet he left them unasked. For a long time he did nothing but hold her, and for then it was more than enough.

She fell asleep, and woke chilled. Riley was awake still, and when he saw her tremble, he pulled up the covers, then gathered her close into his arms once again.

"Why?" he asked her, his voice deep and impatient.

Hannah could think of no way to explain. At least not with words. Tilting back her head, she brushed her lips over his, loving the velvet feel of his mouth and tongue.

"That doesn't explain a whole lot."

"I know." She had no answers for him. The emptiness was back—reality so harsh and brutal that she couldn't bear it a moment longer. Not knowing any other way to ease it, she raised her arms and brought his mouth down to hers and kissed him once more. He wanted answers, not kisses, but soon his physical need overpowered everything else and he made love to her a second time.

Hannah woke at dawn, sick with guilt and self-recrimination, and quietly slipped from the room. It was the last time she'd seen Riley Murdock.

She lay in bed, eyes open wide as she stared at the ceiling. The time had come for her to quit fooling herself. The week before, she'd bought a home pregnancy test at the local drugstore, hiding it under a magazine until she'd reached the checkout stand. It was in her underwear drawer now.

Reading the instructions carefully, she did as they said and waited the longest fifteen minutes of her life for the results.

Positive.

She was pregnant. By her best calculations, almost three months. Dear God, what was she going to do? Hannah had no answers. None. If her mother had been alive she might have been able to confide in her, seek her advice. But her mother had died when she was thirteen.

By rote Hannah set a roast in the oven and waited for her father to return from the church service. At twelve-thirty he walked in the back door, and his gentle eyes brightened when he saw her sitting at the kitchen table.

"So you're feeling better?"

She offered him a feeble smile and clenched her hands together in her lap. "Daddy," she whispered, her eyes avoiding his, "I . . . I have something to tell you."

Chapter Two

Riley Murdock had been in one bitch of a mood for nearly three months. He'd done everything within his power to locate the mysterious Hannah and cursed himself a hundred times over that he hadn't thought to ask for her surname.

Once he found her, he didn't know what the hell he intended to do. Strangling her seemed like a damn good idea. The woman had driven him crazy from the moment she first stumbled into him on the festive Seattle sidewalk.

When he'd woken to find her gone that morning, he'd been devastated with self-recrimination. Then he'd grown furious. In the weeks since, his wrath hadn't diminished. He didn't know what game she was playing, but by heaven he intended to find out.

If there was anyone to blame in this fiasco, Riley noted, it was himself. He'd known from the first that she wasn't like the other women who frequented waterfront bars. The story she'd told him about a couple of men following her was true. She'd been genuinely frightened, trembling with anxiety. The look in her eyes—damn, but she had beautiful gray eyes—couldn't easily be fabricated. Why she had opted to approach him, he didn't know. The woman was full of surprises.

If he was astonished by the fact she'd chosen to sit at his table, then he should have been a candidate for a heart transplant when he discovered she was a virgin. As many times as Riley had analyzed what happened between them, nothing added up right.

She'd approached him. She'd been the one to kiss him. Hell, she'd practically seduced him. Seduced by a virgin. No wonder the tally kept coming up inaccurate. He should have realized, should have figured it out. Instead, he'd been left to deal with this incredible sense of guilt. If only she hadn't disappeared without explaining. Anger tightened his stomach every time he thought about waking up that morning and finding her gone. He'd damn near torn apart the desk manager trying to find out about her. But apparently no one had seen her go.

Riley blamed himself still. He feared he'd frightened her so badly that she'd fled in horror. Had he hurt her? She'd been so tight and so small. It was all he could do not to slam his fist into the wall every time he thought about their brief encounter, which was damn near every minute of every day. What had happened to her since? Was she sick? Alone? Frightened? Pregnant?

He'd been in control of their encounter until she'd kissed him. Now it was weeks later and he still reeled at the memory of the gentle, shy way in which she'd pressed her lips to his. He cursed how he could close his

eyes and continue to taste her. How sweet she'd been.
How warm and delicate. Her lips had molded to his,
and her flavor reminded him of cotton candy. That
alone was enough to torment him, but it wasn't all. Her
fragrance continued to obsess him. It wasn't a commercial one he could name. The only way he could
think to describe it was to imagine walking waist-deep
in a field of wildflowers.

The woman had somersaulted into his life, sent his
senses cartwheeling, and then, without a thought,
without a care, had vanished, leaving him bitter and
confused.

The hell with her, Riley decided rashly. He'd wasted
enough time, energy and expense trying to find her.
He'd return to his well-ordered life and forget her.
Which was obviously what she intended to do with him.

If only he could forget her.

"Dad," Hannah pleaded softly, fighting to hold back
a sob, "say something."

The truth was out, and Hannah hung her head waiting for the backlash of anger and disappointment. It
was what she deserved and what she expected.

To her surprise, her father said nothing. He sat in the
chair and stared into space, his face devoid of expression. Then he stood, laboriously, as if he were feeling
old and beaten. Without a word he walked out the back
door.

Tears filled Hannah's eyes as her gaze followed him.
He stood on the porch for several moments, his hand
wrapped around the support beam, and stared into a
cloudless October sky. Then, stepping off the porch,
once again with slow and strained movements, he
crossed the parsonage lawn and entered the old white

church. Hannah sat at the kitchen table and gave him fifteen minutes before she followed him.

She found her father kneeling at the front of the church, before the altar, his head and shoulders slumped forward. Her heart constricted painfully at the sight of him there on his knees.

"Daddy," she whispered, speaking to him as she'd done as a frightened child. She *was* frightened. Not of what he'd say or of what he'd do, but because the circumstances surrounding this pregnancy were so complex.

George Raymond opened his eyes and straightened. Placing his hand on his knee, he rose awkwardly to his feet. His gaze rested on her, and she watched as his Adam's apple moved up and down his throat while he struggled to restrain the emotion. He tried to smile, a weak attempt to comfort her, then took her hand and together they sat in the front pew.

Hot tears brimmed in Hannah's eyes, threatening to spill over. The lump in her throat felt as large as a basketball, making swallowing nearly impossible. Her father had every right to be angry with her, to rage at her for her stupidity. What she'd done had been the height of irresponsibility. In her anguish she'd rebelled against everything she'd been raised to believe—an incredible departure from anything she'd ever done.

If she could offer any excuse, it was that she hadn't been herself. The hours she'd spent with Riley had been the first in days, in weeks, in which she wasn't suffocating in her grief. She'd reached out to him, a stranger, needing his touch, needing to be held and loved and protected. Needing a reprieve from her pain to ease the frustration of having been cheated from this experience with Jerry, the only man she'd ever truly loved.

She'd been despondent, and in her anguish she'd sought the comfort of a stranger. It had been sheer stupidity on her part. And now she was faced with the knowledge that the one major indiscretion of her life was about to bear fruit.

Even if she hadn't gotten pregnant, even if she'd been able to bury the events of that night for what remained of her life, she had changed. Not only in the physical sense. It had taken her several weeks to realize the physical aspects of her experience were only a minor portion of their lovemaking. Her emotions had become involved. She didn't know how to explain it or what to make of it. She'd assumed that once she left the hotel room, she'd never think of Riley again. But she did, almost constantly, against every dictate of her will.

"I'm sorry, Dad," she whispered brokenly. "So sorry."

Her father wrapped her gently in his arms. "I know, Hannah, I know."

"I was wrong. . . . I was so angry at God for taking Jerry. I loved him so much."

With a tenderness that pitched knives at her heart, her father brushed the hair from her face. "I needed a few moments alone to think through this situation. I've been reminded that God doesn't make mistakes. This child growing under your heart was planted there for a reason. I don't know why any more than I understand the reason God took Jerry home. Nevertheless you are going to have a baby, and the only thing we can do is make the best of the situation."

Hannah nodded, not knowing what to say. She didn't deserve so wonderful a father.

"I love you, Hannah. Yes, I'm hurt. Yes, I'm disappointed in your lack of judgment. But there is nothing you could ever do that would change my love for you or the fact you're my daughter.''

Hannah closed her eyes and breathed deeply, clinging to her father's strength and his love.

"Now, tell me his name,'' he said, breaking away from her.

Keeping her gaze lowered, she whispered, "Riley Murdock... We met only once—the night of the torchlight parade. He's in the Navy, but I don't have a clue where he's stationed.'' Finding him now would be impossible, which was just as well. Hannah didn't want to think about what Riley would say or do once he found out she was carrying his child. Frankly, she wondered if he'd even remember her.

Her father gripped her hand in both his own, and once again Hannah noted how frail he looked. The lines around his eyes and mouth had formed into deep grooves and there was more gray than reddish brown in his thick thatch of hair. Funny how she hadn't noticed that earlier. The changes had come since Jerry's death, but she'd been so consumed by pain and uncertainty that she hadn't noticed he'd been dealing with his own grief.

"The first thing we have to do,'' he said gently, "is make a doctor's appointment for you. I'm sure Doc Hanson will be able to see you first thing Monday morning. I'll give him a call myself.''

Hannah nodded. Unwilling to face the truth, she'd delayed contacting a physician longer than she should have. Doc Hanson was a friend of the family and could be trusted to be discreet.

"Then,'' Hannah told him, drawing in a deep sigh, "we'll need to decide where I should go.''

"Go?" Her father's dear face darkened, the age lines becoming even more pronounced.

"I won't be able to continue living here," she said, her tone weary. She wasn't thinking of herself, but of her father and of Jerry's memory.

"But why, Hannah?"

She inhaled deeply. "Everyone will assume the child is Jerry's." With everything in her heart she wished her fiancé had fathered her child, but she had to deal with the cold, harsh facts. Riley Murdock—a stranger from the Seattle waterfront—was the father. Although it was tempting, very tempting, to allow her church family and friends to believe she carried Jerry's child, she couldn't have lived with the lie. Not when he'd always been so morally upright.

"We'll simply explain to everyone that the child isn't Jerry's," her father stated with one hard nod of his head, as if that alone would set everything right.

"Do you honestly think the congregation will believe me?" she asked him, the words tight in her throat. "I have to leave, Dad," she said firmly, unwilling to compromise.

For her father's sake she must leave Seattle. He'd been such a loving and kind parent, and there were sure to be those in the church who would malign him for her wrongdoings. There would be an equal number who would stand beside them both with loving support, but Hannah couldn't bear to see her father suffer because of her mistakes.

"I'll go live with Aunt Helen until after the baby's born...."

"And then what?" her father demanded, sounding uncharacteristically alarmed.

"I . . . don't know. I'll cross that bridge when I reach it." So many questions and concerns were coming at her, like a spray of rocks from a speeding car. Hannah didn't feel capable of fending off a single one, at least not now.

"We don't need to decide anything yet," he assured her after a moment. But he wore a thoughtful frown as they walked back to the house, where Hannah had left dinner simmering.

The frown didn't seem to leave her father's features from that moment forward. Hannah had been in to see Doc Hanson, who confirmed what she already knew. He ran a series of tests and prescribed iron tablets and vitamins because she was anemic. He'd been gentle and kind and didn't ply her with questions, for which she was grateful.

It was Friday afternoon nearly two weeks after Hannah had first told her father about the pregnancy. Exhausted from her day's work as an underwriting assistant for a major insurance company, she walked into the house and discovered her father waiting for her in the living room. He sat in his favorite chair, his hands curved around the faded upholstered arms, his gaze fixed straight ahead. Hannah called it his "thinking chair." To discover him resting in the middle of the afternoon was highly unusual.

"Good afternoon, Dad," she greeted with a smile, and walked across the worn beige carpet to kiss his weathered cheek. "Is everything all right?"

"It's just fine," he said, returning her smile with an absent one of his own. "Keep your coat on. We're going out."

"We are?" Offhand, Hannah couldn't think of any appointment she'd made. Only infrequently did she accompany her father on house calls, and those were generally scheduled for Tuesday and Thursday evenings. George Raymond made it a point to visit every family in his congregation at least once a year.

His hand protectively cupped her elbow as he led her out the front door and down the steps. The station wagon was parked in the driveway.

"Where are we going?" Hannah questioned. Rarely had she seen her father look more resolute. It was as if he were marching with Joshua, preparing to face the walls of Jericho.

When he didn't answer, she assumed he hadn't heard her and she repeated the question. That, too, was ignored.

He drove silently for several minutes before he reached the freeway, and then he headed south toward Tacoma. The car was warm, and although she was curious as to what was happening, Hannah soon found her eyes drifting closed. Her head bobbed a couple of times as she struggled to remain awake. If only she'd get over this depressing need for extra sleep. It seemed she couldn't last through the day without napping. Lately she'd taken to heading for bed nearly as soon as she'd finished the dinner dishes. She shifted positions and opened her eyes when they crossed the Narrows Bridge and headed toward the Kitsap Peninsula.

She woke when her father made a sharp turn and eased to a stop in front of a guard house. He rolled down the window, and a blast of cold air alerted Hannah to the fact they'd arrived at their destination. She straightened and looked around. Although she'd never been on one before, she recognized immediately that they were entering a military compound.

"Dad?" she quizzed. "Where are we?"

"Bangor," he announced a little too loudly. "We're meeting Riley Murdock."

In Chaplain Stewart's office Riley sat, ramrod straight, across the room from Hannah Raymond and her stern-faced father. Riley's gaze narrowed as he fired a look in her direction. Not once did she deign to glance his way. She sat, her back as rigid as his own, but although she held her head high, her gaze refused to meet his. Perhaps it was just as well.

First thing the previous morning, Riley had been called before his commanding officer. When he arrived, he'd discovered Chaplain Stewart and Lieutenant Commander Steven Kyle.

"Do you know a woman by the name of Hannah Raymond?" the chaplain had asked him.

Riley had reacted with surprise. For three months he'd been frantically searching for her, spending every available weekend combing the Seattle waterfront, asking if anyone had seen a woman of her description. He'd followed the leads, but each one had led to a frustrating dead end. He'd gone so far as to contact a detective agency, but they'd offered him little hope. All Riley knew about her was her first name and the fact she had shiny brown hair and dove-gray eyes. There simply hadn't been enough information, and the agency had been discouraging.

"I know her," Riley admitted.

"How well?"

Riley had stiffened. "Well enough."

"Then you may be interested to learn she's pregnant," Chaplain Stewart stated abruptly, looking at Riley as though he were the spawn of the devil.

Riley felt as if someone had knocked his feet out from under him, and then, when he was laid low, viciously kicked him.

"Pregnant," he repeated, stunned, as though he'd never heard the word before.

"She claims the child is yours," his CO explained. "She maintains it happened during Seafair, which means she'd be about three months along. Does that time frame gel with you?"

Fury and outrage twisted inside Riley until he couldn't speak. All he could manage was a sharp nod. He clenched his powerful fists at his sides until he was sure he'd cut off the blood supply to his fingers.

"At Seafair?" the commanding officer pressed.

Again Riley nodded. "That would be about right." The woman had put him through three months of living hell, and he wouldn't soon forget or forgive that. "When did she contact you?" he asked his CO.

It was Chaplain Stewart who answered. "She didn't."

"Then who did?" he demanded.

"George Raymond, Hannah's father. He's had an extensive investigation done on you, as well."

Great. Wonderful. Now Riley was going to be left to deal with an irate father. That was exactly what he needed to start his day off on the wrong foot.

"George and I attended seminary together," the chaplain had continued, and it was clear from the way he spoke that the two men had been good friends. "When Hannah confessed that the father of her unborn child was in the Navy, George contacted me, hoping I'd be able to help him locate you."

Riley couldn't believe this was happening. The desire to wring Hannah's scrawny neck increased by the minute.

Hannah was pregnant! If he had any luck, Riley swore, it was all bad. Okay, so he was being mildly unreasonable. But she was the one who'd come on to him. He'd assumed, at least in the beginning, that she must be using protection. If he'd believed otherwise he would have taken care of the matter himself. It wasn't until after he'd discovered she was a virgin that he had briefly wondered. And worried. He'd admit now that the deed was staring him in the face.

"What does she want?" Riley demanded. Support, medical bills, maybe even an allotment to cover her expenses while she was unable to work. Riley had no intention of sloughing off his duty. He was the one responsible and he'd own up to it.

Chaplain Stewart stood and walked across the room. He paused and then rubbed his hand along the back of his neck, as if he needed extra time to shepherd his thoughts.

"As I told you earlier, George Raymond is a minister. In his mind there's only one thing to be done."

"And that is?" Riley demanded, remembering he'd left his checkbook at his apartment.

"He wants you to marry his daughter."

"What?" Riley was so shocked he nearly laughed out loud. "Marry her? Hell, I don't even know her."

"You know her well enough," the chaplain reminded him, throwing Riley's own words back in his face. "Listen, son," he continued thoughtfully, "no one's going to force you to marry the girl."

"You're damn right about that," Riley returned
heatedly, slightly amused that he'd gone from Satan's
spawn to "son" in a matter of a few minutes.

"Hannah's not like other women."

Riley didn't need to be reminded of that, either. No
one else he'd ever kissed tasted half as good as she had,
or smelled so fresh and lovely. No other woman had
loved him nearly as well, Riley reminded himself re-
gretfully; her untutored responses haunted him still.
He'd felt engulfed by her tenderness, awed by her
beauty and jolted by her hungry need. She'd been so
tight and so hot that even now, he couldn't think about
their night together without wanting her again.

"You have to understand," Chaplain Stewart went
on to say, "Hannah's been raised in the church. Her
mother died when she was in her early teens, and she
took over the family responsibilities then. Her older
brother's in the mission field in India. This young
woman comes from as traditional a background as you
can imagine."

That was all fine and wonderful. She'd cared for her
family, and he didn't doubt she possessed more than
one admirable trait, but Riley wasn't convinced marriage would be the best solution to the problem. Not
only weren't they acquainted, Hannah's life couldn't
have been less like his own had they sat down and drawn
up a composite of opposite family types.

"Wanting to protect those she loves, not wanting to
shame her family, Hannah's apparently opted to move
away."

"Where?" Riley demanded, instantly alarmed. He
had the feeling he was going to end up following this
woman halfway across the country before this was over.

"I'm hoping her leaving the area won't be necessary," Chaplain Stewart said pointedly.

"What the chaplain is saying," Lieutenant Commander Kyle stressed, "is that if you married the young lady it would solve several problems. But I want it understood, that decision is yours."

Riley stiffened. No one was going to force him into marrying against his will. He'd rot in jail before he'd be pressured into wedding a woman he didn't want. At his silence, Riley's CO leafed through his file, which was spread open across the top of his desk. Riley would be up for Senior Chief within the next couple of years, and the promotion was important to him. Damn important.

"Think about what Chaplain Stewart has said," Lieutenant Commander Kyle urged. "The Navy can't and won't force you to marry the woman."

"That's true enough," the chaplain added. "But from everything I've seen and heard, I believe it's the only decent thing you can do."

Both men were looking at him as if he'd enticed Hannah Raymond into his bed. They weren't likely to believe she'd been the one who'd seduced him!

Riley had brooded over the meeting with Lieutenant Commander Kyle and Chaplain Stewart all night. Hannah was pregnant with his child and the chaplain was breathing down his back like monster dragons exhaling fire. Although his CO hadn't said it, Riley had the impression his promotion might well hang in the balance. Everyone else seemed to know what he should do about it. Everyone, that is, except him.

Now that he saw Hannah again, Riley was even more uncertain. He remembered her as being a lovely creature, but not nearly so delicate and ethereal. She was

thin—thinner than when he'd met her that July night—
and so pale he wondered about her health.

Riley feared the pregnancy had already taken its toll
on her, and he couldn't help being concerned about her
well-being. The urge to protect and care for her was
strong, but Riley pushed it aside in favor of the anger
that had been building within him for the past several
months.

He had damn good reason for being furious with her.

"Are you convinced the child is yours?" Chaplain
Stewart directed the question to Riley.

The room went still, as though everyone were on
tenterhooks anticipating his reply. "The baby's mine,"
he answered firmly.

Hannah's soft gray gaze slid to his as if she longed to
thank him for telling the truth. He wanted to leap to his
feet and remind her that she'd been the one to run out
on him. It hadn't happened the other way around. If
anyone's integrity was to be questioned, then it should
be hers.

"Are you prepared to marry my daughter?" demanded the thin, graying man Riley could only assume
was Hannah's father.

"Dad?" Hannah gasped, pleading with her father.
"Don't do this, please." Her voice was soft and honest, and Riley doubted that many men could refuse her.

Reverend Raymond looked at Riley as if he fully expected him to sprout horns and drag out a pitchfork. If
that were the case, it was ironic that the minister was
demanding that Riley marry his daughter.

"As your father, I insist this young man do right by
you."

"Chaplain Stewart," Hannah said, coming to her
feet, ignoring her father. "Could Riley and I talk for a

few minutes...alone?'' The last word was added pointedly.

The two older men seemed to reach a tacit agreement. "All right, Hannah" the Navy chaplain agreed, coming to his feet. "Perhaps that would be for the best. Come on, George. I'll pour us a cup of coffee and we'll leave these two to sort out their problems in their own way. I have faith young Murdock means well."

Riley waited until the door had closed before he leaped to his feet. He glared across the room at Hannah, not knowing what to do first—shake her until her teeth rattled or gently take her in his arms and demand to know why she was so deathly pale. Before he had the opportunity to speak, she did.

"I'm terribly sorry about all this," she murmured. "I had no idea my father had contacted you."

"Why'd you leave?" he bit out the question between clenched teeth, still undecided about how he was going to deal with her.

She frowned as if she didn't understand his question. Her brow creased until she understood, and then it creased even more. "I suppose I owe you an apology for that, as well."

"You're damn right you do."

"I didn't mean for any of this to happen."

"Obviously," he retorted, trapped in his anger. "No one in their right mind would do this to themselves. The question is, what the hell are we going to do about it now?"

"Oh, don't worry. It isn't necessary for you to marry me. I don't know what ever made Dad suggest that."

She seemed so damn smug about it, and that riled him all the more.

"Apparently your father feels differently. He seems to think my marrying you would salvage your honor."

She nodded. Her hair was tied at her nape, giving Riley a clear view of the delicate lines of her face. As pale as she was, she resembled a porcelain doll, fragile and easily breakable. She looked dangerously close to that point right then.

"My father is an old-fashioned man with traditional values. Marriage is what he would expect."

"What do *you* expect?" His tone was less harsh, his concern for her outweighing his irritation.

Hannah placed her hand on her smooth stomach as though she longed to protect the child. Riley's gaze dropped there, and he waited a moment, trying to analyze his own feelings. A child grew there. *His* child. Try as he might, he felt nothing except regret mingled with a healthy dose of concern.

"I . . . I'm not sure what I want from you," Hannah answered. "As I tried to tell you before, I feel terrible about dragging you into this mess."

"It takes two. You didn't create that child on your own."

Her smile was shy. "Yes, I know. It's just that I never meant to involve you . . . afterward."

That didn't set any better with Riley than the implied threat from his commanding officer. "So you intended to run off and have my child without telling me?"

"I . . . didn't have a clue as to how to find you," she argued.

"Your father didn't seem to have much of a problem."

She looked away as though she wanted to avoid an argument. "I didn't know if you wanted me to contact you."

She sure the hell had a low opinion of him. It rankled Riley that Miss High-and-Mighty would make those kinds of assumptions about him.

"Next time don't assume anything," he barked. "Ask!"

"I apologize—"

"That's another thing. Quit apologizing." He held both hands to his head, hoping the applied pressure to his scalp would help him think.

"Are you always this difficult to talk to?" she asked. He was pleased to hear a little mettle in her voice. It told him he hadn't been wrong about her. This woman had plenty of spirit. It also assured him her health wasn't as bad as he suspected.

"I am when I've been backed into a corner," Riley stormed.

She stood and reached for her coat. "Then let me assure you I'm not the one forcing you into a marriage you obviously don't want."

"You're right. It isn't you. It's the United States Navy."

"The Navy? I ... don't understand."

"I don't expect you to," Riley barked. "It's either do right by you or kiss a promotion I've been working toward for the last several years goodbye." Lieutenant Commander Kyle had implied as much in a few short words.

"Oh, dear. I had no idea."

"Obviously not." He rammed all ten fingers through his hair, then dropped his hands to his sides. "My career could be on the line with this one, sweetheart."

That was an exaggeration, but in some ways Riley felt it could be true.

Hannah grimaced at the derogatory way in which he'd used the term of affection. "But surely if I spoke to them . . . if I were to explain . . ."

Riley laughed shortly. "Not a chance. Your father made sure of that."

"I didn't know."

"The way I see it," he said with thick agitation, "I don't have a hell of a lot of choice but to go ahead and marry you."

Hannah's head snapped up at that. "You . . . can't seriously be considering going through with a wedding."

"I've never been more serious in my life."

Chapter Three

In a matter of hours, Hannah was scheduled to become Mrs. Riley Murdock. She sat on the end of her bed, wrestling imaginary crocodiles of doubt and indecision. They might as well be real, she mused, clenching and unclenching her hands. She felt as though there were powerful jaws snapping at her, jagged teeth tearing at her confidence and determination.

It was Jerry she loved, not Riley. Nothing would ever make the hard-edged sailor into another seminary student. Hannah wasn't foolish enough to believe the Torpedoman Chief was likely to change. One look at his cold, dark features the afternoon of the meeting at Bangor reminded her what a rugged life he led. There was nothing soft in this man. Nothing.

The day of the meeting, he'd been both angry and restless, stalking the room, thundering at her every time she attempted to apologize. In some ways she was convinced he hated her.

Yet it was his child growing within her womb. Hannah flattened her hand across her abdomen and briefly closed her eyes. Despite the complications this pregnancy had brought into her life, Hannah loved and wanted this baby.

Hannah knew that Riley wasn't marrying because of the pregnancy. By his own admission, he was doing so for political reasons. Both her father and Chaplain Stewart had seemed relieved when Riley had announced they had agreed to go through with the wedding.

Hannah had agreed to no such thing. She'd been trapped into it, the same way Riley had. She wasn't sure even now, sitting in her room, dressed for her wedding ceremony, that she was making the right decision.

They were so different. She didn't love him. He didn't love her. They'd barely spoken to each other—and it was because they had nothing in common except the child she carried. How a marriage such as theirs could ever survive more than a few weeks, Hannah didn't know.

"Hannah," her father called after politely knocking on her bedroom door, "it's time we left."

"I'm ready," she said, standing. She reached for the two suitcases and dragged them across the top of her bed. This was all she would bring into their marriage. The pot-and-pan set, the dishes, silverware and other household items she'd collected over the years were gone. She'd donated them to the Mission House the evening she'd met Riley. The irony hadn't been lost on her. Nor had she forgotten how Reverend Parker had announced that God works in mysterious ways. Her entire life felt like an unsolved mystery, and she'd long since given up on deciphering the meaning.

She opened the bedroom door and found her father standing on the other side, waiting for her. He smiled softly and nodded his approval. "You look beautiful."

She blushed and thanked him. She didn't feel beautiful in her plain, floor-length antique-white dress, but having her father smile and tell her so lent her some badly needed confidence. The fact he seemed so sure that marrying Riley was the right thing helped a great deal. She'd always trusted her father and had never doubted his wisdom.

George Raymond took the suitcases from her hands and led the way down the stairs. As he loaded the luggage into the back of the station wagon, Hannah stood on the porch and glanced around her one last time. Bright orange, gold and brown leaves blanketed the sloping lawn, and the skeletal limbs of the two chestnut trees that ruled the front yard rose toward the deep blue sky. She would miss all this, Hannah realized, wondering how long it would be before she returned.

The ride to Bangor took almost two hours. Her father did most of the talking. He seemed to sense how nervous Hannah was and sought to reassure her.

Chaplain Stewart, Riley, and a man and woman Hannah didn't recognize were waiting for them in the vestibule of the base chapel. The chaplain and her father broke into immediate conversation. From the other side of the room, Riley's eyes found hers. His facial expression didn't alter, and he nodded once.

He looked tall and distinguished in his white dress uniform, and although it was little comfort, Hannah realized, that she was marrying a handsome man. In the days since their last meeting, she'd had repeated nightmares about him. In her dream he came at her like a huge monster, eager to devour her. Seeing him now produced a shiver of apprehension.

"If you'll excuse us," Hannah said, her voice barely audible, "I'd like a few minutes alone with Riley."

The conversation came to an abrupt halt as Chaplain Stewart cast an accusing glare in Riley's direction. If the other man's censure disturbed him, he gave no indication. Silently he led the way to the opposite end of the room.

"You've changed your mind?" His tight features told her nothing of his thoughts. Perhaps that was what he was hoping she'd do.

"Have you?"

The corner of his mouth lifted slightly. "I asked first."

"I'm...willing to go through with the wedding, if you are."

"I'm here, aren't I?"

He didn't look any too pleased about it, and she decided against saying so.

"You wanted to talk to me?" he demanded gruffly.

"Yes. I thought we should reach an understanding regarding...the sleeping arrangements before we...you know...before we..."

"No, I don't know," he returned impatiently. His gaze narrowed sufficiently. "Listen, if you're saying what I think you're saying, then the deal's off. If I'm going through the hassle of marrying you, then I want a *wife,* not a sister. Do I make myself understood?"

Hannah lowered her gaze, clenching her hands tightly together in front of her. "Do I have to be your...wife right away?" Her voice was soft and low.

He was silent for so long that she wasn't sure he'd heard her. "I don't suppose it would hurt any if we took some time to get to know one another better first."

"That's what I thought." She raised her head and looked up at him, relieved that he was willing to give her the time she needed to adjust to their marriage.

"How long?" he demanded.

She blinked at the sharpness of the question. "Ah . . . I'm not sure. A few weeks at any rate. Possibly a couple of months."

"A couple of months!"

Hannah was convinced the entire chapel heard him roar and would immediately guess the gist of their conversation. Her face filled with boiling color. "Couldn't we just . . . well, let it happen naturally?"

His face had tightened into a brooding frown. He wasn't pleased and didn't bother to pretend otherwise. "I suppose."

"Of course, we'll be sleeping in separate bedrooms until such time that we're both comfortable with that aspect of . . . our marriage."

"Right," he returned caustically before turning away from her. "Separate bedrooms."

Separate bedrooms! The words repeated themselves in Riley's mind throughout the brief wedding ceremony Hannah's father officiated. The fact that he didn't give Riley the chance to kiss the bride wasn't lost on him. What he hadn't figured out was why the old man had demanded Riley marry his daughter in the first place. His father-in-law was as straitlaced as they come. It remained a mystery why George Raymond had insisted Riley marry Hannah. Hell, if it came down to it, Riley wasn't entirely sure what had prompted him to go through with the wedding himself. What his CO claimed had carried some weight, that was true enough, but Riley knew himself well. No one could have forced him into marrying Hannah if he'd been completely opposed to the idea. Which obviously meant, he reasoned, he wanted her as his wife.

Glancing at her now, sitting by his side as they drove to his apartment in nearby Port Orchard, gave him further cause to wonder. She hadn't said more than a handful of words since the ceremony. He hadn't a clue what she was thinking, but he figured she was looking for some way to get out of this.

"It was very nice of Chaplain Stewart and Lieutenant Commander Kyle to arrange housing on the base for us, wasn't it?" she asked softly.

"Very nice," he repeated. He wondered how many strings his CO had had to pull to come up with that. The news had come as a surprise to Riley, who'd lived in a small apartment complex for the past two years.

"When will we be moving?"

"Soon."

"How soon?"

Hell, first he couldn't get her to talk, now he couldn't shut her up. "Next weekend."

"Good. Packing will give me something to do while you're gone during the day. Once we've moved, I'll look for a job."

"I don't want you doing any lifting, you hear?" She flinched at his harsh tones, and he regretted speaking so forcefully. He'd recently bought a book on pregnancy and birth, and it had stated that lifting anything heavy should be avoided. Riley was surprised at the overwhelming urge he felt to protect Hannah and the baby.

"But I want to help."

"We'll do the packing together." He left no room for argument.

"But what will I do every day?"

"What you normally do."

"I've always worked."

He was silent at that, not knowing what to tell her. He didn't want her out looking for a job. It was plain the pregnancy had already taken a toll on her health. "Relax for a while," he suggested after a moment. "There isn't any need for you to rush out and find a job now."

She sighed and closed her eyes, leaning her head against the back of the cushion. "I think I could sleep for a week."

She looked as if she'd do exactly that, but not in his bed, Riley noted bitterly. Not in his bed.

Riley's apartment was on the second floor of a complex overlooking Sinclair Inlet. The *Nimitz*, an aircraft carrier, and several other large Navy vessels were moored along the piers of the Puget Sound Naval Shipyard. Standing on the balcony, Riley pointed out each ship for her, telling her its classification and type. Most of the information went over Hannah's head, but she found the aircraft carrier easy to distinguish from the others.

The apartment itself was compact. It was clear he'd made an effort to clean up the place a bit. The fact pleased her. The living room had been straightened and newspapers neatly stacked in the corner. The carpet was olive green and blended well with his furniture, which consisted of a black recliner and a three-quarter-length sofa.

"You thirsty?" he asked, taking a beer out of the refrigerator.

Hannah's gaze fell on the alcoholic beverage as she shook her head. She had the feeling he'd offered it to her for shock value. "No, thank you."

Riley shrugged, twisted off the cap and guzzled down half the contents in a series of deep swallows. His Adam's apple bobbed with the action. Hannah turned away from him, and looked back at the narrow waterway.

"We have a minor problem," he said, joining her at the wrought-iron railing.

"Oh?" It was barely four, and already the sky was darkening.

"The apartment only has one bedroom."

Hannah's heart sank. "I see."

"Lieutenant Commander Kyle assured me the place on the base would have two, but for now we're here. What do you want to do about the sleeping arrangements?"

Hannah didn't know. At least not right then. "I could rest on the sofa, I guess."

Riley snickered at that and turned away from her, pausing at the sliding-glass door. "You'd better come in before you catch a chill."

That wasn't likely with her wearing her full-length wool coat, but she didn't want to argue with him. He closed the door behind her, finished the beer and tossed the brown bottle into the garbage. It made a clanking sound as it hit against a glass object, probably another beer bottle. Hannah had never been around a man who regularly indulged in alcoholic beverages and she wondered if this would become a problem between her and her husband.

"You don't approve of drinking, do you?"

That he could read her thoughts so clearly came as a shock. "Would it matter if I did?"

"No."

"That's what I thought." She hesitated, then couldn't resist asking, "Do you do it often?"

"Often enough" was his cryptic reply. He moved past her to lift her two suitcases, which he'd set down just inside the front door, and carry them into the lone bedroom.

Curious to see the rest of the apartment, Hannah followed him down the narrow hallway. The bedroom was the only room on the left. The drapes were closed and the double bed was poorly made. Hannah guessed that he didn't often bother to make it in the mornings.

He placed her suitcases on top of the bed, then sat on the end of the mattress. "You won't get much sleep on that sofa. It's old and lumpy. In case you didn't notice, it's also short."

"I'll manage."

"I'm not a monster, you know."

She blushed, remembering the dreams she'd had the past week about him springing horns and giant teeth. "I know."

"You don't sound all that convinced." He flattened his hands and leaned back, striking a relaxed pose. "If you recall the night we met, you were the one who—"

"Please, I'd rather not talk about that night." She abruptly left the room, walking into the kitchen. He followed her just the way she knew he would.

"In case you've conveniently forgotten, you were the one who seduced me."

"I . . . prefer to think we seduced each other," she returned boldly.

"Naturally, that's what you'd choose to think."

Her face felt fire-engine red. "Do you mind if we change the subject?"

"Not in the least. Answer me one thing, though. What do you expect will happen if we share the same bed? You don't want me to touch you, then fine, I wouldn't dream of it. You have my word of honor."

Hannah ignored the question and the man. Opening the refrigerator, she removed a head of lettuce and a package of half-frozen hamburger. "How does taco salad sound for dinner?"

"Fine, for tomorrow night."

Her gaze flew to his, not understanding him.

"We'll be dining out this evening."

"We are?"

"Right," he said, grinning at her, his look almost boyish. He seemed to enjoy teasing her, bringing up details that would embarrass her, possibly because he fancied seeing her blush. "Far be it for you to tell Junior how you were forced to cook on our wedding day."

"Junior?" Funny, but she'd never given the sex of their baby any thought. The fact that he had, warmed her heart.

"We'll call him that for now, unless you'd rather not."

Her eyes met his, and for the first time that day she felt like smiling. "I don't mind, although I think you should be prepared for a juniorette."

"Boy or girl, it doesn't matter to me. A baby is a baby."

His matter-of-fact attitude stole a little of her good cheer, but she didn't let it show.

"It's ladies' choice tonight. What's your pleasure?"

Hannah hesitated. She'd been craving seafood for weeks, but it was expensive and she didn't want him to think she was extravagant. "Any place would be fine."

"Not with me. It isn't every day a man gets married. How would you feel about a seafood buffet? It's a bit of a drive, but there's a wonderful restaurant on Hood Canal that serves fabulous lobster."

"Lobster?" Hannah's eyes rounded with pleasure.

"And shrimp. And oysters and scallops."

"Oh, stop," she said with a laugh. "It sounds too good to be true." This man had the most incredible knack of reading her mind.

He reached for her hand, and grinning, he led her out the front door and down the stairs to where his red CRX was parked. The drive took the better part of an hour, but once they arrived and were seated, Hannah realized it had been well worth the effort. The smells were incredible. The scent of warm bread mingled with garlic and freshly fried oysters.

Hannah piled her plate high with steamed clams and hot bread. As soon as she was finished, she returned for a slice of grilled salmon and barbecued shrimp, balancing a cup of thick clam chowder on the edge of her plate. The waitress came by with a glass of milk, which Riley had apparently ordered for her. She was pleased to note that he chose coffee for himself.

"This is wonderful," she exclaimed, after returning to the buffet table for the third time. She took a sampling of finger lobster and some oysters.

Riley was openly staring at her.

"Is something wrong?" she questioned, after adjusting the napkin on her lap.

"I would never have guessed one person could eat so much."

Hannah gazed at her plate. "I've made a glutton of myself, haven't I?" She rebounded quickly and smiled up at him. "You have to remember, I'm eating for two."

"You're eating as if you're expecting triplets," he teased, but the way his mouth lifted up at the corners told her he was pleased.

Breaking off a piece of bread, Hannah reached for the butter. "Is there anyone you want to tell about the wedding?" she asked conversationally.

"Who do you mean?" Her question appeared to displease him.

"Family," she said, not understanding his mood.

"I don't have any family."

"None?" It seemed incomprehensible to Hannah, who was so close to her own.

"My father ran off when I was eight, and my mother... Well, let's put it this way: she wasn't much interested in being a mother. I haven't had any contact with her in years."

Hannah set the bread aside. "I'm sorry, Riley. I had no idea... I didn't mean to bring up unhappy memories."

"You didn't. It's in the past and best forgotten."

"How'd you end up in the Navy?"

He seemed to find her query amusing. "How else? I enlisted."

"I see." It had been a stupid question, and she grew silent afterward.

They left the restaurant a few minutes later. A full stomach and the warm blast of air from the heater lulled her into a light sleep. She was only mildly aware of Riley turning on the car radio, switching stations until he found one that specialized in Easy Listening.

Hannah woke when he stopped the engine. It took her a second to realize her head was resting against his shoulder. She straightened abruptly as though she'd been caught doing something wrong. "I'm sorry, I didn't realize—"

"Don't be," he said brusquely, as though she'd displeased him far more by offering an apology than using his shoulder as a support.

He came around and helped her out of the car and cupped his hand under her elbow as they walked up the flight of concrete steps to his apartment.

Once they reached the top, Riley unlocked the door. Shoving it open, he turned to Hannah and without a word calmly lifted her into his arms.

Taken by surprise, she let out a small cry of alarm. "Riley," she pleaded, "put me down. I'm too heavy."

"Let me assure you, Hannah Murdock, you weigh next to nothing." With that he ceremoniously carried her over the threshold, gently depositing her in the leather recliner.

Hannah smiled at him, a little breathlessly, although he'd been the one to do all the work. This man was full of surprises. All week she'd been convinced she was marrying a monster, but Riley had gone out of his way to prove otherwise. Perhaps this marriage had a chance to survive, after all.

Riley turned on the television and reached for the evening paper and, after a few minutes, Hannah excused herself and began unpacking a few of her things. Since they would be moving within a matter of days, she only removed items she'd be needing.

Since Riley seemed wrapped up in something on television, she decided to bathe. The water was warm and soothing, and as she rested her head against the back of the tub, she traced her index finger over her stomach. There was no evidence her body was nurturing a child—at least not yet—but she hadn't reached the fourth month of her pregnancy. The doctor had told her to expect to feel movement at any time, and the prospect thrilled her.

When she'd finished, she dressed in a thick flannel gown and brushed her hair away from her face. Riley was still in the living room, sitting on the edge of his cushion, punching his arms back and forth. She noticed he was watching a boxing match, and she cringed inwardly.

He must have noticed her, because he reached for the television control and turned down the volume. His eyes widened as he assessed her.

"Is something wrong?" she asked, glancing down at herself.

"You normally wear *that* to bed?"

"Yes." He made it sound as if she'd donned sackcloth and ashes.

He nodded and punched the control, turning up the volume. "Then my guess is Junior will be an only child."

Hannah bristled; then, not knowing what else to do, sat down and tucked her feet under her. The fight taking place on the television screen was violent, with two boxers slugging it out as though they had every intention of badly maiming each other. Hannah winced and closed her eyes several times.

"Why would anyone fight like that?" she asked during a commercial break.

"Ten million might have something to do with it."

"Ten million dollars?" Hannah was incredulous. Standing, she looked around for something else to do.

She walked into the kitchen and poured herself a glass of water. The evening paper was on the floor next to Riley's chair. She picked it up and read through it.

"Would you like to go to church with me tomorrow?" she invited.

"No." His eyes didn't stray from the screen.

She set the paper aside and yawned.

"Go ahead and go to bed. I'll wake you when I come in."

Hannah was skeptical, but the fight was only in the sixth round and it looked as if it could continue for a good long while. "You don't mind?"

"Not in the least," he answered, and waved her toward the bedroom.

Hannah found an extra blanket in the hall closet and wrapped that around herself as she lay on top of Riley's bed. It would have been presumptuous of her to crawl beneath the covers when she fully intended to sleep in the living room after Riley had finished with his program.

Although she was exhausted, Hannah had a difficult time falling asleep. What an unusual day she'd had. She'd married a man who was little more than a stranger to her, and discovered in the short time they'd spent alone that he was easy enough to like. She sincerely doubted that she'd ever grow to love him the way she had Jerry, but then Jerry had been a special man. It wasn't likely that she'd ever find anyone like him.

Riley was rough around the edges; she couldn't deny that. He drank beer as though it were soda and enjoyed disgusting displays of violence. Yet he'd gone out of his way to see to it that she had a wonderful wedding dinner. He appeared to be trying.

She smiled at the memory of how he'd hauled her into his arms and carried her over the threshold, then immediately frowned when she recalled the way he'd looked at her in her nightgown and announced that Junior would be an only child.

With a determined effort, Hannah closed her eyes. She knew she wouldn't sleep, but lying in bed was a hundred times more appealing than being subjected to the boxing match.

Hannah stirred, feeling warm and comfortable. Her arm was wrapped around a pillow, although now that she thought about it, this particular pillow was anything but soft. Her eyes fluttered open, and she found a pair of intense eyes staring back at her. She blinked, certain she was seeing things.

"What are you doing here?" she asked.

"The question, my dear wife, is what are you doing clinging to me as if you never intend on letting me go?"

Hannah immediately removed her arm and bolted upright. To her surprise, she was beneath the covers. "How'd you do that?" she asked, noticing at the same moment that he wasn't.

"Do what?" Riley asked with a yawn. He sat up and stretched his hands high above his head and growled as though he were an injured bear stalking the woods. The sound was so fierce it was all Hannah could do not to cover her ears.

"You said you'd wake me," she reminded him, not the least pleased with this turn of events.

"I tried."

"Obviously you didn't try hard enough." Primly, she tossed aside the covers and leaped out of bed. "You had no right . . . We agreed—"

"Hold on a minute, sweetheart, if you're—"

"Don't call me sweetheart. Ever." She hated the way he said it. Jerry had always spoken it with such tenderness and love, and she wouldn't have this man who was her husband desecrate the few precious memories she had of her fiancé.

"All right," Riley said, holding up his palms. "There's no reason to get bent out of shape. For your information, I did try to wake you, but it was obvious you were in a deep sleep. It was either haul you into the living room or leave you be. I chose the latter."

Hannah glared at him. She'd risen quickly and neither the baby nor her stomach appreciated the abrupt change of position.

"Hannah, you're looking pale. Are you all right?"

"I'm perfectly fine," she lied. The all-too-familiar sensation was taking root in the pit of her stomach. Her brow broke out in a cold sweat and her knees grew weak.

"There's no reason to be so upset," Riley continued, undaunted. "I did the gentlemanly thing and slept on top of the covers. Our skin never touched, I promise you." He paused. "Hannah . . ."

She didn't hear whatever he intended to say. With her hand over her mouth, she rushed down the hallway, making it to the toilet just in time to empty her stomach.

Riley helped her to her feet when she'd finished, and gently wiped her face with a damp cloth. "I didn't mean to upset you. Damn, if I'd known you were going to get sick, I'd have slept on the sofa myself. I'll tell you what—you can take the bed and I'll camp out there until we move."

He was so gentle, so concerned. Hannah raised her fingertips to his cheek and offered him a feeble smile.

"My being sick didn't have anything to do with being upset. It's the baby."

He was silent for a moment. "How often does this happen?"

"It's better now than the first few months."

"How often?" he repeated firmly.

"Every morning in the beginning, but only once or twice a week now."

"I see." He released his hold on her and handed her the washcloth. "In that case, forget what I just said. If you want to sleep on the sofa, be my guest."

Chapter Four

"Hannah!" Riley bellowed as he walked inside the apartment. He startled her so much she nearly dropped the box she was carting. "How many times do I have to tell you, you aren't to lift anything?"

"But, Riley," she protested lamely, "this one isn't the least bit heavy."

"I don't care. Your job is to stay out of the way. Once we're into the other house you can start unpacking. If I see you touch a single one of those boxes again, I'm going to lock you out on the balcony. Is that understood?"

It was understood three apartments over, Hannah was sure. Riley had been surly all morning. He'd left before dawn to pick up the rental truck and returned in time to find her hauling boxes from the kitchen into the living room. She was only trying to help, and he'd made it sound as if she should be arrested.

They'd been married a week now, and if these past seven days were any indication of how their lives would blend together, Hannah wasn't sure they'd last the month. Riley seemed to be under the impression that she was one of his men—someone he could order about at will.

With so much to be done before the move, it was ridiculous that he expected her to do nothing.

The afternoon he'd returned to find a neatly organized row of packed boxes stacked in the corner had resulted in a tirade that had left Hannah shaken and pale. No one had ever stormed at her the way Riley did. He seemed to think she should laze around sampling bonbons while watching daytime television.

He regretted his outburst later and offered an abrupt apology, but by then it had been too late; Hannah could barely tolerate looking at him. She escaped into the bedroom and closed the door.

If only he wasn't so unreasonable. He didn't want her cleaning for fear the solvents would harm her or the baby. Nor did he want her painting, although he was often up till the early hours of the morning. In the evenings when he returned from the base, he wouldn't even take time to eat the meals Hannah had so carefully prepared. Generally he grabbed a few bites on the run while she sat at the table, napkin in her lap, determined to ignore him as he shouted warnings at her about doing this or that.

The doorbell chimed, and Riley took the box from her arms, set it aside and answered the front door. Three men of varying sizes and shapes casually strolled inside. The first was dressed in jeans and a sweatshirt, the two others in football jerseys and sweatpants. The trio paused just inside the door when they noticed Hannah.

Riley stepped over to her and looped his arm around her shoulders, drawing her close to his side. "Hannah, this is Steve, Don and Burt," he said, nodding toward each one. "They're my friends. Guys, this is my wife, Hannah."

"Your wife?" the tallest of the three echoed, obviously stunned.

"My wife," Riley repeated brusquely. "Do you have a problem with that, Steve?"

"None." Riley's friend glanced apologetically toward Hannah. "It's just that good friends are generally invited to the wedding, if you know what I mean."

The one in the University of Miami sweatshirt rubbed the side of his jaw as he blatantly stared at Hannah. "Is this the gal you spent all that time—"

"Are you going to stand around here all morning gawking, or are you going to help us move?" Riley demanded, lifting a box and shoving it into Don's arms.

Don let out a loud grunt as the box was shoved against his chest, then cast the others a rueful grin before carrying it out the front door to the waiting van.

The four soon formed a small caravan, carting furniture and boxes. Within less than a half hour, everything in the kitchen and living room was neatly tucked inside the moving van.

In the bustle of activity, Hannah was left to her own devices. Before she misplaced her purse, she carried that down the stairs along with a bag of cleaning supplies and set them on the floor of the truck, locking the door. As she stepped away, she heard Burt murmur something to Riley about a woman named Judy. The short, stocky man who wore a Seahawk football jersey number twelve seemed concerned and abruptly stopped speaking when he noticed Hannah.

Riley turned and frowned, as though anxious she might have heard something he'd prefer she didn't.

"You weren't carrying anything, were you?" he demanded when the silence seemed as loud as thunder.

"My purse," she returned softly, and hurried up the stairs, pressing herself against the railing halfway up when Don and Steve walked past her, each holding one end of the mattress. As soon as they were safely past, she rushed up the steps, pondering what she'd overheard.

Judy.

From the way Burt and Riley behaved, it was apparent they hadn't wanted her to hear. Their reaction led her to only one conclusion: Riley had been involved with the mystery woman. The fact he was married had certainly come as a surprise to the very men he'd labeled his friends.

So Riley had a woman friend; it shouldn't come as any surprise. He was a virile man, and not once had she believed he'd lived the life of a hermit.

A weary feeling came over her when Hannah entered the apartment. Naturally Riley wouldn't tell his friends about their marriage. No man would want to admit, even to the best of friends, that he'd been forced into marriage. Hannah swallowed at the growing lump in her throat. She'd been a fool not to realize Riley would be involved with someone else. Not only had her night of folly wreaked havoc in her own life, it had disrupted several others as well. Recriminations pounded at her like tiny hammers, and she sucked in a giant breath as she battled with her renewed sense of guilt.

Brushing the hair away from her face, Hannah walked over to the sliding-glass door that led to the balcony. Several long-legged cranes walked along the pebbled beach, their thin necks bobbing as they sauntered along the edge of the shallow water. Hannah folded her arms around her middle as she stiffened her spine. It had been Riley's choice to marry her, she recalled. He'd insisted. She might have been able to dissuade her father from this marriage, but when Riley concurred, Hannah had agreed, too weak to battle the pair of them. Riley had chosen to marry her of his own free will, whatever his reasons, and despite the fact that he was currently involved with someone else.

Judy. Hannah was shocked by the hard fist of resentment that struck her as she mentally repeated the other woman's name. Recognizing she was being utterly unreasonable didn't help. It wasn't as though her marriage was a great love match. Riley had never led her to believe it would be. No doubt he'd been with any number of women over the years.

The four men walked into the apartment, diverting her attention for the moment. Riley paused when he found her in the kitchen. His blue eyes searched her as if to read her thoughts, and when she offered him a weak smile, he seemed genuinely relieved.

Doing her best to stay out of the men's way, Hannah did what she could to help the loading go as smoothly as possible. Generally, this consisted of directing traffic and answering minor questions.

It amazed her how smoothly everything was going. She'd assumed it would take most of the day to move, but the four men worked well as a team and handled the burdensome task with an economy of effort.

When the apartment was nearly empty, Hannah moved into the bedroom to push some boxes into the center of the room. She wanted to do something, anything other than stand idle. Never in her life had she stood by, wasting time while watching others work. It went against the very grain of her personality, and she deeply resented it now.

"Hannah!"

"I'm only trying to help," she cried. "You're treating me like an old woman."

"I'm treating you like a *pregnant* woman," he countered sharply, gripping her by the shoulders. Despite the anger in his voice, his touch was light. Hannah raised her gaze to his, and when their eyes met, something warm and delicate passed between them. The silence swelled, filling the room. It was a comfortable silence that chased away the doubts she'd experienced earlier.

Whatever his reasoning, whatever hers, they were married now; and each in their own way seemed determined to make the best of the situation. If Riley had lost his love, then it was behind him now. She, too, had loved another.

Riley's hands inched their way from her shoulder, caressing the sides of her neck. His eyes continued to hold hers, then with excruciating slowness, he lowered his gaze to her mouth. Hannah felt her stomach tighten. The soft throaty sound that slipped from between her lips came as a surprise to her. Her face was flooded with color as she realized she'd practically begged Riley to kiss her again. The very thought mortified her. After all, she'd been the one to lay the ground rules in this relationship, and that had included no touching, at least not for a while. To his credit, Riley had respected her wishes all week. They'd lived as brother and sister—or, more appropriately, as drill sergeant and draftee.

A smile captured his eyes as he lazily rubbed his moist lips over hers. His kiss was gentle and undemanding. Their lips clung as his mouth worked against hers, deepening the pressure and the intensity. Hannah found herself opening up to him. Her hands slid up the hard wall of his chest as she leaned into his strength, absorbing it. Fire danced in her veins as a welcome, foreign excitement filled her.

Riley ended the kiss abruptly, dragging his mouth reluctantly from her. "I don't want you helping anymore. Understand?"

"But, Riley..."

"That's my baby you're carrying."

No sooner were the words out when Steve walked into the room. The other man's gaze shot from Hannah to Riley and then back to her again, as though he weren't sure he'd heard correctly. He didn't comment, but it was apparent the information came as a shock, for his gaze grew deep and troubled.

"I can't stand around doing nothing," Hannah protested heatedly, biting into her lip. Riley might have announced her condition with a bit more diplomacy, instead of dropping it like a hot coal in his friend's lap a few minutes after introducing her as his wife.

A flustered Steve grabbed a box and left the room. Tears of embarrassment filled Hannah's eyes as she abruptly moved away from her husband. Silly tears, she realized. There was no need to hide the fact she was pregnant; it would become obvious to all soon enough, and everyone would know the real reason Riley had married her.

"Hannah?" Riley's tone was gentle, concerned. "I'm sorry. I didn't mean to be so tactless."

Assuming he'd left with his friend, Hannah stiffened and kept her back to him as she smeared the moisture across her cheek. "I overreacted.... I guess I'm just a little tired is all."

"You're doing too much."

Hannah couldn't help smiling at that. She'd barely lifted a finger all morning. Once again his hands rested on her shoulders; and he gently turned her into his arms. As before, his touch was tender. His breath mussed the soft brown curls that had escaped the scarf that held the hair away from her face. Closing her eyes, she soaked in the comfort she felt in his arms, which seemed to outweigh the revelations of that morning.

"Steve and the others would have figured it out sooner or later."

Unable to resist, she flattened her hands against his hard chest and rested her head there for several seconds. "You're right. It's probably best this way. It's just that—"

"You'd have preferred for my friends to digest one piece of information at a time. You needn't worry that they'll judge us, you know. Friends wouldn't." He smiled down on her and then leaned over to brush his mouth against hers once again.

Hannah blinked as he moved away from her, lifted a heavy box upon his shoulders and seemingly without effort carted it out the door.

She stood for a moment and pressed her fingertips to her mouth. These few brief kisses were the first they'd exchanged since that fateful night. It had been incredibly good. Incredibly wonderful.

Once the truck was loaded, Riley came for Hannah, escorting her down the stairs and unlocking the van door before helping her inside the cab. Coming around the front, he hopped into the driver's seat, started the engine and then grinned over at her. "You ready, Mrs. Murdock?"

His smile and mood were infectious, and she nodded and grinned herself. "Ready."

Switching gears, he gripped the steering wheel and started whistling a catchy tune. It was the first time in a week or so, it seemed, that they hadn't been at odds with each other; the first time that Hannah felt that her husband wasn't going to storm at her for some imagined wrongdoing. Thus far into their relationship, he seemed more like a caretaker than a husband.

He continued whistling, smiling over at her every now and again. His hand reached for hers, and he linked their fingers together. He stopped whistling long enough to raise her hand to his mouth and kiss her knuckles.

"Who's Judy?" The question was out even before Hannah realized she was going to ask it. Her timing might be lacking, but she was relieved to have the subject out in the open.

Riley stopped whistling; his happy sound was cut off abruptly as a weary silence filled the cab.

"What makes you ask?" He merged with the flow of traffic as they followed the highway that curved around Sinclair Inlet, his gaze not wavering from the roadway.

"I'm not stupid, you know," she returned, resenting his attitude. "I heard you and Burt talking. If you were involved with someone else, the least you could do is give me fair warning."

Riley's frown deepened. "Judy and I are not involved—at least not the way you're implying."

"I wasn't implying anything," she answered primly. "I was just trying to save myself from future embarrassment."

"Future embarrassment?"

"Yes. It's obvious your friends know nothing about me, and others might share the same concern as Burt had about…Judy. I don't mean to make a federal case out of it." Indeed she deeply regretted bringing up the subject. "All I want to know is if someone is going to give me weird looks and then inconspicuously inquire about Judy when you introduce me."

"All Burt did was ask a simple question. One, by the way, that was none of your business," Riley returned shortly. His hands tightened around the steering wheel.

"None of my business," she repeated calmly. Obviously she was traipsing across ground he had no intention of mapping. "I see."

"It's obvious you don't. Damnation, woman, you're making a mountain out of a molehill."

"I most certainly am not," she replied, doing her best to hold back the flash flood of anger that threatened to drown her. "If anyone is being unreasonable, it's you. Apparently the subject is a touchy one and best dropped. I'm sorry I said anything."

"So am I."

It seemed that Riley wasn't watching the road as well as he should have been, because a car shot past them and the driver hammered on the horn as he sped by. Her husband muttered something under his breath that Hannah pretended not to hear.

"Are there others?"

"Other what?" Riley shouted. His frustration with her was clearly getting the best of him.

"Women," Hannah explained serenely. "I should know about them, don't you think? It might save us both a good deal of embarrassment."

"Are you asking for a list of every woman I've ever made love to? Is that what you want? Are you sure that'll be enough to satisfy you? I married you, didn't I? What the hell more do you want? Blood?"

The knot that formed in Hannah's throat was so large it made swallowing difficult and conversation impossible. So he and this Judy had been lovers. He'd implied as much by suggesting he list his affairs for her. Tilting her chin at a regal angle, she stared out the side window and dropped the subject entirely. He seemed relieved at the silence, although it grated sharply on Hannah's nerves.

Once they had passed through the gates at Bangor, Hannah watched with interest as they wove their way through a maze of streets toward the assigned housing. The long rows of homes were identical, painted gray and adorned with white shutters.

Riley pulled the van into the driveway of a corner lot and leaped out. He came around and helped Hannah down, then sorted through his keys until he found the one he was looking for.

"The house is quite a bit larger than the apartment," he said as he unlocked the front door, his eyes avoiding hers. He paused, then added, "The second bedroom is considerably smaller than the other." He seemed to be waiting for her to comment.

"I don't mind taking the smaller one."

Her answer didn't appear to please him, and after the door was opened, he stalked back to the truck and lowered the tailgate so the others could start to unload.

Left to her own devices, Hannah walked inside alone. It was a pleasant home, clean and well maintained. The living room was spacious, and had a brick fireplace and thick beige carpet. The kitchen was more than adequate with a raised counter for stools. The bedrooms were as Riley had explained—one larger than the other.

As she'd agreed, Hannah chose the smaller one for herself, leaving the door open. When Burt appeared carrying her two suitcases, she directed him into the room.

"I thought these were your things?" he said, and from the confused look he wore, he was sure he'd misunderstood her.

"Yes, please. The bedroom set I ordered will be delivered sometime this morning."

Burt looked over his shoulder, as if he fully expected Riley to appear and jerk the suitcases out of his hands and deposit them in the master bedroom.

"You're sure about this?"

"Positive," she answered with a gentle smile.

Riley happened upon them just then. He hesitated when Burt scratched the top of his head, set down Hannah's luggage and walked out of the smaller bedroom.

"Did you have to make such an issue of the fact we're not sleeping together?" he asked between clenched teeth.

"I wasn't making an issue of it," she returned sweetly. "Truly, Riley, I wasn't."

Grumbling, he stalked out of the house.

Riley returned to the van where his friend Steve was standing on the back lifting out the cardboard boxes for the others to haul inside.

"So you and Hannah aren't sharing a bedroom," he teased, taking delight in doing so. "I never thought Riley Murdock would allow any woman to lead him around by the nose."

Riley didn't deign to comment. He'd wanted to tell his three best friends about the marriage. The slight hadn't been intentional. There'd been enough to do in the past week, getting ready for the move, without worrying who knew about his marriage and who didn't. It wasn't as though he were trying to keep it a secret, and he regretted his lack of foresight now.

Matters weren't going well between him and Hannah. The woman was more stubborn than anyone he'd ever known. He'd insisted she not lift anything, concerned for her health and that of the baby. Every day, it seemed, she took delight in defying him. Invariably he lost his patience with her. She never argued with him, not once, but his tirades left her pale and withdrawn. Afterward, Riley felt like a heel. On more than one occasion he hadn't been able to live with himself and he'd gone to her and apologized, feeling like a brute for having chastised her. Just when things seemed to be working out between them, Burt had mentioned Judy Pierce. His friend certainly hadn't helped his cause any.

Judy was a friend—nothing more. But Riley sincerely doubted that he'd ever convince Hannah of that. The two had dated a few times over the past several years, but nothing had developed from it. His friends might have drawn a few conclusions about the relationship, conclusions that Judy herself might have implied. It didn't matter what Judy had told the others; she meant nothing to him and never would.

There hadn't been another woman in Riley's thoughts, night or day, from the moment he'd met

Hannah. She'd had him twisted up in knots for months. Riley had never experienced frustration the way he had since meeting her. Attempting to locate her after she'd run out on him had demanded time, effort and money. When everything he knew how to do had failed, he'd resigned himself to never seeing her again, only to have her thrust back into his life like a sharp knife. A double-edged one, at that. She was his wife now, but he might as well have entered a seminary, for all the good it did him to have spoken marriage vows.

Frankly, Riley didn't know how much longer he was going to last under this insane arrangement. If anyone had told him he would go more than a week after his wedding without making love to his wife, he would have sworn they were crazy. He'd agreed to Hannah's terms for one reason only. Perhaps it was a bit conceited of him, but he'd firmly believed he'd have her in his bed within a matter of days. After that first night, when he'd upset her so badly by sleeping at her side, he hadn't even tried. Hannah certainly hadn't gone out of her way to encourage his attentions. The kiss they'd shared in the apartment had been his first sign of hope in days. Once they got moved in and settled down a little, he'd work on getting her into his bed. If everything went right, it shouldn't take long.

The furniture and boxes were nearly unloaded when the truck from the furniture store arrived. The two men delivered the oak frame, mattress and nightstand and within a matter of minutes were promptly on their way.

Riley had hoped their timing would have been a little more to his advantage, but since Hannah had already let the others know they weren't sharing a bedroom, it didn't much matter.

The last of the furniture was in place and Riley was unloading what remained of the boxes when Don approached him, looking apologetic.

"What's wrong?" Riley asked. "Did you break something?"

"Not quite." The electrician pushed up the sleeves of his shirt, glanced up at Riley and shrugged. "I'm sorry, man, I didn't mean anything."

"What the hell did you do?" Don wasn't exactly known for his tact.

"I called Hannah...Judy. I swear it was a mistake.... I just wasn't thinking."

Riley groaned. "What did she do?"

"Nothing. That's just it. She corrected me and then went about organizing the kitchen. It was the way she looked—so, hell I don't know, fragile, I guess, like she didn't have a friend left in the world. It got to me, man. It really got to me. I tried to apologize, but everything I said only made it worse."

Riley knew from experience the look Don was talking about. He'd been the recipient of "the look" several times himself this week. Riley wondered if his wife realized she possessed this amazing talent for inflicting guilt. It wasn't anything she said, or even did, but when she lowered her eyes and her bottom lip jerked, it was all he could do not to fall to his knees and beg her forgiveness. To his credit, he hadn't given in to the impulse. At least not yet.

"I think you ought to go talk to her. Clear the air about Judy before someone else makes the same mistake."

Riley nodded.

"We'll wait out here," Steve suggested. Since he was the only one of the four who was married, Riley readily agreed. Women were known to be unreasonable about the silliest things. He should have explained about Judy when Hannah had asked, but something inside him had hoped she might be a little jealous. Keeping her in the dark about an old girlfriend could help his cause. Apparently he was wrong again. Damn, but he wished he'd paid closer attention to women's feelings when he was young.

He found her in the kitchen, unpacking dishes. She glanced up at him, and her gaze narrowed into cold slits. Riley paused. He'd never seen her wear that particular look before, and instinct cautioned him.

"Hannah." He said her name gently.

She slammed a pan on the stove and winced at the crashing sound it made. For an instant he thought she was going to apologize, she looked so shocked. She surprised him once more by straightening out her arm and pointing at him as though he were in a police lineup and she was identifying him for the authorities. Her mouth opened and closed twice before she spoke.

"We might not be sleeping together, but there's something you'd best understand right now, Riley Murdock."

She braced her hands against her hips, digging her fists into her waist. Her slate-gray eyes flashed like nothing he'd ever seen. Her hair had pulled free of its tie and soft brown waves spilled haphazardly over her shoulders. Riley had seen Hannah frightened, humbled, browbeaten and mussed from lovemaking, but he'd never seen her like this. She was so damned beautiful, she took his breath away.

"Is something wrong?" he asked innocently, almost enjoying her outrage.

"Yes, something's very wrong. I want one thing understood: I will not tolerate infidelity. If you're in love with this Judy, then I'm sorry, but it's me you're married to and I fully expect . . . no, I *demand* that you respect our wedding vows."

To the best of his knowledge, Riley had never given her cause to believe he intended to do otherwise. He wasn't sure what Don or one of the others had implied, but he'd best clear up the misconception now, before matters got out of hand.

"I'll honor my vows."

She hesitated as if she weren't entirely sure she should trust him. After a long moment, she nodded once and mumbled something he couldn't hear.

"Tell me," he said, walking toward her, fully intending to take her in his arms; a couple of kisses might reassure her even more. "You wouldn't happen to be jealous now, would you?"

"Jealous?" She threw the word back in his face as though he'd issued the greatest insult of her life. "If you can honestly mistake integrity and principles for jealousy, then I truly wonder what kind of man I've married."

With that she turned and walked into her bedroom and closed the door. Hannah had probably never slammed a door in her life, he realized.

Air seeped between Riley's clenched teeth. He'd done it again. Just when he was beginning to make headway with her, he got cocky and said something stupid. It was becoming a bad habit.

He let a few moments pass, then decided to try once again. He knocked on her bedroom door, but didn't wait for her to answer before turning the knob and walking in. A husband should be allowed certain rights. Hannah turned and glared at him accusingly.

"I didn't mean what I said."

She held a blouse to her front and stared stonily back at him. "I see. So you fully intend to cheat on me."

"No, dammit." He jerked his fingers through his hair. "You're purposely misconstruing everything I say." His patience was wearing paper-thin. "I shouldn't have said anything about you being jealous. Judy doesn't mean anything to me. I haven't seen her in weeks. We may have talked twice in the last three months. I've been trying to cool the relationship. She resented that."

Hannah deposited the blouse in the closet with the others. "I see."

"I don't wish to argue with you, Hannah. Can we drop the subject of Judy now?"

She lowered her gaze and nodded. "I...I didn't mean to shout earlier. I don't generally get angry like that.... It must be the pregnancy."

"I understand what you're saying."

"You do?" Her beautiful gray eyes leveled with his.

He nodded. "You see, I've had this problem for several months now," Riley admitted, stepping across the room. "There's been this woman on my mind."

Her eyes were unbelievably round, and she was staring up at him. Her moist lips immobilized him, and in that moment he knew he had to taste her again. His need was beyond reason, beyond his control. He reached for her, barely giving her time to adjust to his embrace before his mouth smothered hers. He caught her unaware and used it to his advantage to slip his tongue into her mouth. He expected her to protest the unfamiliar invasion, but she surprised him once more by giving him her own. Their mouths played with each other, danced, sang, rejoiced in the intimacy they shared.

Sliding his hands down the length of her spine, he drew her to him, pulling her into the heat of him. For an instant she resisted, and Riley feared he had gone too far, frightening her when that was the last thing he wished. He wanted to make love to her, the way he'd been dreaming about doing for nearly four months. Every minute she made him wait seemed like an eternity.

Hannah wasn't like any other woman he'd known. She was delicate and sweet and deliciously provocative, innocently provocative. He couldn't hold her without experiencing the sensation of walking through a field of blooming wildflowers. With his hands at her hips, he dragged her closer, letting her feel the heat rise in him. He edged his way toward the bed, thinking if he were able to get her on top of the mattress, he might be able to remove her blouse. The thought of tasting her breasts, of holding them in his hands once more, was so powerful he lost his balance. He caught himself and her, before they went crashing to the floor. It was then that he noticed the framed picture lying on top of an unpacked box.

He stopped abruptly as a cold chill raced over him. His eyes narrowed as he looked down on her. "Who's that?" he demanded.

Chapter Five

"Who is he?" Riley demanded a second time. Instinct told him the photo wasn't one of a relative. He knew he was right when Hannah's gaze shot toward the box in question. The look that came over her features was incredible, a mixture of pain and of love so strongly mingled that it was as if she were no longer aware of who or where she was.

"Jerry Sanders," she answered in a voice so low Riley had to strain to hear. "We were engaged."

"Engaged?" Riley repeated the word, not because the news shocked him or because he didn't believe her, but because... if she'd been engaged to Jerry Sanders, then why the hell had she been a virgin? Furthermore, why had she gone to bed with him? Questions came at him like exploding rockets.

"He...died a...few months back...in a car accident." It was apparent that even speaking of her former fiancé was painful for Hannah.

Suddenly everything clicked into place for Riley. The way she'd stared at him that night on the waterfront. The ethereal look about her, the pain and uncertainty he'd read in her eyes. No wonder he'd felt this overwhelming urge to take her in his arms, hold her, protect her, love her. She had been walking around emotionally wounded, absorbed in her grief.

"When?"

She understood his question without him having to elaborate. Tears crowded her eyes, and when she spoke it was with difficulty. "July second."

A sick, sinking sensation landed with a hard thud in the pit of his stomach. Three weeks. Seafair, when he'd met Hannah, had been a scant three weeks following Jerry's death. No wonder she'd come warm and willing to his bed. She'd been in such grief she hadn't a clue what she was doing. This also explained why she'd run from him early the following morning.

Closing his eyes, Riley roughly plowed his fingers through his hair. When he opened his eyes, he found Hannah staring at him. "Do you love him?" he asked, his heart pounding like a giant hammer inside his chest. It wasn't in Hannah to lie. Of that, Riley was certain.

She looked away and nodded.

Riley didn't know why he felt compelled to ask. Seeing the reverent way in which she'd gazed at the other man's picture had told him everything he needed to know. The fact she was married to him was damn little comfort.

"You've got your nerve talking about fidelity to me," he said forcefully, battling the dual demons of anger and pride. Their entire marriage was a farce, only he hadn't been smart enough to figure it out. How incredibly stupid he'd been. Exhaling sharply, Riley felt like the world's biggest fool. For months, she'd had him dangling by a thread, toying with his mind; had him worrying about her, frightened about what had become of her. Their time together, those brief hours he'd treasured beyond all others, had meant nothing to her. Not one damn thing. She'd been looking for him to give her what her fiancé never had; perhaps pretending he was another man the entire time they'd been making love.

She'd used him.

The sickening feeling in his stomach intensified.

"Keep the damn thing out of sight!" he shouted. "You're married to me now, and I won't tolerate having another man's picture in my home. Is that understood?"

Hannah stared at him blankly, her features so pale and drawn he couldn't look at her.

"Throw it away." If she didn't do it, by God, he would. Riley would be damned before he'd allow another man to haunt his marriage. When she didn't immediately comply, he stalked across the room and reached for the photograph.

Hannah let out a small cry, scrambled across the bed and jerked the frame from his reach. From the way she reacted, he might as well have been coming toward her with a chain saw.

"No!" she cried, holding the photograph against her breasts as if it were her most valuable possession. "I'll keep it out of sight . . . I promise."

He stared at her, wanting with everything in him to smash the photograph to the ground, and with it destroy the memory of the man she loved. He would have done it, but one look told him Hannah would fight him like a wildcat to see that nothing happened to her precious photograph.

He scowled, then turned sharply and walked out of the bedroom and the house, not stopping until he was outside where his three friends were waiting. He forced himself to smile and loop his arms over the shoulders of Burt and Don. There had never been a time in his life when he felt more like getting fall-down-on-his-face drunk.

Hannah raced to the window in time to see Riley pull away. Tears streaked her face and she brushed them aside with the heel of her hand, feeling wretched. From the first, she'd meant to tell her husband about Jerry, but never like this. Never like this.

He'd made her so angry suggesting she was jealous over Judy. The very idea was ludicrous. Good heavens, she'd never even met the woman. Riley had infuriated her and she'd reacted in spite, knowing he'd eventually notice Jerry's picture. Once he did, she'd reasoned, then he would realize she couldn't possibly care one way or the other about his former lady friends.

What was important to her was the sanctity of their marriage. They'd spoken vows before God and man, and the promises they'd made to each other were meant to be taken seriously. The circumstances surrounding their wedding weren't ideal—Hannah would be the first one to admit as much—but they'd agreed to make an effort to do whatever they could to ensure this marriage worked. If they were to have any chance of that, a fundamental trust had to be implanted early in their relationship. It was for that reason alone that Hannah had brought up the subject of fidelity. Certainly not because she cared one whit about Riley's on-again/off-again relationship with the mysterious Judy.

A deep, painful breath tore through her chest. The stone-cold way in which Riley had glared at her stabbed at her heart. She knew her confession had wounded him deeply.

Her husband wasn't a man who often betrayed his feelings. A hundred times in the past week she'd attempted to read him, tried again and again to understand this man with whom she'd vowed to spend the rest of her life. She'd found the task nearly impossible. He was often quiet, more often withdrawn. Other than to order her about, he'd rarely spoken to her.

Every once in a while she'd find him studying her, but when their eyes would meet, gauging his thoughts had been impossible. That wasn't the case when he'd found Jerry's picture, however. Riley had been murderous. His eyes, his features, everything about him had spelled out his fury. And his pain. Hannah would give anything she owned to have kept Jerry's picture safely tucked away in a drawer.

The sardonic way in which Riley had glared at her clawed at her tender heart. Hannah wanted Riley to know about Jerry, but it had never been her intention to hurt him.

Then again, maybe it had.

He was so unreasonable. So demanding. First he'd taunted her about another woman and then he'd infuriated her. In her anger she'd struck back at him, but she hadn't meant to hurt him. Never that.

She reached behind her and tugged free the scarf that tied the hair away from her face. Regret ebbed over her.

As soon as Riley returned, she'd apologize. She owed him that much.

When he hadn't come home several hours later, Hannah became concerned. She'd unpacked and systematically arranged the kitchen to her liking. That took what remained of the morning. Once she was finished, she made herself lunch, then wandered into the living room, holding the sandwich in her hand. Pausing at the window, she looked out, hoping, praying she'd find some sign of Riley. Her pulse accelerated when she noted his car was parked at the curb, but then she remembered he'd returned the truck to the rental agency and was apparently with one of his friends.

Discouraged, she went back to the kitchen and finished her glass of milk. The sandwich had lost its appeal, and she dumped it in the garbage. Looking around her, she went into the bedrooms, making up the beds.

It was well past dark when Hannah finished straightening up their little house. She surveyed her efforts, standing in the middle of the living room, hands on her hips. The transformation was a little short of amazing. What had seemed like a barren shell of walls and empty space now resembled a home.

Her brother's photograph rested on the fireplace mantel along with one she found of Riley. She guessed that it had been taken several years earlier, soon after he'd enlisted in the Navy. She'd stumbled upon it while unpacking a box of books and spent several moments studying the intense young face staring back at her. She hoped to gain an insight into her husband, but she'd found the photograph as difficult to read as the man.

It had taken a good deal of effort to arrange the furniture the way she wanted, and she was likely to incur her husband's displeasure for having worked so hard, but that wasn't anything new. What did he expect her to do while he was away hours on end? Twiddle her thumbs?

After stacking the empty boxes in the patio off the kitchen, Hannah fixed herself a bowl of clam chowder for dinner. She soaked in a hot bath once she finished the dishes.

Riley's disappearance was beginning to irk her. The least he could do was phone—only they didn't have one, not yet. She was concerned, but hadn't wanted to admit as much. The urge to contact her father was compelling. Not because she was willing to admit she'd made a mistake—which she was strongly beginning to believe—but so that she could hear the sound of his voice. In his own quiet manner, George Raymond would lend her encouragement, which she needed so badly just then. But again they had no phone. Hannah had rarely felt more cut off from those she loved, or more alone.

By ten, she made her way into her bedroom, weary to the bone, both mentally and physically. The urge to weep was nearly overwhelming. Her marriage couldn't be going any worse.

Hannah stirred at the sound of Riley crashing around the house. Checking her clock radio, she noted that it was nearly three in the morning. Tossing aside her blankets, she leaped out of bed and rushed down the hallway to discover Riley awkwardly straightening a kitchen chair he'd knocked to the floor. He seemed to be having trouble keeping his balance.

"Riley." She was so pleased to see him, so excited, she ran directly into his arms. "Thank God you're home..." She hugged his middle, pressing her flushed face to his chest and squeezing tightly. The hours he'd been away had seemed like an eternity.

Although she'd labored most of the day, setting their house to order in an effort to put him out of her mind, it hadn't worked. She'd been worried. All evening her mind had played tricks on her, listing the places he might have gone, the people he could be with, until everything had crashed together in regret and confusion.

Apparently she'd caught Riley by surprise, and he stumbled backward until he collided with the kitchen counter. His arms supported Hannah, and when she looked up at him, fearing he might be hurt, he caught her chin with his hand. His eyes clouded for an instant as if he were surprised to find her in his home, then without warning, without giving her any indication of what he intended, his mouth came crashing down on hers.

The kiss was hard, almost brutal as he lifted her from the floor. The hand at the back of her head held her prisoner, although she didn't struggle. He'd taken her so completely by surprise that for a moment she was numb with shock. This was a Riley she didn't know. One that frightened her with his fierce, hungry demand.

"Riley," she said, pulling her mouth free. "No..."

He answered her by kissing her again, dragging his mouth back to hers. Gone was the gentleness she'd always found in him, the tender concern. Instead she was met with desperate need. He tasted of restless passion. Against her will, against her pride, Hannah felt herself responding. Her hands clawed at his shirt as she clung tightly to him.

Riley moved his hands to her face, covering her ears as he worked his mouth from one side of her lips to the other. She wanted to protest, but the instant she opened her mouth, his tongue was there, boldly claiming the right to taste, to possess any part of her that he wished. The few times Riley had kissed her in this manner, he'd gently stroked the inside of her mouth. Now he used his tongue ruthlessly, sweeping it in and out from between her lips, plunging, probing, swirling it over her own, over and over until she was so weak she would have slumped to the floor without his support.

"No more," she said forcefully, pushing against him, needing to be free. Free of the warm, delicious sensations he was capable of making her feel. Free of the endless hours of worry and regret. Free of the past that clung like tentacles around her heart.

Riley's breathing was labored as he buried his face in the curve of her neck, kissing her there while his hands roved at will down her back and over her buttocks.

Again, Hannah made the effort to free herself. "You're drunk!"

She felt his smile against the hollow of her throat. "You mean it took you this long to figure it out?" he asked with a weary laugh. "You really are an innocent, aren't you?"

"May I remind you I was an innocent until I met you!" she cried, backing away from him. In his present mood, he might drag her into his bed and have his way with her and not even realize what he was doing.

"Don't look so worried," he said with a slurred laugh, reaching for her. "You're safe. Even if I wanted to make love to you, I'm so drunk, I doubt I could do anything about it." He laughed once more, but there was no humor in the sound. No humor and no amusement.

With some effort she managed to untangle his arms from her. In her eagerness to right the wrong she'd committed against him, she hadn't even noticed his condition.

"I'm not your precious Jerry," he said with a sneer. "But you can pretend. That's what you did that night in Seattle, isn't it? Pretend I was him." He waved his index finger back and forth in front of her face. "You didn't think I'd figure it out, did you?"

"Stop it," she cried, tears blurring her eyes.

"Well, go ahead and pretend all you want, my sweet. I don't mind playing a few pretending games myself. But ask yourself this, who shall I pretend you are? Judy, perhaps?"

Hannah felt sick to her stomach, nauseous and dizzy both at once. Unable to listen to another word, she turned and rushed into the bedroom, slamming the door. Not sure if she could trust him to leave her alone, she shoved the chair across the carpet and propped it under the handle.

He must have heard her efforts because he paused outside her door and gave a slurred, sick-sounding laugh. "Don't worry, my sweet. You're safe for tonight."

Riley woke the following morning with a compound headache. His temple throbbed like a giant piston firing inside his head. The pain was complicated by the sounds of Hannah in the kitchen. From all the racket she was making, it sounded like ten women instead of one.

Holding his head between his hands, he staggered out of his bedroom. "What the hell are you doing?" he demanded, grimacing at the sound of his own voice.

Hannah turned around and glared at him as though he were the devil incarnate. When she did deign to answer, she did so with a lofty tilt of her chin, as though speaking to him were beneath her. "I'm cooking breakfast."

"At this ungodly hour?"

"It's after nine." She set the cast-iron skillet down on the burner with enough force to break it in two. "But for those who choose to... to carouse to the wee hours of the morning, nine must indeed be an ungodly hour."

"Indeed," he echoed. If his head wasn't hurting so damn much, Riley might have been able to enjoy her tirade. Unable to understand why she was so angry, he watched as she slapped a piece of bacon in the pan, then jabbed it with a fork as though it needed to be killed before frying.

"Did you want something?" she demanded, when he continued to stand in his underwear in the middle of the kitchen.

"Peace and quiet," he suggested hopefully. "I don't suppose that would be so much to ask, would it?"

"Not in the least." With a flair for the dramatic, she turned off the stove, removed the pan and tossed the fork into the sink. Jerking the apron free from her waist, she hurled that at him, hitting him full in the face. By the time he'd managed to remove it, Hannah had walked out the front door, slamming it with enough force to shake the windows.

"Hannah!" he shouted, storming after her. He stopped abruptly when he reached the porch, realizing he couldn't very well traipse after her in his skivvies.

"Get back here right this minute," he ordered, pointing his finger at the ground.

She tossed him a defiant, mocking look and continued down the sidewalk. A suffragette couldn't have stepped with any more conviction than his wife, Riley noted wryly.

His first instinct was to let her go. If she was going to behave like a shrew, then to hell with her. His head was spinning, his ears rang and frankly he wasn't in any mood to deal with her temper tantrums.

As he was walking back to his bedroom, intent on ignoring Hannah and her outburst, it struck him how unusual it was for the sweet, gentle-natured Hannah to rage at him or anyone.

Holding his hands to his head, he tried to remember what he'd said to her to get her so irritated. Briefly he remembered their encounter from the night before. She'd shocked him by the eager way in which she'd raced into his arms and hugged him. They'd kissed, and the need he felt for her had all but consumed him. Then she'd pulled away from him just as she had every time he'd touched her since that night in Seattle, and he'd gotten angry with her. What had he said? Riley couldn't remember, not for the life of him.

He released a swearword and reached for his pants, urgently jerking them up his long legs. He couldn't let her traipse down the street alone. Hell, she hadn't even taken a sweater with her. In her condition, she might harm herself and the baby if she were to catch a chill.

Riley grabbed a jacket on his way out the door, jogging after her, furious with her and outraged at himself for letting her leave the house.

It amazed him how far she'd gotten by the time he reached her. She didn't slow her pace until his steps matched hers, and even then she continued walking, ignoring him.

"Hannah?" He spoke her name softly when he noticed the moist trail of tears that streaked her face. "Would it help any if I told you I was sorry?" He didn't know what he was apologizing for, but it was apparent he'd hurt her, and knowing that didn't sit right.

She stopped and looked up at him through narrowed, suspicious eyes.

"Whatever I said, I didn't mean it," he tried once more.

"You don't remember?" She sounded incredulous.

"No," he admitted, reaching for her hand. "Come back to the house and we'll talk about it. All right?"

She seemed to be trapped with indecision. He raised his hands to her face and gently rubbed the tears from her cheeks. Each one was an accusation against him. His heart constricted at how pale her features were, how fragile she looked. It demanded every ounce of control he possessed not to take her in his arms and beg her forgiveness. He was a reckless bastard to inflict his drunkenness on so delicate a soul, and he silently vowed never to do it again.

"Come on," he urged, wrapping his arm around her shoulders and steering her back toward the house. She resisted momentarily.

"You aren't wearing socks," she apparently felt obliged to point out.

"I didn't have time to slip them on. My wife took off on me," he said as a means of making a small joke. "I had no idea where she was headed."

"Church," she admitted in a tight whisper.

"Church," he repeated wryly as the fear evaporated within him. From the determined way in which she was running away from him, Riley had been convinced she was walking out of his life. He'd rushed after her, nearly paralyzed with the fear that she was going to disappear again. He couldn't allow that—not if it was within his power to stop her.

"Come back with me?" he asked, looking down the street to their house.

"I'll... I suppose I could attend the second service," she answered softly.

He kept his arm around her as they strolled back to the house, savoring those few moments that he could hold her in his embrace. There were so few opportunities to feel close to her. It wasn't a comfortable feeling, needing Hannah, wanting her. She'd have done them both a favor if she'd chosen someone else that night; but despite everything, he was pleased she hadn't.

"How's Junior this morning?" he asked, wanting to make light conversation.

"Fine."

"And Junior's mommy? How's she feeling?"

"About as good as Junior's daddy."

Riley grinned and rubbed his chin across the top of her head. "That bad?"

"I... I didn't sleep much last night."

"We'll both take a nap this afternoon," he promised, and in his mind he was thinking how good it would be if he could convince her to lie down with him.

The first week after they'd settled into their new home was a busy one for Hannah. She scheduled her first appointment with the Navy physician and went looking for a part-time job.

It was a rainy, cold morning on Thursday, and Hannah had just put some kidney beans on the stove to soak, thinking she'd make a batch of chili for dinner, when there was a knock at the front door.

She opened it to find a tall, slender woman with bright brown eyes standing on the other side. "Hello," she said, grinning broadly. "I know I'm supposed to wait for our husbands to introduce us, but I couldn't stay away a minute longer. I'm Cheryl Morgan, Steve's wife." She extended her hand to Hannah.

They exchanged a brief handshake while Hannah led the way into the kitchen. "Steve," she repeated, then remembered. "He helped us move."

"Right," Cheryl said with quick nod. "I would have come along, too, but I was working." Hannah noted they were around the same age and knew immediately that she was going to like Cheryl Morgan.

"When Steve came home and told me Riley was married, I couldn't wait to meet you. I hope you don't mind me stopping in unannounced this way."

"Of course not. I've been bored to tears all morning." Hannah put the teapot on to boil and brought down two cups and saucers. "I suppose...Riley's marriage must have come as a shock."

"I'll say," Cheryl agreed, reaching for one of the sugar cookies Hannah had set on the table and crossing her long legs. "I plied Steve with questions, but he seemed rather close-mouthed about the whole thing."

Not wanting to explain their marriage and the pregnancy both at once, Hannah busied herself readying the tea, attempting to disguise her uneasiness. "It happened quickly."

"A whirlwind courtship. How romantic."

Hannah wasn't sure how to respond to that. A whirlwind was right, but it hadn't been much of a courtship. Not with her father and Chaplain Stewart running the show.

Once the water was boiling, Hannah added it to the teapot, leaving it to steep a few moments before pouring. "I'm so pleased you stopped by. I was beginning to wonder if I was going to meet anyone on the base."

"I'm glad I stopped by, too." Cheryl paused and slowly shook her head. "That Riley is a sly dog. He had me worried sick he was going to marry—"

"Judy," Hannah supplied for Cheryl when she stopped abruptly. For a moment her newfound friend looked as though she wanted to stand up and grab back the words.

"Then you know about her?"

Hannah nodded without elaborating. She knew her name and that Riley claimed she didn't mean a thing to him, but beyond that she was in the dark.

Cheryl slapped her hand over her chest. "You'll have to forgive me. I have this terrible habit of saying whatever's on my mind. I can't seem to stop myself."

"Don't worry. You haven't offended me." Hannah smiled as she added sugar to her tea and stirred lightly. "I'll admit I don't know a lot. Riley hasn't said much. But from what I gathered, they'd been seeing each other regularly."

"They were pretty thick in the beginning of the summer," Cheryl explained, sipping from her cup. "Then the relationship cooled. Judy is...nice, don't get me wrong. But she's accustomed to getting what she wants, and she'd set her sights on Riley. I don't think she took kindly to his sudden loss of interest."

Hannah wasn't sure how to comment, so she simply nodded, hoping that would suffice.

"I know why Riley married you," Cheryl said, not unkindly.

Hannah dropped her gaze as color crept up her neck. Naturally Steve would have told his wife about the pregnancy; that only made sense. Cheryl was probably also aware Hannah and Riley weren't sharing a bedroom, too.

"You're perfect for someone like Riley."

"I...am?" It came out in the form of a question rather than the positive statement she'd intended.

"Absolutely perfect. He's this rough-and-tough macho guy. The strong, silent type who's too stubborn for his own good. I'm sure you know what I mean."

Hannah was quick to agree with a nod.

"For a long time after I first met Riley, he made me uncomfortable," Cheryl admitted, glancing anxiously toward Hannah. "He isn't an easy man to know. It's impossible to figure out what he's thinking. He keeps everything to himself. Even though Steve's probably his best friend, he didn't know about you."

No one knew about her, but Hannah understood what Cheryl was saying. Riley kept most of his thoughts to himself. It was what had made these past few weeks so difficult. They'd sit down across the dinner table from each other and he'd ask her a few questions about her day and share nothing of his own. Her few attempts at drawing him into conversation had been met with silence. Yet he was genuinely concerned about her. Solicitous. Hannah knew he was trying as hard as he knew how to make everything right for her.

Sunday morning had been a turning point. They'd both seemed to regret the events of the day before and worked hard at overcoming the hurt they'd inflicted on each other. Riley had driven her to church and then returned later to pick her up. They'd talked more that day than the entire previous week. When she'd set dinner on the table, he had raved about her efforts and then insisted upon doing the dishes himself.

"It took me a year or more to feel at ease with Riley," Cheryl continued.

A year! Hannah groaned inwardly. They maintained a fragile peace even now. He was concerned about her health and that of their baby. He was the one who insisted she make a doctor's appointment and that she schedule it at a time when he could go in with her. He hadn't argued with her about finding a job, but she knew from his lack of enthusiasm that he'd prefer it if she remained home. But he hadn't insisted she not look for employment.

Thus far, her efforts had been restricted to part-time office positions at the base. Several were available, and she'd gone in to fill out the paperwork and was told she'd be contacted for an interview sometime soon. For now, all she could do was be patient.

"As I said earlier, you're a perfect complement to Riley," Cheryl remarked, munching on her second cookie. "You're gentle and sweet. What I want to know is how that crusty hardheaded sailor ever met someone like you."

Chapter Six

"How we met?" Hannah repeated slowly. Rather than confess the truth, she glanced shyly in Cheryl's direction and said, "That's rather an involved story, and if you don't mind, I'd prefer to leave it for another time."

"Of course," Cheryl returned, easily appeased. She glanced anxiously at her watch. "I've got to be at the hospital in an hour. If I'm not careful, the time will slip away from me."

"You work at the hospital?"

Cheryl nodded. "In Labor and Delivery."

Hannah brightened. "Really? That must be interesting work."

"Believe me, it is. I find it incredible how many babies decide to be born while Daddy's out to sea. Speaking of which," she said, waving her hand as she hurriedly finished a sip of tea, "isn't it the pits Riley and

Steve are leaving for that training session? I hate it when
the Navy does this, but then I should be accustomed to
the way the military works by now. Steve isn't any more
thrilled about this than I am, and I bet Riley feels the
same way."

Hannah hadn't a clue what Cheryl was talking about,
but she didn't want the other woman to know it. If Riley
was going on deployment, he hadn't shared the news
with her. Hannah felt lost in the dark, groping around,
searching for meaning. She forced a smile when she
noticed Steve's wife anxiously studying her. "The pits
is right."

"So soon after you two are married."

"Do they know exactly when they'll be going?"
Hannah hoped she effectively disguised the eagerness in
her voice. She felt hollow inside, as if a giant void had
opened up and exposed what a farce her marriage really
was. It hurt more than she thought possible for Riley to
have hidden this from her.

"It looks like they're scheduled to head out Monday
morning, but I doubt it'll be a full cruise. At least, that's
what the scuttlebutt claims. They should be home before Christmas, at any rate, although I fully expect them
to be gone the entire seventy days this spring."

Seventy days. Hannah's mind went blank. Spring was
when their baby was due. Alarm gripped her chest, and
she struggled to conceal the apprehension. It was bad
enough being cut off from her father and friends and
from all that was familiar to her, but knowing she'd be
facing the birth of her baby without Riley terrified
Hannah. She pushed her fear aside, determined to deal
with it later.

"I wish I could be here Friday night," Cheryl added,
downing the last of her tea. "I would have been con-

tent to meet you then, but I'm scheduled to work. The next time the guys get together for poker, the two of us will have our own night out.''

Hannah managed a smile and nod. "That sounds like fun."

They spoke a few minutes more, then Cheryl had to leave for the hospital. Hannah saw her to the door and impulsively hugged her, grateful Steve's wife had taken the time to stop by and introduce herself. Their conversation had been a fruitful one.

For hours afterward Hannah felt numb. A disquieting, uncomfortable knot lodged itself in her stomach. In three short days Riley would be leaving for a lengthy patrol, and he had yet to say a word to her about it. Nor had he mentioned it was likely he'd be at sea during the birth of their child. Surely a wife should be entitled to such information. Hannah felt she had a right to know. Every right.

She was frying up hamburger for chili when Riley walked into the house two hours ahead of schedule. He hesitated when he saw her. "You're not ready," he said, his tone lightly accusing.

"For what?" She had a difficult time burying her sarcasm. Perhaps there was something else he'd purposely forgotten to mention. He seemed to think she was a mind reader.

"The doctor's appointment."

"Oh . . . dear." After her conversation with Cheryl, her appointment with the Navy physician had completely slipped her mind.

Flustered, she headed toward the bathroom. "I'll only be a minute." She ran a brush through her hair, applied a fresh coat of lip gloss and changed her top all within five minutes. When she returned to the kitchen, she found Riley adding the cooked meat to the simmering kidney beans. He replaced the lid on the Crockpot.

As they drove to the clinic, Hannah glanced over at her husband several times, amused by how well his personality was portrayed in his facial features. His chin was nothing short of arrogant. His jaw was as sharply chiseled as his pride. His eyes and nose and mouth—every part of him gave the overall impression of strength and power. Yet he was a stranger to her, sharing little of his thoughts and even less of himself. She felt like an intruder into his life, extra baggage he was forced to drag around with him.

Riley must have felt her scrutiny, and when he returned her look, she blushed and dropped her gaze to her lap, then waited a moment before nonchalantly glancing at him again.

She felt dangerously close to repeating everything she'd learned that morning from Cheryl Morgan. She would have if she hadn't been anxious to learn how long it would take Riley to tell her of his plans. She was his wife, although she was more certain than ever that he didn't want her in his life and only tolerated her presence. No, Hannah decided, she'd say nothing. She would play his waiting game.

Riley was anxious about Hannah's health. He'd never known anyone could be so pale. Her coloring had something to do with it; but it was more than that, far more, and he was concerned. He intended on talking to the doctor, to reassure himself she'd be all right while he was out to sea.

The fact he'd be gone for a few weeks didn't sit well with him, either. He hadn't broken the news to her yet, delaying the inevitable as long as possible for fear of upsetting her. There'd been enough upheaval in their lives in the past few weeks without this. When it came right down to it, Riley realized he'd rather not leave Hannah, but the training schedule wasn't optional. Damn little in the Navy was.

Riley loved the sea, loved life aboard the nuclear-powered submarine, the USS *Atlantis*. But he didn't want to leave Hannah. Not so soon. Not yet.

He'd had several days to assimilate what he'd learned about her and her former fiancé. It didn't sit well with him that Hannah loved another man. He tried not to think about it, to push the other man to the far reaches of his mind and pretend Jerry had never existed. It was the only way Riley could deal with knowing Hannah might be married to him, but she would never truly belong to him.

Hannah made Riley feel vulnerable. He didn't understand what it was about her that touched him in ways no other woman ever had. One hurt look from her had the most curious effect upon him. It was as though someone had viciously kicked him in the solar plexus. The irony of it all was that the person Riley sought to protect her from most was himself. His insensitivity. His pride. His anger.

If what he felt for Hannah was love, Riley couldn't say. His brushes with the emotion were best described as brief. He cared about her in ways that had never concerned him with others. That was understandable, though; no other woman had ever carried his child. He was anxious about her health; she was a fragile thing, delicate and rare. It seemed all he could do was make her as comfortable as possible, and that felt like damn little.

Other than a few slips, Riley was working hard at gaining her trust. Convincing her to share his bed was motivation enough. He longed to have her by his side, to rest his head upon her stomach and feel for himself the new life her body nurtured. Every once in a while he'd lie awake and grow wistful, dreaming of the time she would willingly turn into his arms and snuggle her lush womanly body next to his own. Marriage had made him fanciful, Riley decided. He'd enjoyed the physical delights a woman's body could give him from the time he was in his teens, but he seldom spent the night with a woman. Hannah had been an exception from the first. He'd wanted her the night he met her in Seattle, and nothing had changed. The fact she was in love with another man didn't seem to matter.

The time Dr. Underwood, the obstetrician, spent with Hannah added to Riley's concern about his wife's pregnancy. The doctor took several minutes to talk to them both, and ordered blood tests for Hannah.

Riley's concern must have registered because Dr. Underwood took a few extra minutes to explain the reasons for the additional tests. He strongly suspected Hannah was still anemic, and as soon as the results were available he would write a prescription for a higher dosage of iron tablets. There were several questions Riley had, as well, although it was apparent Hannah felt it irrelevant to have Riley bring up her sleeping habits and the fact she still suffered from occasional bouts of morning sickness.

Riley was silent on the short drive back to the base. His mind was digesting the answers the doctor had given him. If the truth be known, he was worried. Damn worried.

"You're being awfully quiet," she said as they exited the freeway. "Is something troubling you?" Casting anxious glances his way, she seemed to be waiting for him to make some declaration. Riley hadn't a clue what she wanted him to say.

"I'm fine," he answered shortly.

She gazed out the window then, turning her head away from him. Feeling bad for the brusqueness with which he'd responded to her, he reached for her hand, lacing her fingers with his own. "I'm concerned you're not eating the way you should be," he said as an explanation.

"I'm very conscious of everything that goes into my mouth."

"You pick at your food. I swear you don't eat enough to keep a bird alive."

"That's ridiculous."

Riley swallowed a tart reply. The last thing he wanted to do was argue with her, although she seemed to be looking for an excuse herself. They'd done too much of that in the past few days. He didn't want to leave for the training exercises with matters strained between them— at least not any more strained than they already were.

"I've gained two pounds since I was in to see my family doctor," she said, apparently unwilling to let the matter rest.

He didn't respond, knowing it wouldn't help to chastise her further. "You promise to take the iron tablets?"

"Of course," she returned, then hesitated before adding, "Junior is my baby, too, you know."

Junior. Riley cracked a smile. He'd nearly forgotten there was a baby involved in all this. His primary concern had been for Hannah, so much so that he'd forgotten the very reason she was sitting at his side.

When they got back to the house, there was a message on the answering machine informing Hannah of a job interview scheduled for the following afternoon. If she couldn't make the appointment, she was to contact the personnel office first thing in the morning.

Hannah's eyes brightened as she listened to the message, and she smiled over at Riley.

"The job's right here on the base," she said, sounding pleased.

"Doing what?" In an effort to disguise his uneasiness about the whole issue of her working, Riley opened the refrigerator and brought out a chicken leg, munching on it although he wasn't the least bit hungry.

"Secretarial work. I...was employed at an insurance agency before...before we were married."

Riley nodded. "Is the position you applied for full-time?"

"I...I think so. It must be."

"I see."

Hannah glared at him as though he'd attacked her family's heritage. "Why'd you say it like that?"

"Like what?" He pretended not to understand, although he had a fair idea what she was talking about. He wasn't keen on her taking on a forty-hour workweek—not when her health was so delicate. Riley swore he never knew anyone who required nine hours of rest a night the way she did, although Dr. Underwood claimed this need for extra sleep would soon pass.

"Like...like you don't approve of my working."

"I don't." There, he'd said it, bold as could be. "I don't happen to think it's a good idea."

"Why not?" Hannah demanded. "Because of the baby?"

"Yes. And other factors."

"What other factors?"

Riley sighed. Already their voices were raised, and he could see he wasn't going to be able to extract himself from this easily. He tossed the chicken leg into the garbage and washed his hands, carefully considering his words. Hannah was staring at him, impatiently waiting. "You claimed you needed some time to adjust to our marriage."

"What's that got to do with anything?"

"I feel you should put your efforts into our relationship."

She took her own sweet time to digest his words, but when he looked in her direction, he noticed she didn't seem pleased with his straightforward answer.

"In other words, if I agree to sleep with you, you'd approve of my working."

That wasn't what he'd meant in the least. Yes, he'd been honest enough to admit he wanted to make love to her. He'd made that fact abundantly clear on their wedding day. A brother-and-sister relationship didn't interest him then, and it appealed to him even less now.

"Well?" she asked, demanding a response from him.

"I don't want to quarrel over this, Hannah." He was smart enough to recognize a loaded question when he heard one. Smart enough to extract himself as best he could, too. "All I'm saying is that I'd prefer it if you invested as much time in our relationship as you would in a job. There are only so many hours in a day. You can't do everything, you know."

"In other words you wouldn't be willing to help with the cooking or the housework?"

Riley was quickly losing his grip on his patience, which had always been in short supply. Hannah seemed to be looking for an excuse to pick a fight with him by tying him up in verbal knots. She had been from the moment he'd arrived home. Hell if he knew what he'd done that was so terrible now.

"I'd be willing to help with the cooking and house-work." He fully expected his answer would take the starch out of her arguments. How willing he actually would be to help around the house was another question entirely. Having her there when he walked in the door after a long day with dinner prepared and waiting was a luxury he could easily become accustomed to enjoying.

"What about the times you're out at sea?"

"What about them?" Frankly he couldn't understand why that would make any difference. If anything, it was a strong argument to keep her home. With him away, no one would be around to make sure she wasn't overworking herself.

"I'll . . . be bored without a job."

"What makes you say that? The other wives seem to have plenty to do to occupy their time. You will, too."

Once again she seemed to need time to assimilate his words. For several minutes she said nothing. Then, as if by rote, she stepped over to the cupboard and brought down dishes and began to set the table.

"Do you want any help?" He felt downright noble asking. It seemed like a husbandly thing to do.

"No," she said softly, shaking her head. "Dinner will be ready in a few minutes."

Apparently this was the end of their discussion. "What about the job interview?" he asked, trying not to let his feelings on the issue leak into the question.

True, he'd rather she didn't work, but he wouldn't stop her if that was what she truly wanted. Once again he felt the fleeting twinge of being truly virtuous.

"I . . . I'm not sure what I intend to do about the job yet."

Riley felt encouraged by that. At least she wasn't going to openly defy him, and was willing to take his concerns into consideration. Other than a few rocky places, their marriage was coming along nicely. They were learning the give-and-take necessary to make any relationship work, and Riley couldn't help feeling good about that.

Dinner was ready twenty minutes later. There was a batch of steaming corn-bread fresh from the oven, and the tureen of hot chile con carne. All homemade. All delicious. Riley eyed the table with appreciation, complimenting her.

They ate in silence, and once again Riley noted how she continued to glance his way several times, as though expecting something. What, he wasn't sure. He complimented her once more on the excellent dinner and made some fleeting remark about never having eaten better, which was true. Before he'd married Hannah, dinners had consisted of microwave specials or something he could grab on the run. Nothing like the home cooking he'd enjoyed since their marriage.

When they'd finished, he helped clear the table. He rinsed the dishes and set them in the dishwasher. With only the two of them, the task was complete in a matter of minutes.

Hannah stored the leftovers in the refrigerator and wiped down the counters. The evening news was on, and Hannah sat on the chair across from Riley's recliner and picked up her knitting. The sight of her needles working the soft pastel yarn into a blanket for their child had a curious effect upon his heart. It warmed him in ways he was only beginning to understand. It dawned on him suddenly that she loved and wanted this baby.

Glancing up, Hannah found his eyes on hers. She openly glared at him before looking away, as though she deeply resented it was him sitting across from her and not Jerry, the real love of her life. The good feelings he'd experienced a few moments earlier drowned in a sea of resentment.

A heavy dose of anger simmered in him for several minutes before he stood and made himself a cup of instant coffee. Reaching for the evening paper, he worked the crossword puzzle.

"I'd like to visit my father over Christmas," Hannah said, working the knitting needles with a vengeance. She jerked hard on the ball of yarn, then looked up at him as if she fully expected an argument.

"Fine." He rarely made plans for the holidays. Frankly, they didn't mean that much to him. "Am I included, or would you rather I stayed away?"

Once again she glanced upward, obviously surprised by his question. "Included, of course. We are married."

Riley didn't know what to read into that comment, if anything.

Following the brief snatch of conversation, the only sound in the entire house was the gentle hum of the dishwasher and the noise coming from the television. Riley thought of several topics he wanted to discuss, but dismissed them all. It was apparent Hannah wasn't in any mood to chat.

Looking away from her, Riley realized that despite everything, he wanted this marriage to work. For their

child's sake, for Hannah's sake, for his own peace of
mind, Riley was determined to do everything he could
to ensure its survival.

He'd taken the biggest gamble of his life by agreeing
to marry Hannah. He'd done it without realizing he was
playing with a loaded deck, but he was coming to grips
with her love for Jerry. The stakes were too high to back
down now. Something told him, something deep and
primal, that Hannah and their child represented his one
chance for finding happiness, and he was taking hold of
this opportunity with both hands and holding on tight.

By eight-thirty, right on schedule, she was yawning.
Although he pretended an interest in a television program, Riley was aware of Hannah with every fiber of
his being. He'd hoped by this time to be able to kiss and
hold her whenever the mood struck him, which he knew
would be often. Looking at her now, busy tearing out
several rows of stitches, her back ramrod straight, Riley
marveled that in two weeks of marriage that he'd been
allowed to kiss her as often as he had. She'd never
looked more untouchable than she did at this moment.

"A penny for your thoughts." Riley couldn't believe
he'd said that. He hated the ineptitude he experienced,
attempting to deal with his wife. He felt like a bungling
youth when it came to understanding her moods.

"You don't honestly want to know what I'm thinking," she replied stuffing her knitting into the wicker
basket resting on the carpet next to her chair.

"I would," he countered sharply.

She stared at him, and Riley was shocked to read the
stark emotion marred by a glistening veneer of tears.
Although she battled to conceal the stubborn pride, it
burned from her eyes. With some difficulty, she managed to keep the tears at bay. "I . . . I was just thinking

I'd adjust to our marriage a whole lot easier if you behaved more like a husband.''

Riley didn't have time to react before she stood and hurried to her bedroom, closing the door. He intended to follow her when he heard the lock slip noisily into place. Sharply expelling his breath, he stood alone in the living room, wondering what the hell she'd meant by that. Maybe, he mused, he would start acting more like a husband when she started behaving like a wife.

The interview went poorly. As childish as it seemed, Hannah would have liked to blame Riley for that. She'd slept fitfully all night and felt nauseous the moment she lifted her head from the pillow. The bouts of morning sickness had all but disappeared of late, and she delayed getting out of bed as long as she could. By sheer determination she managed to hold down her breakfast until Riley left for work. The last thing she needed or wanted was him fussing over her.

Hannah wasn't proud of the way she'd acted the night before. She'd been cranky and unreasonable and on the verge of weeping. Her emotions were playing havoc with her, and she hated being so thin-skinned. Riley had hurt her. He didn't know or understand that, which only complicated matters. If only he'd tell her he was leaving. She'd done everything she knew to prompt the information out of him. It hadn't worked, and she battled a deep sense of betrayal and regret.

Although she felt physically wretched, she dressed carefully for the interview and went into the office with high expectations. Her credentials were excellent, as were her skills, but as soon as the interviewer learned she was pregnant, everything had taken a turn for the worse. It seemed the office was interested in someone older. In other words, a secretary beyond her child-bearing years.

Riley was home by the time she returned. He stood when she walked in the door, glancing anxiously in her direction.

"I didn't get the job," she announced on her way through the living room. Her voice shook slightly, and she did her level best to ignore him. Dealing with one disappointment at a time was her limit.

He followed her into the kitchen. "What happened?"

"It seems they aren't interested in a secretary after all. They want a ... a grandma."

"A what?"

"Someone who isn't pregnant," she explained tersely. "Only they dressed it in more delicate terms. I could sue them."

"There'll be other job interviews."

Hannah had fully expected Riley to gloat when he learned she hadn't gotten the job. He didn't want her working, and had said as much. Having him gently re-assure her only served to confuse her. Her throat thick-ened—something she'd always hated because it was a sure sign she was close to tears. Hannah hated to cry. Some women had perfected the art of weeping with a natural feminine grace. That wasn't the case with Han-nah. Her skin got blotchy, her nose ran, and if she tried to speak, her words sounded as though they were com-ing out of a pepper grinder.

"I'll never get a job," she said, hating it when her voice cracked.

"Sure, you will."

Hannah glared at Riley. She was depressed and mis-erable. The last thing she wanted was for her pragmatic husband to pretend to be Mary Sunshine, especially when she was fully aware of the fact he didn't want her to take the job in the first place.

"I . . . I find your optimism to be downright hypocritical." She tossed the words at him with a vengeance.

"Hannah, whether you decide to take on an outside job is entirely up to you. I voiced my concerns and left the matter in your hands. Better than anyone, you know how much you can or cannot do."

"You're singing a different tune than you were yesterday."

He nodded. "I talked it over with a friend."

"Steve, I suppose. After all, Cheryl's employed full-time, isn't she?"

His eyes flew to hers. "How'd you know . . . ?"

"She stopped in the other morning to introduce herself." Hannah refused to look away, hoping he could see the pain that was in her heart. She was doing everything she knew to be the best wife she could to Riley Murdock. More than anything, she longed for this marriage to work, but they didn't stand a chance if her husband insisted upon keeping her emotionally at arm's length. He should have told her he'd be leaving for six weeks the minute he'd learned that he'd been assigned sea duty. It cut deep slices against the grain of her pride whenever she realized how short a time they had left to be together. In a matter of hours he was scheduled to leave for heaven only knew how long—weeks, possibly months—and he hadn't seen fit to so much as tell her. But then she was holding him at arm's length herself, refusing to make love with him.

"I'm pleased you had a chance to meet Cheryl. I'm hoping the two of you will be friends."

"I'm sure we will be."

Riley glanced anxiously at his watch. "Listen, Steve reminded me of something this afternoon. I apologize that I didn't have time to talk it over with you, but apparently it's my turn to host the poker game."

"The poker game," she echoed, playing innocent.

"Yeah. Four of us from the *Atlantis* get together every other week or so and play low-stakes poker. With the wedding and the move, the game completely slipped my mind. Steve mentioned it this afternoon. I couldn't very well cancel it on such short notice."

"In other words, you'd like for me to disappear for the next several hours?"

"Not at all. You can stay, if that's what you want." But his words didn't sound the least bit sincere. "Only..."

"Yes?" she prompted.

"The guys aren't used to having a woman around. Steve's the only one who's married, so there might be some objectionable language. I'll do my best to be sure the guys tone it down."

"I see." Hannah could picture it already. She'd be as out of place at her husband's poker party as she was the night she rushed into the waterfront tavern. No doubt if she stayed she'd be wheezing cigarette smoke and picking up countless empty beer bottles.

"We generally drink a few beers, too, but not enough to get drunk," he added, confirming her suspicions.

"I get the point, Riley," she said, reaching for her coat and purse. "How long should I be gone?"

Her husband wasn't a man to hesitate. He didn't do it often but he did so now. He exhaled sharply and jerked his fingers through his hair. "I wish you wouldn't look at me like that. I feel like enough of a heel as it is.''

"One movie? Or should I plan on taking in a double feature?" she asked stoically.

"I forgot about the stupid game, all right? There've been other things on my mind lately. If you want to crucify me for that, then go ahead."

She took her own sweet time buttoning her coat. "Do you need me to fix you something for dinner before I leave?"

Riley shook his head. "No, thanks."

"All right then, I'll go now. I assume you have no objections to my taking the car?"

"Of course not."

"Fine. Then I'll plan on being back as late as I can."

He closed his eyes tightly. "Why do I feel so damn guilty?" he shouted. "I forget about a stupid poker game and—"

"Perhaps it's the other thing you're forgetting that's troubling you," she announced calmly. Her heart was pounding at double time, but for all outward appearances she was the picture of serenity. A deep blue mountain lake couldn't compare with the tranquillity she faultlessly portrayed.

"The other thing?" he yelled. "Damn it all to hell. There's nothing I hate more than a woman who refuses to talk straight. If you have a problem, I suggest you spell it out right now, because I refuse to play guessing games with you."

"Guessing games?" she returned flippantly. "I don't like playing them myself." With a scornful tilt of her head she tapped her finger against her lips. Until she'd married Riley, Hannah hadn't known it was in her to be so sarcastic. "Now let me see, when will Riley be shipping out next? I do wonder."

His mouth tightened. "Cheryl told you."

"No," Hannah cried, battling fury and pain. "She assumed I knew...assumed any husband would tell his wife. Only I'm not any wife, am I? You want me about as much as you want this marriage. You couldn't have spelled it out any plainer than this. Well, I don't want this marriage, either."

The crescent-shaped lines around Riley's mouth went white. His eyes, sharp, clear, intense, cut into her as effectively as a hunting knife. It was all too apparent he was having difficulty holding on to his composure. "We'll discuss this later."

"There's nothing more to discuss," she retorted. "You've already told me everything I need to know. I'm an encumbrance in your life. You don't want to be married to me. Trust me, it doesn't come as any shock. I didn't want this marriage, either—you were the one who insisted. I don't understand why. I never intended to drag you into this. I never even intended for you to know about the baby. You were the one... Why, Riley, why did you insist upon marrying me? I have a right to know that much."

Her demand was met with stark, naked silence. She rubbed the heel of her hand down her face, wiping away evidence of her tears. She stared at him, damning him for being there that fateful night. How much simpler her life would have been if she'd called a cab. She'd been such a fool, and her stupidity was ruining three lives.

"Why did I insist upon marrying you?" he repeated hoarsely. "Because I didn't want my son to grow up a bastard the way I did."

Chapter Seven

A hard knot tightened Riley's stomach as the color drained from Hannah's pale features. He felt raw and angry; the pain of years past clawed at his nerves. "I was two years old before my mother got around to marrying Bill. He didn't last long, though. None of my mother's men friends ever did."

Hannah's gaze met his. Damn, but he wished she'd say something. Anything. Until she'd demanded to know why he'd insisted on marrying her, Riley hadn't given the matter much thought. The answer was complicated by a multitude of other factors. Rather than stick his reasons under a microscope, Riley preferred not to think about them. Marriage was the best solution, or so it had seemed at the time. Riley wasn't sure of that any longer.

Unshed tears glistened in Hannah's dove-gray eyes. She'd never looked more frail, as though it was all she could do to remain upright. He noted how ragged her breathing was as she edged her way past him. Riley reached out to her, wanting with everything in him to ease her mind in some small way, but she flinched and snatched her arm from him before he could touch her.

He stood numb and empty. The power of her silence wounded him deeply. He was aware, too, of her pain; and knowing he was the one responsible cut unmercifully at his heart.

Riley watched her move down the hallway, her steps like those of a sleepwalker. As she opened the door to her room and walked inside, he experienced a weighty sadness. He was standing there trying to decide what to do, if anything, when the muted sounds of her sobs reached him. Riley wasn't sure who she wept for—him or for herself. Perhaps her sorrow was for their unborn child.

Unable to listen to her anguish and do nothing, Riley reacted to his instincts. God as his witness, he'd never meant to hurt Hannah. Her door wasn't locked, and for that much he was grateful. She was curled up in a tight ball on top of her bed, her soft dark hair cascading over her face and neck. Her shoulders were racked with sobs.

Led by impulse, Riley moved to her side and sat on the edge of the mattress. With gentle fingers, he brushed the hair from her face, fearing she'd pull away from him again. He couldn't have borne it if she had. As strange as it seemed, he needed her at that moment as much as she needed him, although he was certain neither would be willing to admit as much.

Not knowing how to relieve her anxiety, or his own, he lay down beside her, resting his head on the same pillow as hers. For long moments he simply watched her, hoping his being there would lend her comfort.

After a while her tears abated and she opened her eyes. They were round and weary, as if mirroring her soul. Her innocence and her beauty stirred him, and without examining the sudden, fierce need that flamed to life within him, he kissed her.

Riley intended for the kiss to be uncomplicated, a gesture of apology, a form of absolution for the hurt they'd inflicted upon each other. But once his mouth met hers, all was lost. Moaning, Hannah opened to him. He reached for her, entwining his fingers in her hair, dragging her closer to him. Deepening the kiss, he sought her tongue with his own.

When she shyly moved her tongue against his, Riley felt as though the bed had fallen out from under him. They kissed again, and it was slow and gentle, so damned gentle that it produced an overpowering ache. Not a physical ache, as Riley would have expected, but an emotional one, buried so deep that at first he couldn't identify it. He felt close to Hannah, closer than he had in all the time they'd been married. The walls of misunderstanding and pride were down, broken, shattered by a newfound willingness to help each other.

His hands caressed her cheeks and tenderly brushed aside the stray tendrils of hair from her sweet face. Their gazes met in a rush of need and longing. The questions were there, as bold as ever, but they didn't bother with words, didn't bother with explanations.

Riley had never known a silence so blissful. A contented silence. The sweetest silence he'd ever known. Precious moments of tenderness unlike anything he'd ever experienced.

Shyly, Hannah leaned forward and kissed him, curling her tongue around his. Heat against heat. Hand against hand, fingers entwined. Their mouths dueled in a love-starved battle as though they had an eternity to do nothing but savor one another. Wherever his life would lead him, whatever happened between him and Hannah, Riley realized he would always treasure these few, precious moments with her.

Ending the kiss slowly, Riley buried his face in her shoulder and dragged several deep breaths through his chest. He dared not look at her when he spoke, afraid of what he would read in her eyes.

"Can you feel Junior move yet?"

"I . . . don't know," she whispered back, her smile evident. "Sometimes I'm sure I do, but then I convince myself it's all part of my imagination. The doctor said I should feel him kick any time now."

"Can I feel?"

She smiled and nodded. Taking his hand, she pressed it against her stomach, holding it there. Her hand over his. His hand over her abdomen. Riley lifted his gaze until it met hers, waited for movement, then sadly shook his head. He was barely able to distinguish the slight thickening at her waist, and only then because she was so thin.

"There . . . are other changes," she whispered.

Once more he raised questioning eyes to hers, not sure he understood.

"My breasts are fuller."

Risking all, Riley gently cupped his hands over her glorious breasts, lifting them, allow them to fill his palms. Touching her so intimately had an immediate effect upon him. The hardness eloquently portrayed his plight. He wanted her. He needed her. It would be weeks before he'd be able to hold her and touch her again, and knowing that lent an urgency to his desire. For two weeks he'd been patient, doing nothing to pressure her, but he needed her now as he never had before. So much so that he was willing to broach the forbidden subject.

"I want to make love to you." Riley had always been direct. He might have dressed up his desire with a bunch of fancy words, or drugged her with kisses until she willingly submitted. But he wasn't willing to do either. When Hannah came to his bed, he wanted her to be fully aware of what she was doing and with whom.

A long moment passed, and he was encouraged by the indecision he felt in her. At least she was considering it, which was a giant step from the sharp rejection she'd given him the day of their wedding.

"Why?"

If she needed a little inducement, Riley was more than willing to supply it. "I'm going to be away six weeks. That's a hell of a long time for a husband to be without his wife...."

"No," she said flatly, and pushed herself free from his grasp. Sitting up on the edge of the bed, she brushed the hair away from her face, using both hands. He was surprised to realize she was trembling.

"Hannah, for the love of heaven, we're married!"

"Six weeks without making love must be some sort of record for you. Your pressure tactics aren't going to work with me."

"Pressure tactics!" Riley exploded. He could have had her, could skillfully have brought her to the point of desperate physical need. Instead he'd taken a more direct route and in the process robbed himself of the very love he craved. "Before you start accusing me of anything, you'd best examine yourself."

She blushed and looked away. "I don't know what you're talking about."

"My breasts are fuller," he mimicked in a high fal-setto voice. "Sweetheart, you were asking for it."

Hannah's face went fire-engine red. "That's ridiculous!"

Riley gave a short, disbelieving laugh. "What's so wrong about us making love? I don't know of any place where it's a crime to sleep with one's wife."

Her gaze narrowed. "If I'm your wife why didn't you tell me you were leaving? A . . . a stranger comes to my door and tells me my own husband will be gone for several weeks—a *stranger*, for the love of heaven."

"I thought I was doing you a favor."

"Spare me any more of your favors."

Riley swore he'd never known a more unreasonable woman. What had he done that was so unforgivable? His crime had been to delay letting her know about the training cruise so she wouldn't fret about him going. He was being kind. Thoughtful. Just as a husband should be. Instead, the whole thing had blown up in his face.

Riley was prepared to argue with her when the door-bell rang. For a split second he couldn't decide if he should answer it or not. In the end he decided it wouldn't do any good to talk sense to Hannah. She was bent on thinking ill of him, and he wasn't likely to say or do anything that could change her mind.

The weekend passed in a haze for Hannah. Riley barely spoke to her, which was just as well since she worked equally hard to avoid any contact with him. The tension in the house was as thick as a London fog; thick enough to slice up and serve for dinner, although it would have made bitter fare.

Hannah spoke only when asked a direct question. Riley was constrained and silent. No unnecessary words passed between them. Nor looks, and certainly no touching. He camped in one area of the house and she in the other, and they both went overboard to be certain their paths didn't cross.

Monday morning Hannah heard her husband rummaging through the house several hours earlier than normal. Realizing he was probably preparing to leave for the *Atlantis*, she lay in bed, trying to decide if she should make the effort to see him off properly.

Her preference was to leave matters as they were, but soon the decision was taken from her. Riley politely rapped against her bedroom door just loud enough to wake her if she were sleeping, but not enough to frighten her. She sat up, holding the blankets protectively against her breasts, although it was unnecessary since she wore a thick flannel nightgown and the possibility of him viewing any part of her anatomy was highly unlikely.

"Yes?" she called out, working hard to put a frosty tone in her voice.

He opened the door, and his six-foot frame was stiffly silhouetted against the light that spilled into the hallway from the kitchen. He didn't move into the bedroom and continued to hold on to the door handle. "I'll be leaving soon."

She nodded, confident there was nothing she could add to the announcement.

"I left two phone numbers on the kitchen table for you. If a problem arises and you need anything, call either one of those numbers." His words were heavily starched and devoid of emotion. He might have been discussing the weather, for all the feeling he displayed.

"All right."

He dropped his hand away from the door and hesitated for a moment. "Goodbye."

"Goodbye," she returned just as tautly.

He closed the door, and with willful determination, she laid her head back down on the pillow. Closing her eyes, Hannah stubbornly decided to go back to sleep and ignore her husband the way he'd ignored her. She supposed she should consider herself lucky he'd taken the trouble to bid her farewell.

An achy heaviness weighed down her chest, and Hannah realized she was on the verge of tears. She hated the wetness that rolled down the sides of her face, dampening the pillow. She hating Riley for making her feel so loathsome, as though she'd done something very wrong. It felt wrong to have him leave for six weeks of sea duty when so much remained unsaid between them.

Rolling onto her side, she was determined to ignore her husband, the Navy and her conscience. Closing her eyes, she waited for the void of sleep to willingly claim her once again. If there was ever a time in her life when she was looking for the escape of slumber, it was now. Instead, the painful weight pressing against her breast threatened to suffocate her with every breath she drew.

Tossing aside her covers, she sat on the edge of the bed, her pride battling her conscience. If she rushed out to him, what could she possibly say? Hannah didn't know. That she was sorry? The words would have lacked conviction, and Riley would know immediately and would use it against her. She didn't want him to leave like this, but she knew of no way to end the tension and keep her pride intact.

It was while she was debating with herself that she heard the front door close. Hurriedly shoving her feet into her slippers, Hannah rushed into the living room.

NO COST! NO OBLIGATION TO BUY! NO PURCHASE NECESSARY!

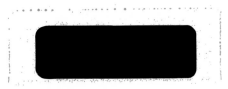

PLAY "LUCKY 7"
AND GET AS MANY AS SIX FREE GIFTS...

HOW TO PLAY:

1. With a coin, carefully scratch off the silver box at the right. This makes you eligible to receive one or more free books, and possibly other gifts, depending on what is revealed beneath the scratch-off area.

2. You'll receive brand-new Silhouette Special Edition® novels. When you return this card, we'll send you the books and gifts you qualify for *absolutely free!*

3. If we don't hear from you, every month we'll send you 6 additional novels to read and enjoy. You can return them and owe nothing but if you decide to keep them, you'll pay only $2.92* per book, a saving of 33¢ each off the cover price, plus only 69¢ delivery for the entire shipment!

4. When you join the Silhouette Reader Service™, you'll get our subscribers'-only newsletter, as well as additional free gifts from time to time, just for being a subscriber.

5. You must be completely satisfied. You may cancel at any time simply by sending us a note or a shipping statement marked ''cancel'' or by returning any shipment to us at our cost.

This lovely Victorian pewter-finish miniature is perfect for displaying a treasured photograph— and it's yours absolutely free—when you accept our no-risk offer.

Just scratch off the silver box with a coin.
Then check below to see which gifts you get.

YES! I have scratched off the silver box. Please send me all the gifts for which I qualify. I understand I am under no obligation to purchase any books, as explained on the opposite page.

335 CIS ADEW
(C-SIL-SE-10/91)

NAME

ADDRESS   APT.

CITY   PROV.   POSTAL CODE

7	7	7	WORTH FOUR FREE BOOKS, FREE VICTORIAN PICTURE FRAME AND MYSTERY BONUS
🍒	🍒	🍒	WORTH FOUR FREE BOOKS AND MYSTERY BONUS
●	●	●	WORTH FOUR FREE BOOKS
🔔	🔔	🍒	WORTH TWO FREE BOOKS

SILHOUETTE "NO RISK" GUARANTEE
- You're not required to buy a single book—ever!
- You must be completely satisfied or you may cancel at any time simply by sending us a note or a shipping statement marked "cancel" or by returning any shipment to us at our cost. Either way, you will receive no more books; you'll have no obligation to buy.
- The free books and gifts you receive from this "Lucky 7" offer remain yours to keep no matter what you decide.

If offer card is missing, write to:
Silhouette Reader Service, P.O. Box 609, Fort Erie, Ontario L2A 5X3

Business Reply Mail

No Postage Stamp Necessary if Mailed in Canada

Postage will be paid by

SILHOUETTE READER SERVICE
PO BOX 609
FORT ERIE, ONT.
L2A 9Z9

DETACH AND MAIL CARD TODAY

She reached the front window and parted the drapes in time to watch Riley climb into his friend Burt's battered blue pickup. Burt must have said something to Riley about seeing her at the window, because Riley's gaze reluctantly returned to the house.

Her heart demanded that she do something. Raise her hand in a gesture of farewell. Press her fingers to her lips in an effort to let him know he'd be missed. Something.

Hannah, however, did none of those things. Unshed tears burned her eyes, and still she stood there, wanting to blame him, blame herself for ever having agreed to this farce of a marriage. No more than a few seconds passed before the pickup pulled away and the opportunity was lost.

Two weeks into the training cruise, Riley was convinced he was the biggest heel who'd ever walked the face of the earth. If he'd plotted the ruin of his marriage, he couldn't have done it with any more expediency.

He'd wanted to talk over their problems with her before he shipped out, but a man has his pride. Everything he'd done or tried to do, she mistrusted. Okay, so he'd made a mistake by not telling her he had orders for the training cruise. Surely a man was allowed one small error in judgment. The least she could do was cut him some slack; he was new to this husband thing.

Not Hannah. Not his dear, sweet wife. She'd settle for nothing less than blood.

He'd made the mistake of viewing her as a timid soul. His wife, he soon learned, had more fight in her than some tigers. Misjudging her wasn't a mistake he planned on making again.

Personally, he didn't think withholding information from one's spouse was grounds for placing him in front of a firing squad. Hell, Hannah might as well shoot him for all the good he was doing the Navy. Riley had never felt emotionally lower in his life. It showed in his attitude and in everything he did. If this was the way matters went, he didn't know how the hell he was ever going to last. . . .

Six weeks had never seemed so long to Hannah. Two of those weeks had slipped by with sluggish disregard for her remorse. Not an hour passed when she wasn't thinking about Riley, regretting the way they'd spent their last few days together. They'd wasted those precious hours when so much could have been resolved. Instead she was left to wait day after day, week after week, for his return just so she could tell him how terribly sorry she was.

They were both so damned proud, so damned stubborn. Neither one of them had been willing to give an inch. Their stubborn pride was like a cancer that had eaten away at their better judgment. Both were at fault. Above everything else what was troubling her was the knowledge that if they continued to feed the mistrust and the doubts, in time it would destroy them. There was too much at stake to play such cruel games with each other: their child's future, their future.

When two people are married, Hannah reasoned, no matter what the circumstances, they must learn to make concessions. She'd been so willing to find fault with Riley, so willing to place the blame on . . .

Her. Riley openly acknowledged as much after a month of missing Hannah. Never again would he leave her behind with unsettled business between them. This time apart was pure torture because he'd been too damned stubborn to talk out his feelings. She accused him of not being a husband, and he'd found her lacking as a wife. Four long weeks had softened the tough hide of his arrogance, and he willingly admitted his mistake. He'd never been strong on relationships, preferring to live his life independent of others. Caring for another, putting her needs before his own was new to him, and he'd committed several blunders.

His damn pride was the crux of the problem. Hannah was carrying his child, and if she was a bit sensitive over some matters, the least he could do was to be a little more understanding.

His inexperience in dealing with the opposite sex posed other problems. Riley had never lived with a woman. He didn't know what to expect or how to act toward her. They both needed time to adjust to each other, make allowances. This infernal need to look for the bad instead of the good in their marriage was destined to doom them.

They'd made mistakes aplenty, but that was to be expected. They were both new to this marriage business. For years Hannah had assumed she'd be marrying Jerry Sanders, a seminary student. It was little wonder she was having a difficult time adjusting to life with a beer-drinking, poker-playing sailor.

Despite all that, they were physically attracted to each other. The child Hannah carried was testimony of that. The desire he felt for Hannah hadn't changed. Riley dreamed of the day she would willingly share his bed. Closing his eyes, he could almost smell the sweet scent of wildflowers that was hers alone. Dear sweet heaven, he missed her—more than he'd ever dreamed it was possible to miss anyone. He'd gotten impatient, wanting to make . . .

Love. Riley hadn't been unreasonable that night. What he'd said about a husband and wife sharing a bed had struck a raw nerve with her. Waiting to make love until she was more comfortable with their relationship had seemed like a good idea to Hannah when she had first mentioned it. She'd since altered her opinion. Mingled with the other regrets she was suffering since his deployment was the fact she had never spent the night in his bed. Riley wasn't a brute. He would never have forced her. His kisses were gentle and thorough, speaking more of commitment than passion. His touch, so warm and special, conveyed all the wonderful things a man and woman, a husband and wife, could expect in a loving, long-lasting relationship. He'd never pressured her or rushed her, and had been willing to grant her all the time she required. Her anger and pride had pushed him away, leaving her to brood six torturous weeks over what might have happened.

Never again, Hannah promised herself, would she send Riley off to sea the way she had this last time. When the USS *Atlantis* docked, he'd know how sorry . . .

He was. Riley was determined to make up for this rocky start with Hannah. Never again would he give her reason to doubt him. He was committed to her, committed to their marriage, committed to their child; and God willing, he fully intended to prove it.

"You're sure I don't look too fat?" Hannah asked, carefully watching Cheryl's reaction to the maternity top. There was no disguising the soft swell of her abdomen any longer. She'd changed in other ways, as well. Her thick brown hair fell past her shoulders, the ends curving under naturally. She'd pulled the thick waves away from her face, locking them into place with two gold barrettes.

"Oh, Hannah" Cheryl whispered, her voice lowering slightly, "you look so... beautiful."

Drawing in a deep breath, Hannah sincerely hoped her friend was right. The USS *Atlantis* was due to dock that afternoon, and she'd spent a good portion of the morning preparing herself and the house for this homecoming celebration with Riley.

Everything was ready, right down to the last-minute details. Thick steaks were marinating in the refrigerator; a homemade apple pie, Riley's favorite, was cooling on the kitchen countertop. A single bottle of beer was resting in a bucket of ice along with a soda for her. The table was set with a lace tablecloth and dishes. The centerpiece of carnations and candles was ready to be lit. The only thing needed to make the celebration complete was her husband.

Although she'd had six long weeks to work out what she planned to say to him, Hannah could think of no words that could adequately voice what was in her heart. She was anxious about this meeting, concerned, longing for everything to be as perfect as she could make it. She had missed him dreadfully and sought to prove how much by planning every aspect of his homecoming.

"I doubt that Riley will be able to keep his eyes off you," Cheryl told her. In the weeks that their husbands had been out to sea, the two women had become good friends. "His hands, either," Cheryl added. "Trust me, I know what I'm talking about. When Steve comes off a cruise, he can't leave me alone for two or three days straight. Not that I'm complaining, mind you."

Hannah found speaking so frankly about one's love life slightly embarrassing. Especially when her and Riley's marriage had yet to be consummated. Looking away from her friend, Hannah smoothed the maternity top over her hips in an effort to disguise her uneasiness.

"I'm showing now.... I wasn't when he left.... Do you think he'll notice?"

"No," Cheryl admitted, laughing. "He won't be able to take his eyes off those beautiful eyes of yours long enough to realize you're into maternity clothes now. Besides, Riley isn't going to be looking at your stomach."

"He'll notice." Of that Hannah was sure. "I can barely button my coat." She wasn't even six months pregnant, and already she felt like a blimp. The baby was so active now, no longer leaving her guessing when he chose to thrash about. The love she experienced for her unborn child overwhelmed her. Often when she sat, she flattened her hand over her abdomen, reaching out to her child, reassuring him. At night in bed, she spoke to him, telling him about his father and all that she was doing to prepare for his arrival. When she'd first suspected she might be pregnant, Hannah had tried to ignore the pregnancy, push it from her mind, unable to cope with the fruit of her night spent with Riley. Now, the baby dominated every thought and action.

The day was bright and cold, Hannah noted as they rode down to the waterfront. The nuclear-powered submarine was docked at Delta Pier, the largest of the three wharves at Bangor.

Other family members of the *Atlantis* crew were crowding the waiting area by the time Cheryl and Hannah arrived, although they were several minutes early. The air was thick with excitement and anticipation as wives and children anxiously looked for signs of their loved ones.

The early-December wind cut through the front of Hannah's coat, but she was too nervous to think about being cold. She stuffed her hands in her pockets and turned her back to the intermittent gusts.

As the men started down the gangplank, Hannah bit into her lower lip as the waiting crowd hurried forward to greet their husbands and fathers. A small pain gripped her stomach, but she ignored it, certain it must be nerves; certain everything would be all right the instant she caught sight of Riley.

"There's Steve!" Cheryl exclaimed, pointing out her tall, lanky husband, then waving the small bouquet of flowers she'd brought as a welcome-home gift. "Oh, damn, I'm going to cry," Cheryl added, smearing the moisture across her cheeks. "I hate it when I do this. His first look at me in weeks and I'll have mascara streaks running down my face. I'll look like a zebra."

Hannah smiled at her friend's joke, impatiently watching as the men of the *Atlantis* disembarked, eagerly searching through a sea of unfamiliar faces, hoping to find the one that was.

"Riley's three men behind Steve," Cheryl said, pointing him out to Hannah. It took her a moment to locate him, but when she did, her mind spun at a feverish pace, attempting to make sense of all that was happening to her. Her heart thudded. After all these weeks of torturous waiting, she was about to come face-to-face with the man who'd overshadowed every waking moment of her thoughts. All that she'd done, everything she'd bought, every place she'd gone, every person she'd talked with receded into the background as she focused her attention on Riley.

He paused at the top of the gangplank and seemed to be searching through the crowd. He didn't see her, Hannah knew, just by the way he squared his shoulders and shoved his duffel bag over his shoulder. There wasn't any reason he should expect her. The only means of communication between the submarine crew and family members during deployment was family grams, and Hannah hadn't known what those were until it was too late to send one. Even if she had known, she wasn't certain what she could have said in a few short lines.

As Riley stepped onto the pier, Hannah hurried forward, scooting around several other women and children. Riley seemed oblivious to the heartwarming scenes going on around him, determined to make it off the wharf as quickly as possible. She thought to call out to him, but her throat was so tight she would have choked on his name.

Riley stopped midstep when he saw her, his brow pleating into a look of surprise and wonder. The duffel bag slipped from his fingers seemingly without notice.

Hannah smiled and ran into his arms, closing her eyes as she savored the feel of his powerful arms when they surrounded her. He was warm, and even through several layers of clothing she could feel his heart pound against her own until it seemed that the two had merged and beat as one.

His hands were in her hair and his lips were searching out hers. His mouth was rough and urgent as he claimed her lips with a tender violence.

"Hannah . . . Oh, God. I'd hoped you'd come," he whispered between kisses. "But I didn't expect it."

"I'm sorry, so sorry for everything," she sobbed.

His mouth covered hers, halting her words. "Shh," he pleaded, kissing her face, her neck, bouncing his lips off hers as though he weren't certain even now that she was there with him and that she was actually in his arms.

Hannah had to pinch herself to know it was real. Nothing could have prepared her for the kaleidoscope of wild emotions that burst to life within her. It was as if she'd lain dormant the entire time Riley had been to sea. Only upon his return could she feel again, and feel she did: warm and loved and needed. Tears splashed down the side of her face.

"We'll talk later," Riley promised. "But for now let me kiss you."

"Yes," she cried, "yes." She slipped her arms around his neck, standing on her tiptoes as she nestled her face in the curve of his neck. For now there was no mired past, only the present, which felt incredibly right, incredibly good.

Several minutes sped past. It might have been hours, for all Hannah knew. Riley gently eased her away from him as he carefully studied her. His eyes widened when he noticed how nicely round her stomach had become. Silence stretched into silence.

Hannah pushed the knotted emotion from her throat enough to be able to speak normally. "As you can see, I've been eating well."

His gaze rested on the strained buttons of her coat, and a gloating, happy smile curved up the corners of his mouth. "How are you feeling?"

She grinned. "Never better."

"And Junior?"

"He's growing like a weed. I...I think we might have a soccer champion on our hands."

Riley laughed outright. "So he's doing his share of kicking these days?"

Hannah nodded. "You'll be able to feel him now."

"Good. I'll look forward to doing exactly that." He reached for his duffel bag, tossing it over his shoulder with familiar ease. "Shall we go home, my love?" he asked, draping his free arm over her shoulders.

Hannah agreed with a quick nod of her head. Home. Their home. It was where she belonged. Where Riley belonged. The two of them together.

Chapter Eight

In all his years of military life, Riley had never experienced a homecoming more profound. There'd never been anyone waiting at the wharf to greet him before. No wife to rush forward and run into his waiting arms. No one to shout with joy and excitement when he stepped down the gangplank.

Until this day, Riley never realized how much he'd missed. His heart felt full, brimming over with a happiness, a contentment that radiated from deep within his soul.

He couldn't stop staring at Hannah as they drove back to the house. She'd changed, and the transformation left him dumbfounded. Her hair was different—longer, thicker, shinier. She wore it pinned up, away from her face, exposing high, prominent cheekbones and gray eyes so beautiful it was like staring into a darkening winter sky. Her color was back, her cheeks rosy and her eyes clear and bright.

The beauty he saw in her was enough to steal his breath. He struggled for words, wanting her to know what was in his heart; but a hard lump had formed in his throat and it was impossible to speak. He slowed his breathing and swallowed, hoping to ease the pressure so he could say the things he wanted, but for then it was impossible. There was so much he longed to tell her, so much he wanted to explain. He would in time, when he could say it without trembling like a schoolboy.

He'd been starved for the sight of her, rushing through the crowds along the wharf in his eagerness to hurry home, praying she'd still be there, praying she could find it in her heart to forgive him, praying she'd be willing to put the ugly past behind them and start anew. He hadn't dared to hope she'd be at Delta Pier waiting for him with the other wives and families.

Riley parked in front of the house and felt its welcome penetrate him like a hot bath on the coldest day of the year; warmth, love and acceptance awaited him inside. He climbed out of the car, went around to the passenger side and opened the door for Hannah. Together they walked into their home, shutting out the winter.

Riley was struck almost immediately by the changes that greeted him. The house had been living quarters before he was deployed; he returned to a home. It took him a few minutes to ascertain the differences. First he noticed a bright orange, gold and bronze afghan draped over the back of the sofa, with matching pillows tucked at the corners. A large oak rocking chair rested between his recliner and the end table. This, too, was new. But by far the most prominent addition was a large oil painting hanging on the wall above the fireplace. His gaze had been drawn to it almost immediately.

"I wondered if you'd notice that," Hannah said shyly.

"It's beautiful." Rolling hills of blooming blue and gold wildflowers waving in the wind beneath a blue summer sky. Fluffy clouds skirted the horizon. It must have cost a fortune, but Riley didn't care how much she'd spent on it. Wildflowers were damn special to him.

"I'm so pleased you think so," Hannah responded happily, looping her arm around his and pressing her head to his shoulder.

"Where'd you ever find it?"

She paused. "I didn't exactly find it."

"Oh?" He dropped his duffel bag and was removing his coat.

"I painted it myself."

Riley went still, stunned by the richness of her talent. "I didn't realize you painted."

"I didn't, either," she returned with a light, slightly embarrassed laugh. "It was something I'd always longed to do, but had never had the time. I signed up for classes while you were away. Come," she said, her voice bubbling with excitement, "there's something I want to show you." She took him by the hand and led him through the kitchen and down the hallway to the bedrooms.

She opened her door, stepped briefly inside to turn on the light, then stood back proudly for him to see.

Riley glanced inside and turned to his wife, awestruck. "You painted this?" She'd turned one entire wall into a mural for the baby. A long-necked giraffe nibbled foliage from a bright green apple tree heavy

with luscious fruit. In the background two lambs frol-
icked along a hillside, chasing butterflies.

She nodded, smiling broadly. "Do you think Junior
will like it?"

"He'll love it."

"Cheryl and I found this in a garage sale last weekend," she went on, excitement creeping into her voice
as she moved across the room to the closet, opening the
door and retrieving a bassinet. She looked up at him
expectantly.

The white wicker bed seemed more suited to a little
girl's dolls than an infant. "Junior will fit in there?"

"For about three months. Then we'll need a crib. I've
been pricing them," she said as her eyes rose steadily to
his. "Be prepared. I was shocked by how expensive they
are, but," she added quickly, "we might be able to find
a used one that's far more reasonable."

Riley nodded, barely hearing her. His attention was
caught by the stack of tiny clothes and blankets Hannah had put inside the bassinet. He held up one impossibly small T-shirt, amazed that any human could ever
be so tiny.

"I've been picking up a few things for the baby every
paycheck," Hannah explained, running her palm across
the top of the freshly folded cotton diapers.

Riley couldn't understand the hesitation in her voice,
as though she feared he'd disapprove of her spending
his money. He lifted his gaze to connect with hers.

"I...took a part-time job as a legal assistant. I work
fewer than twenty hours a week," she ventured halt-
ingly. "I hope you don't mind."

"Of course not. I shouldn't have been so dictatorial
before. You know far better than I how much you can
and can't do."

She seemed relieved at that, as though she'd been dreading telling him about her part-time employment.

"We'll buy a new crib," Riley stated decisively and, unable to resist, he threaded his fingers through the hair at her temple and gently kissed her there.

She smiled, her eyes as warm as fresh honey. "I was thinking we should...since we'll probably be using it again a few years down the road."

For Riley, the implication was like a silken caress. In time there would be other children.

"Oh," she said excitedly, rushing toward her dresser drawer, "I nearly forgot." She opened the top drawer and pulled out a piece of paper and handed it to Riley, enchanting him with her smile. He had trouble dragging his gaze away from her. He swore he'd never seen anyone so beautiful.

When he could, he looked at the slip of paper for several moments, puzzled by the series of dark circular lines that followed no pattern that he could discern. To him it resembled a sonar reading. "What is it?"

Hannah's sweet, delicate laugh filled the room. "Not what! He...or she. That's Junior."

"Junior?" Riley was amazed.

"It's an ultrasound. The doctor took it on my last visit. See," she told him, pointing out the vague outline of the baby's head and spine. "Oftentimes they can determine the sex of the baby by these pictures."

"And?" He didn't bother to disguise his curiosity.

"Junior was sleeping with his back to us so we can't be sure. Dr. Underwood will probably do another one in a few months."

"We might well be having a daughter, you know," he said, returning to the bassinet and holding up a pale blue sleeper. Nearly everything Hannah had purchased was geared for a boy. For some odd reason, the realization pleased him immensely. Repeatedly he'd told himself the sex of their child didn't matter; but deep down, he longed for a son, although he hadn't admitted it even to himself.

"I'm prepared for that." Her face lit up with pleasure as she dug through the small pile of clothes until she found a frilly pink dress with lace trim. "I couldn't resist this. Isn't it adorable?"

Riley nodded, thinking he'd never seen anyone more adorable than Hannah. Her eyes widened and her gaze shot to Riley. "He's kicking now. Do you want to feel?"

His nod was eager. Sitting down on the edge of the mattress, he flattened both hands against the soft swell of her stomach.

"You might not be able to feel him through all these clothes," she said, pushing aside her pretty green top. Her skin was warm and as smooth as silk as she gripped him by the wrist and pressed his palm just below the elastic waistband of her wool slacks. "Here," she whispered as though she feared she'd disturb their child, sliding Riley's hand to the right. "He's kicking now. Can you feel?"

Riley closed his eyes, concentrating, then with a shrug of disappointment, shook his head. "Not yet."

"You will soon."

He nodded, brushed his lips over the distended roundness at her waistline and then reluctantly righted her clothes. Hannah sighed softly and wrapped her arms around his head, gently laying her cheek over his crown. "Junior and I have missed you so much."

"I missed you, too," he murmured, wrapping his arms around her waist and hugging her close. He shut his eyes, savoring her softness, drinking it in the way a man dying of thirst swallows down a glass of cool, clear water.

They held each other for several moments, swaddled in tenderness and appreciation for what they'd found, for what they'd both come so close to destroying. For the love he'd feared would forever escape him.

Yes, love, Riley realized. He hadn't wanted to admit it until now, but he did love Hannah. He knew so little of the emotion, his acquaintance with it was so brief, that he hadn't recognized what should have been obvious. Some part of him had known it the night they'd met. It should have been obvious later when he spent so much frustrated effort on locating her again, tearing up the city in a futile attempt to find her.

Her hands were in his hair, gently fingering his nape. "Are you hungry?" she asked after a while.

Riley tried to speak, but the words didn't come. His heart, his throat, were too full, so he simply nodded and with a good deal of reluctance released her.

"I've got dinner all planned," she announced happily. "Steak, twice-baked potatoes, fresh green beans with almond bits, and salad."

"It sounds delicious."

"I wanted to bake homemade rolls, but I ran out of time. I did get an apple pie made."

He felt like laughing for no reason and knew she was watching him, hoping he wasn't disappointed. "Apple pie is my favorite."

"I thought it might be."

Hand in hand, they strolled into the kitchen. They'd moved through it earlier, but Riley hadn't had time to notice everything Hannah had done to prepare for this homecoming. His heart swelled with appreciation as he saw the table and centerpiece.

"Can I do anything to help?"

Hannah shook her head and reached for an oven mitt. "No, thanks, I've got everything under control. It'll only take me a few minutes to cook the steaks."

"What about the mail?"

"I...opened some of it—what looked like bills—and paid those when your check arrived. The rest I set on top of your dresser."

He nodded, kissed her cheek and headed for his bedroom.

As she'd promised, dinner was ready in only a few minutes. Riley couldn't remember a meal he enjoyed more. The steak, juicy and succulent, was cooked to perfection. The salad, crammed full of sliced fresh vegetables was a small work of art. The piecrust seemed to melt in his mouth. He complimented her again and again. Hannah blushed with pleasure each time.

Sweet promise filled Riley's heart. Later, perhaps this very night, he told himself, he'd approach her about sleeping in his room. He wouldn't pressure her into anything physical, he promised himself. He'd go out of his way to be sure she understood that he'd be content to hold her in his arms. When she was ready for lovemaking, she should let him know. They'd go slow and easy, and she could write her own ticket as far as the physical part of their marriage went. It sounded reasonable, and he felt good about it, waiting for just the right moment to make the suggestion.

The right moment never came.

About halfway through their dinner something changed. For the life of him, Riley didn't know what. Hannah grew quiet. One moment she was chattering like a magpie and the next she went still and silent. Not understanding what was happening, Riley made up for the lack of conversation, conscious of the abrupt change in her mood the entire time he was speaking. In an effort to cover the uncomfortable silence he told the details of what he was allowed to relate about the cruise and his job, filling in the everyday particulars of his life aboard the nuclear-powered submarine. She seemed genuinely interested in what he described, and asked questions, but he couldn't shake the feeling he'd said or done something terribly wrong.

After dinner she quickly washed up the dishes, refusing his help. "I'm going to bed now," she announced stiffly, then disappeared into her bedroom, closing the door.

Riley was left standing in the kitchen, stunned. Mentally he retraced everything that had passed between them for something, anything that might offend her. He could think of nothing. Not one damn thing. An altar boy couldn't have faulted his behavior. Hell, he was so much in love with her he would have cut out his tongue rather than hurt her.

Walking into the living room, Riley sat in his chair and reached for the evening paper. He scanned the headlines three times without comprehending a word of what he was reading.

Ten minutes, he decided. He'd give her ten minutes to come to her senses, and if she didn't, then he was going in after her. He'd demand to know what the hell he'd done that was so terrible, if it came to that.

The frustration ate at him like acid. Usually, when he arrived home from any length of time at sea, he stopped in at the apartment just long enough to drop off his duffel bag and change clothes. Then he'd meet up with his friends and they'd hit the streets and celebrate. This time, not once, from the moment he'd stepped off the *Atlantis,* had he considered leaving Hannah.

His own ten-minute deadline passed. Tossing aside the evening paper, Riley braced his elbows on his knees and rubbed his hands over his face. So this was what it meant to be married, Riley mused, sighing heavily. To hand a woman his heart and his soul and then have her trample upon it for some imagined wrong.

He knew what she wanted. He hadn't been fooled by her sweet, docile ways. Everything she'd said and done had been computed to convince him of his wrongs. Now she was looking for him to meekly follow her into the bedroom and beg her forgiveness.

Like hell. If he'd committed some terrible crime, then she'd have to tell him face-to-face instead of hiding herself away in her bedroom, waiting for him to come and grovel at her feet. He'd gladly suffer her indignation before he'd lower himself to that.

Riley's heart beat high in his throat as he soared to his feet. It would serve her right if he were to disappear, leave her to wonder and fret while he stayed out half the night, carousing with his friends.

He toyed with the idea, fueling it with angry frustration, when his gaze happened upon the oil painting above the fireplace. His breath came in jagged bursts as he recalled the pride and eagerness that had flashed from her eyes as she'd studied his reaction, so eager for his approval.

Had everything she'd said and done been calculated to bring him to his knees? Riley found it hard to believe. Difficult to fathom. Hannah knew little of subterfuge.

He stepped over to the sofa, his steps slow and measured. Picking up the crocheted pillow, he ran his hands over the surface, admiring Hannah's work. His thoughts were in turmoil, torn between what his heart was saying and what his head was shouting.

Hannah could never love anyone like him. He was too crude, too coarse for someone as gentle and sweet as a preacher's daughter.

Anger and bitterness swelled up inside him, nearly choking off his breath. Venting his frustration, he bunched up the soft pillow in his hands and tossed it back down to the sofa with a fiery vengeance.

So that was love! he decided, feeling neglected and abused, irritated with himself for peeling open the gates of his heart. The emptiness inside him had never seemed more hollow. He was left vulnerable and alone, and his pride gave him damn little solace.

He'd go to her, he determined, if that was what it took. Have this out, once and for all.

Two steps into the kitchen, he found Hannah. Her hands were gripping her stomach, and when she glanced up at him he found tears in her eyes. He'd never viewed such stark terror in anyone.

"Riley," she moaned, reaching out to him, "something's wrong. I'm losing the baby!"

Chapter Nine

Riley's heart dropped to his knees. Without a word he moved forward and swung Hannah into his arms. Not stopping for his coat or anything else he rushed out the front door, slamming it closed with his foot.

Panic clawed at him like a shark's jaws, but for Hannah's sake, he dared not reveal his fear. One look at her ashen features told him she was frightened half out of her mind and a hairbreadth from hysteria.

Once she was safely deposited in the front seat, he raced around the car, jumped inside and started the engine. The tires squealed as he roared down the street, leaving a cloud of black smoke in his wake.

"We're about ten minutes away from the hospital," he said, praying he was able to keep the fear and trembling out of his voice.

"Hurry, please hurry," she begged.

Hannah bit into her lower lip and turned her head away from him, pressing her hands against her stomach, determined to hold on tightly enough to save their child.

"I don't want to lose my baby," she sobbed. "Oh, Riley, I love him so much." She was in terrible pain, he realized. Her breath came in quick rushes, each accompanied by a small animallike cry. His fears became rampant as he worried that she might hyperventilate.

Riley pulled into the emergency entrance at the hospital in record time and slammed on the brakes. Leaping out of the car, he didn't even bother to close his door as he sprinted around to Hannah's side. Scooping her up in his arms, he ran toward the double glass doors that automatically flew open for him.

"My wife!" he shouted when a physician approached. "She's having a miscarriage." An orderly rushed forward with a gurney, and Riley laid Hannah on it, gripping her hand as they raced down the wide corridor.

Once they were inside a cubicle, the emergency-room staff pulled closed the curtain surrounding the bed. The physician, calm and professional, patted Riley on the shoulder. "It'd be best, son, if you waited outside."

Riley looked to Hannah for confirmation, but her eyes were tightly closed and her lips were moving and he knew she was lost in a world of pain and prayer.

"The baby?" Riley pleaded.

"I'll do everything I can," the stocky man vowed. "I promise you." His hands gently pushed Riley from the room.

Feeling helpless and full of despair, Riley staggered down the hall, his heart pounding so loudly it stormed in his ears. He was trembling so badly he had to sit down. The waiting room was deserted, and he mechanically lowered himself into a molded plastic chair.

Over the years, Riley had routinely faced danger. Twice he'd stared death in the face and hadn't flinched. Death had no grip on him, nothing to blackmail him into submission. Whether he lived or died was in the hands of the fates, and he hadn't particularly cared one way or the other.

Now the bitter taste of fear filled his mouth, swamping his senses with dread that went soul-deep. His breathing turned shallow and he balled his fists, clenching and unclenching them as his heart roared louder than a jet engine.

Riley wanted this child more than he'd ever realized. He hadn't given much thought to Hannah's pregnancy while he'd been at sea. He'd been too concerned about his relationship with his wife to think much about their child. Although Hannah's pregnancy had greatly impacted on his life, Riley had experienced no deep emotion concerning their baby. "Junior" hadn't seemed real to him.

It wasn't that way any longer. Riley had touched the bed where his son or daughter would sleep, had held the T-shirt that would warm his or her body. He'd viewed a scrambled photograph, a progress report of his baby's physical development, and had seen for himself the perfection of this young life. His own hand had pressed against Hannah's womb, communicating his love to his unborn infant.

Love Junior he did, with a weight that crushed him. A weight so crippling that tremors of fear pulsed through his body as he waited in agony. Waited for some word, some sign of what was happening behind closed doors. Of what was happening to Hannah, happening to Junior, happening to himself.

Whom did one plead with in instances such as this? Fate? Riley didn't know. Fate had always been a joker to him, playing cruel pranks on him from the time he was born. He wasn't about to plea-bargain with lady luck.

The stark terror he'd read in Hannah's eyes returned to haunt him. He felt so damn helpless. Her desperation was as keen as his own. Her fear and pain had been alive in her eyes. And there hadn't been a damn thing he could do. The last he'd seen before he was forced out of the emergency room was her lips moving in silent, desperate prayer.

God, Riley decided. One spoke with God when there was nowhere else to turn. He wasn't a man accustomed to religion. There'd never been anything or anyone that he'd needed or wanted badly enough to risk going before the Almighty.

Until now.

He rose awkwardly to his feet, standing as he would before a superior officer. His shoulders were back, his eyes straight ahead, his hands dangling loosely at his sides.

A thick tightness gripped his throat as words escaped him. It didn't seem right, somehow, to make so important a request without offering something in return. His thoughts stampeded ahead to what he might possibly have to bargain with, but there was nothing. Nothing.

Unable to hold still, Riley started pacing, his mind and his heart confused. "I don't know why you sent Hannah into my life," he whispered. "But thank you."

He felt a little less inept once he started talking. "I promise you I'll be a good husband to her.... I'm probably going to need some help with that." His intentions had always been good, but he didn't know much about the way women thought, so if God was willing to give him a few pointers along the way, then Riley would be more than happy to receive them.

Now that he'd breached the barrier of his own self-consciousness, Riley found it wasn't so difficult to speak his mind.

"I'm not the kind of man who finds it easy to ask for something," he began again. "It seems wrong to come to You with a request and not be able to give something back in return. It's about Hannah, God, and Junior. I can't do a thing for either of them. It's out of my hands entirely. If you'll take care of them both, I'll tell you what—I'll start attending church services with Hannah." It was the best he could do. Heaven knew that would be sacrifice enough for someone who'd only darkened a church door for weddings and funerals. Twice now, she'd invited him to come with her. That sort of thing seemed important to his wife. But then Riley should have expected that; after all, she was a preacher's daughter.

"If you can think of anything better, let me know," he ended, then in afterthought added, "Amen."

Riley felt a little better after that. He sat back down, analyzing the events of the afternoon. It didn't take long for him to realize Hannah must have started feeling bad sometime during their dinner. She hadn't said anything to him. Nothing. He continued to sort through his thoughts, adding up the obvious, when the physician approached.

Riley rose slowly to his feet, his heart beating so hard his rib cage ached. "How is she?"

The physician smiled. "Fine. The baby, too."

The wild sense of relief Riley experienced was beyond words. He went weak with it.

"You can go see her now, if you like."

"Thank you, sir," he said, reaching for the man's hand and pumping it several times. He started toward the cubicle when the corpsman stopped him.

"Hey, is that car yours? You're going to have to move it."

He nodded, ignored him and raced back to the small examining room where they'd taken Hannah.

Hannah felt like such a fool. She'd been convinced she was losing the baby, and the fear had struck terror in her heart. In fact, she'd been suffering from a bad case of indigestion.

For days she'd been anxiously waiting for Riley's return. They'd parted in anger, and she had no way of knowing what his mood would be once he returned. After the horrible way they'd treated each other, he might wish to end their marriage. The pains had started early that afternoon, long before she'd had anything to eat—small, barely distinguishable cramps that she'd dismissed as nerves, which in fact they were.

It was later, during dinner, that the sharp, hard, contractionlike spasms had started. Not knowing what they were, she'd tried to ignore them, hide them from Riley, hoping they'd go away. Instead they'd grown more intense while she was doing the dishes. Not wanting to alarm her husband, she'd excused herself as soon as she could and gone into her bedroom. If she lay down and rested, she'd reasoned, it might help to ease the pain.

Instead the cramps had grown steadily worse, so piercing and constant that she'd convinced herself she was suffering a miscarriage. Her fear and panic had added to her physical distress—at least that was the doctor's explanation. Nevertheless she felt like such an idiot, frightening Riley the way she had. He'd driven like a madman in his rush to get her to the hospital, and it had been for naught.

"Hannah?" Riley pulled back the white curtain and stepped inside. How pale he looked, colorless and stricken as if he'd aged ten years in the last thirty minutes.

She held her arms out to him, and he hastened to her side, gathering her in his embrace and holding her so tightly against him that he nearly stole her breath.

"You're all right?" he asked, brushing the hair away from her face, examining her as though he could read in her eyes everything he needed to know.

She blushed and nodded. "The baby, too."

He grinned at that. "I heard." He pulled a chair to her bedside and sat down. He took hold of her hand, gripped it in both his own and pressed it to his cheek. "Tell me what happened."

"I... I'm not exactly sure. I started feeling pains earlier this afternoon."

"Why didn't you say something? I'm your husband—you should have told me." He sounded so angry, and with good reason, she supposed; but that didn't restrain the tears from flooding her eyes, brimming and spilling down her face.

"I'm sorry," he added quickly, once he viewed her distress. "I didn't mean to shout. It's just that..."

"I'm the one who's sorry," she said between sniffles. "I feel just dreadful putting everyone through this trouble for. . . for a case of nerves."

"Nerves," Riley bellowed loud enough to shake the windows. He slumped back down into the chair and rubbed his hand down his face. "Nerves," he repeated, as if he hadn't heard her correctly the first time.

"Hey, buddy," the corpsman said, walking abruptly into the room, "I told you before, you're going to have to move your car. You're blocking the roadway."

Riley looked at him as though seeing a ghost, then turned back to Hannah. "Are they going to let you come home?"

She nodded eagerly. "The doctor gave me something to settle my stomach, but he wants to check me in another ten minutes and see how I'm feeling."

"You gonna move that car? Or are you going to force us to tow it away?"

"I'll move it," Riley answered without looking at the impatient corpsman. Riley paused long enough to kiss Hannah, shook his head and then turned and walked away.

She might have imagined it—in fact Hannah was sure she had—but as her husband started out the door, she thought she'd heard him mumble something about indigestion and God not playing fair.

Sunday morning the alarm woke Hannah. She reached out, turned off the buzzer and pulled the blankets over her shoulders, wrapping them around her.

Three days had passed since her episode at the hospital, and she still hadn't forgiven herself for creating such a terrible fuss and alarming Riley the way she had.

He'd taken it all in good humor, teasing her about it, but always in fun, being careful not to embarrass her.

They were much more at ease with each other now. The terrible tension that had existed between them the first awkward weeks of their marriage had disappeared.

As she lay in bed, savoring the warmth, she mulled over the strange events of the past few days. Riley had been so gentle with her, solicitous, making few demands on her.

Too few.

She'd hoped once he'd returned from sea duty that he'd say something or make some token gesture toward inviting her into his bed.

Thus far it hadn't happened. If Hannah were more worldly or a bit more sophisticated, she would have approached him herself. But she'd hoped her husband would make it apparent that he wanted the two of them sharing a bed. Perhaps she'd ruined everything early on when he'd asked her to make love and she'd callously rejected him. A hundred times since, Hannah had regretted it. She'd been so foolish. Her pride was hurting them both.

Perhaps Riley, disgusted by her attitude, didn't intend to ask her again. Perhaps he was waiting for her to voluntarily come to him. She mulled over the thought several moments, wondering how she'd go about it. Should she broach the subject herself? Hannah didn't know how she'd do it without becoming flustered and red-faced.

While he'd been at sea, she'd often gone shopping with Cheryl. One Saturday, a week before the men were due home, the two had gone into a lingerie shop at the Kitsap Mall. Cheryl had bought a skimpy black nightie with a fur hem. She'd joked that the hem was there to keep her neck warm.

While they'd been in the shop, a lovely peach-colored silk gown had caught Hannah's eye. Cheryl had convinced Hannah it was perfect with her coloring, and with a little encouragement from the saleslady, Hannah had purchased the gown.

The night before, she'd trifled with the idea of putting it on for Riley. She hadn't, caving in to her insecurities instead, convinced her pregnancy was too advanced to be sexy.

Sexy. She smiled to herself. Women who were nearly six months pregnant weren't seductive looking no matter what they wore to entice their husbands. No, the peach gown wouldn't work at this late date. She needed something else—something that would convince her husband she wanted him. Only she wasn't sure what.

"Hannah?" Riley knocked politely at her door. "Are you up?"

"Not yet," she answered, surprised that he was.

"You'd best hurry or you'll be late for church."

He was right, although she hated to crawl out of a toasty bed. She didn't have time to dally this Sunday. After Riley had gone to sea, she'd joined the church choir and had been asked to sing a solo for the first service.

With a limited wardrobe to choose from, Hannah shed her nightclothes and slipped the olive-green street-length dress over her head and adjusted the waistband. In another couple of weeks, she wouldn't be able to wear this one, either. Sighing, she ambled out to the kitchen, pleasantly surprised to find the coffee brewed and waiting for her.

"You're up bright and early," she said to her husband, bringing down a mug.

He nodded, more interested in reading the Sunday paper than conversing with her. Hannah watered down her coffee with a generous portion of milk, then carried it into the bathroom with her while she worked her hair into a French plait.

When she'd finished, she went back into her bedroom for her coat. Normally she fixed herself something small to eat—a piece of toast with a piece of fruit—but she didn't want anything to coat her vocal cords before she sang.

Buttoning up her coat, she reached for her purse, prepared to leave the house. As she walked through the living room, Riley set aside the morning paper and stood. He was dressed in slacks and a sweater.

"You ready?" he asked.

"Yes." Hannah wasn't sure she understood. It wasn't until they were in the car that it dawned on her that Riley meant to attend the church service with her.

His wife continued to amaze Riley. He'd been taken by surprise when she had stood in the middle of the church service, following the communion meditation, and approached the piano. She slipped onto the mahogany bench and skillfully ran her fingertips over the keyboard. Riley hadn't had a clue she could sing, any more than he'd been aware that she possessed such extraordinary talent at the piano. As he'd sat back and listened to her hauntingly beautiful voice, his heart had filled with a renewed sense of appreciation for the incredibly gifted woman he'd married. The poignant words of the song had touched him in ways that were completely foreign, and he'd sat for several moments afterward, pondering their meaning.

Following the worship service, he'd suggested they go out to breakfast.

"Why didn't you tell me you could sing like that?"

Hannah finished spreading jelly on her toast before she answered. "You never asked."

He frowned and reached for the syrup. "How long have you been playing the piano?"

She shrugged. "I started lessons when I was about six, maybe seven. I don't remember. My mother was the pianist for the church until she died, and I took over for her."

"I had no idea you were so gifted."

"Oh, Riley. Honestly, you make it sound like I'm another Chopin or something."

"You're damn good. Have you ever thought of doing anything with your music?"

She smiled sweetly up at him and shook her head. "Heavens no. I played the piano because, well, because it was expected of me. Don't misunderstand me. I love it—in fact I miss it quite a lot. But music isn't my life."

Riley thought about this and nodded when the waitress came by with the coffeepot to refill his cup. "Are there any other talents you possess that I don't know about?"

Hannah mulled that over and shrugged once more. "I'm quite a good seamstress."

"Where's your sewing machine?"

"I left it at my father's house when we . . . married. I was hoping to pick it up over Christmas. You might have noticed the stack of material I've been buying lately. It's on the floor in the bedroom. I've got to do something about clothes."

"Buy yourself anything you want," he offered, not understanding why she hadn't before now. It was apparent she was growing out of almost everything she owned.

"It's much cheaper to make them, and I enjoy it."

"Will you have the time?"

"Yes, Mr. Worrywart."

She grinned, and Riley swore he could drown in her eyes. She'd smile, and his heart would melt. She had the uncanny talent for making him feel like a schoolboy— flustered and inexperienced. There wasn't anything he wouldn't do for her. He'd practically given up drinking, and he hadn't even noticed. With the exception of Steve, he was losing touch with his friends. There wasn't anyone he'd rather spend time with than Hannah.

There were problems, however. He wasn't keen on them maintaining separate bedrooms. He wanted her sleeping by his side. Damn it all to hell, that was where she belonged. He just hadn't figured out how he was going to get her there. The first night he'd been home, she'd been rummy with the medication the doctor had given her and had fallen asleep on the return trip from the hospital. The following afternoon he'd been assigned duty and she was in bed asleep by the time he arrived home. Asleep in her own bed.

"If it's all right with you, I thought we'd leave for Seattle about two o'clock Christmas Eve," she said, interrupting his thoughts.

"Sure," Riley answered, cutting a fat link sausage with the side of his fork. "That'll be fine."

"Dad's anxious to see us both. I've missed him."

Riley nodded, preoccupied. "It might be a good idea if we go shopping soon for a crib and whatever else we're going to need."

"Already?"

"I'd like to have everything set up for the baby before the middle of January."

"Why?" She stopped eating, setting her fork down as she studied him.

The apprehension in her eyes ate at him like battery acid. "I'll be away again. This time until April."

She swallowed tightly. "The baby's due the middle of March."

"I know. I won't be here, Hannah. I'd give anything to be with you, but I can't."

"I . . . know," she admitted reluctantly. "But don't worry, I'll be fine. Cheryl volunteered to be my birthing partner . . . but I wish it could be you."

"I wish it could be, too." More than she'd ever know, but it wouldn't do any good to stew about it. Several of his peers had become first-time fathers while out at sea. He'd do it, too, although it didn't sit right with him to have Hannah go through the delivery and birth without him there.

"Would you like to do some Christmas shopping this afternoon?" Riley asked, hoping to lighten the mood.

Her nod was eager. "I love Christmas. I guess I'm just a little kid at heart."

"We all are when it comes to receiving presents," Riley murmured. Until recently he hadn't a clue what he should buy for Hannah, but he'd inadvertently stumbled upon the perfect gift for his wife. Now, all he had to do was keep it a secret for the next three weeks.

* * *

"Dad!" Hannah called out as she stepped into her childhood home, feeling engulfed in its warmth and welcome. "We're here."

George Raymond stepped out from the den, a pair of wire-rimmed glasses perched on the end of his nose. He wore slacks, a shirt and the old gray wool sweater she'd knitted for him several years back. His smile was broad and automatic as he spied Hannah and Riley just inside the front door.

"Welcome, welcome," he greeted, holding open his arms. He gave Hannah an enthusiastic hug and exchanged hearty handshakes with Riley.

"Let me get a good look at you," her father said excitedly, stepping back to examine her.

Hannah couldn't help but blush. She removed her coat and hung it in the hall closet, self-conscious the whole time of how prominent her pregnancy was becoming. A little nervous, as well, knowing she'd be confronting members of her father's congregation. It wouldn't take long for anyone to realize she'd been several months pregnant when she married Riley.

"I'm getting so fat," she murmured, resting her hands on her bulging stomach.

"I don't believe I've ever seen you more beautiful," he told her thoughtfully. "My goodness, girl! You look more like your mother every day."

"Where would you like me to put these things?" Riley asked. He'd returned to the car and had carted back an armload of goods Hannah had insisted they bring.

"Oh, my goodness, I forgot about the pies. In here," she said, directing Riley toward the kitchen.

He followed her into the country-style kitchen and set the flat boxes that contained the pumpkin and apple pies on the countertop. "I swear you packed enough food to feed an army," he chastised. But she noted he wasn't complaining too loudly since she'd baked the apple pie especially for him.

"Dad wouldn't have known what to have ready," she explained for the sixth time. She'd gone grocery shopping the day before, picking up everything they'd need for Christmas dinner. Her father had relied on her to cook the main meal at Christmas for so many years, she doubted that he knew what to have on hand. Rather than leave it to chance, she'd brought everything with her, much to Riley's chagrin.

As Riley and her father carried everything inside, she sorted through the grocery sacks, tucking several items inside the cupboards.

It felt good to be home again, Hannah mused. She felt keenly the warmth of her father's welcome, although she'd had mixed feelings about this visit for several weeks.

Oh, she was pleased to see her father again. They'd spoken regularly on the phone, taking turns contacting each other, and he'd been the one to suggest she and Riley make the two-hour trip to Seattle for the Christmas holiday.

Hannah had agreed without giving the invitation a second thought. It wasn't until much later that she realized it would be difficult to hide her pregnancy. Although most everyone in her father's congregation was kind and loving, there were sure to be some who'd feel it was their God-given duty to point out that she'd married much too quickly and quietly after losing Jerry; and when they noticed her stomach, they'd know why.

Jerry.

Funny, she hadn't thought about her late fiancé in weeks. Although he was never far from her mind, the love she felt for him seemed far removed from the life she shared with Riley now. Jerry would always be someone special in her life and in her heart, but he was gone. Without her ever realizing it, the emptiness she'd experienced in the grief-filled weeks following his death had come to be filled with the love that had flourished for Riley and their child.

Even so, someone was bound to mention Jerry during her visit, and she wasn't sure how Riley would react when it happened.

The weeks since his return from the training cruise had been idyllic—so perfect that she didn't want to risk ruining the fragile peace between them.

"Hannah, my goodness!" her father called out from the living room. "So many gifts."

She left the kitchen to find Riley bent under the Christmas tree, unloading two shopping bags filled with brightly wrapped gifts.

"Ho, ho, ho," he teased, grinning up at her.

"What's that?" she asked, noticing a large square box she hadn't seen before.

Riley tucked it at the back of the tree, out of her reach. "Never you mind."

"The candlelight service is at seven," her father reminded them.

Hannah glanced at her watch. "I'd better change my clothes now," she said, heading toward the stairway.

"I put your suitcases in your old room," her father called out after her. Hannah stopped midstep and glanced back at her husband, her eyes wide with apprehension.

Riley read her look and followed her up the stairs. "What's wrong?" he asked, once they were out of earshot of the living room.

"Dad doesn't know," she whispered, hating the way color crept into her cheeks.

"Know what?"

Rather than go into a long explanation, she climbed to the top of the stairs and opened her bedroom door for him to see for himself. Inside sat two suitcases: one belonging to her and the other to Riley.

"Dad assumes we're sleeping together," she said. "If we don't . . . he might think something is wrong. Would you mind very much, Riley, just for tonight?"

He paused just inside the room, and his eyes slowly found hers. "No, Hannah," he told her after a while. "I don't mind at all."

Chapter Ten

Riley couldn't be more pleased at this turn of events. His own father-in-law had inadvertently laid the groundwork Riley had been impatiently waiting weeks to arrange. Hannah and he would be sharing a bed for the first time since their marriage nearly three months past. It was all Riley could do not to wear a silly grin.

"Will you be joining us for the candlelight service?" George Raymond asked Riley once he was back downstairs.

Personally, Riley hadn't given the matter much thought. He'd been attending services with Hannah for the past few Sundays and was surprised to find church wasn't nearly as bad as he'd assumed. The sermons had practical applications to everyday life. He listened carefully, hoping to gain insight into Hannah's personality. And into his own.

"Hannah told me you'd been going to church with her lately," George added, wearing a proud look, as though he'd always known his daughter would turn Riley's life around. "I'm pleased to hear it."

Riley nodded, swallowing down a sarcastic reply; but one good turn deserved another, and his father-in-law had gotten Hannah into his bed—a feat Riley had been attempting for weeks. Christmas Eve candlelight service, however, seemed above and beyond the call of duty.

It wasn't until they walked the short distance from the parsonage to the white steepled church that Riley understood why George had made an issue of inviting him to the service. It would be the first time Hannah had been home since their wedding. With them married short of three months and her pregnancy apparent, there was sure to be stares and a few harsh questions.

Riley's arm tightened around Hannah's shoulders; he wanted to shield her from gossip and candid looks. He was grateful when they sat toward the front of the church, away from discerning eyes.

Once they were situated in the polished wooden pew, Riley's gaze found the manger scene. The baby nestled in the straw captured his attention, and he couldn't help wondering how Joseph must have felt the night Mary had been in labor. At least he hadn't been out to sea, worrying about his wife, wishing he could be with her. The scene hit too close to home, and drawing a heavy breath, he looked away.

The service started shortly after they arrived. One thing Riley appreciated about church was the music. When they stood and sang Christmas carols, his loud baritone voice boomed through the building, bringing several stares and a few appreciative nods.

Hannah glanced up at him and smiled so sweetly that for a few measures, Riley had trouble singing. Love did funny things to a man, he realized meaningfully. Last Christmas Eve he'd been sitting in a bar, hitting on the waitress. Twelve months later, he was standing in a church singing "Silent Night" at the top of his lungs.

George Raymond moved toward the altar and lit a candle, using it to ignite others. Two men stepped forward and accepted the lighted candles. Protecting the flame by cupping their hands behind the wick, they moved down the center aisle, lighting the candle of the parishoner sitting at the end of the pew. That person shared the flame with the one sitting next to him, who turned to share it with the next person, until the light had been passed all the way down the row. Soon every candle in the church was burning.

There were a few more rousing Christmas carols. George might not have intended them to be sung boisterously, but Riley was in a spirited mood and it felt good to sing loud and strong as if he'd been doing it every Christmas of his life. At least he knew the tunes of these hymns. Some of the others he'd heard in church the past few weeks sounded as though they'd come straight out of the Middle Ages.

The sermon was short and sweet, just the way Riley liked them. He'd wondered what kind of preacher his father-in-law would be, suspecting George Raymond would be the fire-and-brimstone type, but Riley was pleasantly surprised.

There was another carol, and Riley was thinking the service would soon be over. He was mentally calculating how early he could pretend to be tired and urge Hannah to go up to bed. Since it was barely eight, he figured it would take another hour or so.

"This has been a painful year for our church family," George announced, stepping close to the podium microphone. "A year of change and transition. A year of pain and renewal. There seems no better time than Christmas to honor Jerry Sanders."

Hannah went still beside Riley. Still and rigid. She reached for his hand, squeezing it tightly, but Riley had the impression she would have held on to anyone's hand. Her breathing went shallow, and he was left to wonder at her strange behavior. It took a few moments to understand what was happening, to realize the man his father-in-law had chosen to honor was the Jerry Hannah had been engaged to marry.

Once he'd figured it out, it was all Riley could do to remain in the pew. To be forced to sit and listen to the tribute to Hannah's former fiancé was like holding Riley's face underwater and asking him to try to breathe.

"Are you all right?" he whispered to Hannah, wishing there was something he could do to spare her this. To spare himself this.

"Are you?" Her gaze—ripe with meaning, ripe with memories—slid to his.

He nodded, taken aback by her question. No man enjoys being trapped into listening to the limitless virtues of the man his wife loved . . . loved still; but the choice had been taken away from Riley. He tried to relax and let his mind wander.

"I doubt there is a life in this church that Jerry Sanders didn't touch," George continued, his low voice vibrating with grief. "From the time he was in his teens, Jerry felt God's call to the ministry, but he wasn't pious or overly devout. He was a man who loved others and reached out when he saw a need. Once, when Jerry was twelve, he brought a young mother to the church door, explaining that he'd met her outside a gas station. Her husband had abandoned her with a three-month-old child and she had nowhere to turn. Jerry couldn't leave her and do nothing, so he did the only thing he knew how. He brought her to his church.''

Hannah's fingers tightened around Riley's. Her features had gone pale, and Riley hedged, debating how much attention they'd garner if he picked her up and carried her out of the church. Too damn much, he decided reluctantly.

"It wasn't only strangers Jerry helped—he touched all our lives," George continued, and stepped away from the podium. One by one, three men and one woman moved forward, sharing incidents that involved Jerry Sanders.

Riley didn't want to listen, didn't want to hear any of this, but he had no choice. Each story revealed the other man's generosity and love in a new light. As the tales were recounted, Riley realized he'd never known anyone as generous or as kindhearted as Jerry Sanders. What George had said earlier about Jerry not being a goody-two-shoes was right. He'd been real, reacting with indignation to the wrongs committed around him, reaching out to help others even when he faced impossible odds. He was the type of man Riley would have liked to count as a friend.

The realization struck a sharp cord within him. It wasn't an easy thing to admit, even to himself.

No wonder Hannah had loved him, and grieved still. Jerry's death had dealt her a crippling blow. How unfair it must have seemed to her. How wrong that Jerry should be taken from her. He glanced over at her and noticed the tears streaking her face. She struggled to hide them, but it did little good.

Leaning forward, Riley reached into his back pocket and handed her a handkerchief. Slowly, as though she feared what she'd find, her gaze sought his.

Riley hurt. What man wouldn't? But his concern at the moment was more for Hannah. For the loss she'd suffered, for the pain she experienced being forced to rip open the half-healed wounds of her grief.

By the time the testimonials were finished and the plaque unveiled in Jerry's honor, Riley was ready to weep himself. Weep with frustration and anger. Weep because the comparison of his life and Jerry's was so striking. It was all he could do not to haul Hannah out of the church. And escape himself.

He wanted to make a quick getaway, but as soon as the service was over, several friendly folks crowded around them, looking for an introduction. Their eyes were curious as they noticed Hannah's stomach, but no one said anything.

Hannah amazed him with the warm way in which she handled the potentially disastrous situation. She looped her arm around Riley's, smiled adoringly up at him and introduced him with such pride and devotion that she fooled even him. Anyone listening would have thought their marriage was the love match of the century. It was left to him to complete the picture, and for her sake, he did the best he could.

How well he succeeded remained to be seen.

It seemed to take forever before they could escape. Riley turned his back on his father-in-law who stood in the vestibule, bidding the last well-wishers a joyous Christmas.

"I'm going to kill him," Riley muttered under his breath as they walked out the side door of the church.

"How could he do that to you?" The tracks of her tears had left glistening streaks down her cheek.

"I'm sorry, Riley. So sorry."

"What have you got to apologize for?" he demanded brusquely.

"For Dad. He'd never do anything to intentionally hurt one of us. He simply wasn't thinking. I'm married to you now, and he doesn't realize you even know about Jerry. Dad loved and misses him still. Jerry was as much a son to him as my brother, and he's still grieving."

"He might have warned you."

"Yes. I'm sure he intended to, then simply forgot."

Hannah could offer a hundred excuses, but it did damn little good. Riley claimed a few minutes to himself, making the excuse that he wanted to check the car. He did that, then walked around the block until the sharp tip of his anger had worn off. Then and only then, did he return to the house.

George Raymond, his look apologetic, was waiting for him when Riley stepped in the front door. "Hannah's upstairs."

Riley didn't trust himself to say one word. He bounded up the stairs, taking them two at a time. Tapping lightly against the bedroom door, he waited until Hannah answered before letting himself in.

She was sitting on top of the bed, in a sexless flannel nightgown, brushing her hair. She cast her gaze self-consciously downward as he walked into the room and started unbuttoning his shirt after pulling it free from his waist.

He wished she'd say something. She didn't.

Riley sat on the side of the mattress, his back to his wife, and removed his shoes and socks. When he stood to unbuckle his pants, Hannah peeled back the bed-spread.

"I . . . generally read for a while before I turn out the light," she said softly. "You don't mind, do you?"

"No."

With a maddening lack of haste, she walked around the end of the bed and rooted through the suitcase for her book. Bending over the way she did offered Riley a tantalizing view of her long, slim legs. It wasn't more than a fleeting glimpse, but then it didn't take much to get his juices flowing. Riley wondered how the hell he was going to lie next to her all night and not touch her.

Hannah was worried about Riley. In her heart, she knew her father hadn't meant to hurt her. Or Riley. Even now, George Raymond seemed oblivious to what he'd done. Rather than cause a strain in their close re-lationship, she'd silently gone up the stairs following the candlelight service to wait for Riley. He seemed to take forever to join her. Not everything her father did was thoughtless or ill-advised; by chance he'd managed to get her and Riley into bed together, which was a feat she'd been working toward for weeks.

Had she realized they'd be sharing a bed when she packed, Hannah realized sadly, she would have brought her silky peach gown. Pregnancy or no pregnancy, she wanted to view Riley's reaction when she wore it.

Riley was under the covers, lying back, his hands tucked behind his head, staring at the ceiling when she returned with the book she intended to read. He was so far over on his side of the bed it was a wonder he didn't slide onto the floor. He continued to stare straight ahead at the light fixture while she hurried under the blankets, shivering with the cold. Still he remained where he was.

Hannah read for no more than fifteen minutes, then hurried out of bed, turned off the light and rushed back. She rolled onto her side, tucking her knees under her breasts in order to get warm again.

"You all right?" Riley asked in the darkness.

"Yes . . . I'm just a little cold." She hoped he'd snuggle up against her and share his body's heat, but he didn't. The silence was strained, but she didn't know what to say to make it better. Feeling helpless and inadequate, and like the world's worst wife, she buried her face in the pillow to hide the ever-ready flow of tears.

"Hannah?"

"Yes."

"Are you crying?"

"No."

He gave an abrupt, hollow laugh. "You never could lie worth a damn. What's wrong?"

If he wouldn't come to her, then she'd go to him. Once the decision was made, she rolled onto her other side and aligned her body with Riley's, pressing her head to his shoulder. He felt hard and muscular, warm and whole.

Slowly, as though he were going against his better judgment, he brought his arm out from beneath his head and wrapped it around her shoulder. It felt so good to have him hold her, to have him touch her, that she closed her eyes on a deep sigh.

"You have nothing to fear from him, you know," she whispered, once her throat was clear enough to talk evenly, unemotionally. The love she felt for Jerry was far removed from the life she had now.

"You love him."

Hannah couldn't deny it. "A small part of me always will. He was a special man."

Riley grew silent, but she could tell from the even rise and fall of his chest and the steady beat of his heart that he hadn't taken offense, but was mulling over her words.

"When I was little, I can remember my father telling me that when God closes a door he always opens a window. This time he opened two. I don't regret being married to you, Riley. I feel honored to be your wife."

His hand gently stroked her shoulders. The day had been long and emotion packed. Hannah yawned and, nestling her face near Riley's neck, closed her eyes.

A smile curved her lips as she felt his mouth brush a soft kiss at her temple. Within minutes she could feel herself drifting off to sleep.

Until he'd met Hannah, Riley hadn't realized how full of irony everyday life could be. He'd dreamed, plotted, schemed to get her into his bed, and once she was there, he found he was afraid to touch her. Afraid and unworthy. He, Riley Murdock, actually feared her moving close to him, tempting him beyond endurance, snuggling her lush breasts against him. He trembled at the thought of his body, so hard and powerful, filling Hannah's delicate softness. The problem, he recognized, was one of his own making. Knowing that didn't alter the situation, however.

Hannah openly admitted her love for her dead fiancé, and after learning what he had that evening, Riley didn't blame her. Jerry Sanders had been one hell of a man.

A far better man than he'd ever be. Riley had been born on the wrong side of the blanket. By the time he was in junior high, he'd been labeled a troublemaker and a rabble-rouser. His headstrong, rebellious ways had repeatedly gotten him into trouble throughout high school. He was lucky to have escaped reform school, not to mention prison. Actually, he had the Navy to thank for rescuing him from a life of crime.

He'd enlisted the day after he graduated from high school, at the bottom of his class. His cocky attitude hadn't lasted long; by the end of boot camp he'd realized the Navy could well be his one chance to turn himself around. It was up to him to decide.

It had taken him fifteen years to make the transformation from a street-smart, foulmouthed kid with a chip on his shoulder the size of a California redwood to a responsible Navy chief. A few of the rough edges of his personality had been rounded off over the years, but he'd never be the educated, cultured husband Jerry Sanders would have been to Hannah.

Riley would like to hate Hannah's fiancé, challenge him face-to-face for her heart. But everything he'd heard that night in church convinced Riley that, had he known Jerry, he would have liked him. Jerry Sanders had been the kind of man everyone looked up to and admired. A natural leader, a lover and defender of justice. Hell, the man had been near perfect. There wasn't anything to fault him with. He'd been a saint. He must have been, to be engaged to a woman as beautiful as Hannah and restrain from making love to her.

Hannah, who'd been sheltered and protected all her life, was the perfect match for such a man as Jerry. She was generous and sweet, a delicate rose; and by God, she deserved a better husband, someone far more decent than he'd ever be.

The problem was, what would Riley do about it now? Even if he found the courage to leave her for her own good, he couldn't turn away from her now. Not with her six months pregnant with his child.

What was a man to do in such a situation? The hell if Riley knew. He wasn't even close to being good enough to deserve Hannah. She'd crashed into his life when he least expected to meet a woman like her. One night with her had left him frantic with worry, furious and baffled. He hadn't known who she was or where she'd come from; all he had known was that he had to find her again.

He was getting too old, Riley decided. Too tired. Too weary. He was losing his cutting edge. His emotional resilience was gone. He'd like to blame Hannah for that, as well, but he couldn't. The problem was his own. The stark truth of the matter was he'd never been in love before and he'd lost his heart to her that night in Seattle.

His heart and his mind.

All his life he'd been waiting to meet someone like her. He just never expected it to happen in a waterfront bar. He'd seen her and wanted her immediately, not recognizing himself what it was he found so damned appealing about her. After three months of marriage, he knew. He'd been attracted to her innocence, her generosity of spirit and her awesome ability to love. For once in his life, Riley needed a woman to love him. Someone who belonged to him. Someone not bound to a memory.

He couldn't, he wouldn't share her.

But he did already.

As he lay next to Hannah, her measured, even breathing echoing in his ear, the implications of his situation pounded at his temples with the sharpness of a hangover.

He could fight her love for Jerry, do everything he could to wipe out the other man's memory. In essence Riley could shadow-box with a dead man. Or he could accept her love for the seminary student and go on, doing his utmost to be the best husband he knew how to be—always knowing, always conscious that he was a damn poor second choice.

The choice, however, had already been made. The gold wedding band on his finger was reminder enough of that. The child growing in Hannah's womb convinced him there could be no turning back now. That being the situation, the best Riley could hope for was that, in time, she'd be able to look past the hard outer crust he wore like battle armor and come to love him, too.

Love.

No one had told him it was such a painful emotion. Powerful enough to break a man, topple him from his prideful perch and leave him shaken and unsure. Riley loved Hannah and their unborn child beyond reason. Enough to cast all pride aside.

She stirred and rolled closer to him, draping her arm across his stomach. Her bare legs scooted next to his as she drew in a deep, even breath. Lying as she was, her stomach nestled against his side, reminded him how grateful he was that she hadn't lost Junior. He'd never experienced such panic as he had the night he'd driven her to the hospital.

It happened then, and Riley's eyes flew open. The baby kicked, and he'd felt it as strongly as if Hannah herself had poked him. An involuntary grin grew and grew.

"Riley," she whispered, "did you feel him?"

"Yes."

"I told you he was going to be a soccer player."

"He's so strong."

Her smile was evident even in the dark. "Tell me about it." She yawned, holding her hand in front of her mouth. "What time is it?"

Riley read the illuminated dial of his wristwatch. "A little after two."

"Did Junior wake you?"

"No. I was lying here thinking."

"About what?" she quizzed.

She sounded worried, and he sought to reassure her. "About what we should name Junior. I was thinking . . . that if you wanted, we could name him after Jerry."

Her silence confused him. He turned his head toward her, hoping there'd be enough moonlight in the bedroom to judge her expression.

"That's the most beautiful thing you've ever said to me," she murmured, her voice breaking with emotion. She pressed her hand on his shoulder and kissed his cheek. "Actually, I've been giving some thought to a name myself."

"And?" he pressed.

She hesitated, as though she expected him to disapprove of her choice. "There's a Hannah in the Bible. I didn't know if you were aware of that or not."

Riley wasn't, but that shouldn't come as any shock. Now that he thought it over, it made sense that a godly man like George Raymond would give his only daughter a scriptural name.

"She was married and desperately wanted children. She tried for years and years to become pregnant, but was barren."

"So far I don't see any similarities between the two of you," he teased, and was rewarded with an elbow in his ribs.

"Might I continue?"

"By all means."

"Hannah went to the temple to pray, asking God for a child, and soon afterward she found herself pregnant. When her son was born, she named him Samuel."

"Samuel," Riley repeated slowly, testing the name. It had a nice solid sound to it. Samuel Murdock. "I like it, but aren't you taking a lot for granted? We could very well be having a daughter."

"Samantha, then."

"All right," Riley said, gathering her close in his arms, pressing his chin against the crown of her head. "Samuel or Samantha it is."

"Samuel Riley Murdock."

Riley felt his throat thicken. "Or Samantha Hannah Murdock."

"But Riley, that's too awkward a name for a little girl. Samantha Lynn or Samantha Anne would be better."

"It's Samantha Hannah, so don't argue with me."

"In that case I certainly hope we have a son," she muttered under her breath, just loud enough for him to hear. She tugged the blankets more securely around her shoulders and continued to use his chest for a pillow. It wasn't the most comfortable position, with her breasts brushing against him and her thighs rubbing his own, but Riley hadn't the strength to ask her to move.

"Good night, Hannah," he said, closing his eyes, content for the first time in hours. "Good night, Sam," he added, and nearly laughed out loud when a tiny foot or arm jabbed him in the side.

"Oh, Riley!" Hannah cried as she pried open the lid to the large rectangular box he'd squirreled away beneath the tree. "Oh, Riley," she repeated, tears brimming in her eyes as her gaze shot over to him. With infinite care, she removed a soft pink maternity dress from the tissue wrapping and held it against her waist. "How'd you know?"

"You mean other than the fact you went back to the clothes rack four times to look at it?"

"But it's much too expensive.... I could probably sew one like it for half the price. But I'm so pleased I don't have to! I've only got a couple of things I can wear to work as it is. Oh, Riley, I love it so much. Thank you." She rushed to his side, threw her arms around his neck and hugged him hard.

"Tears, Hannah," her father teased.

"Don't worry, I get emotional so easily now. Dr. Underwood said it was to be expected."

"Your mother was the same way. She'd start to weep over television commercials when she was carrying your brother and you." His eyes grew warm at the memory as he leaned back in his chair and smiled down on his daughter.

"Riley, open my gift next," she said, breaking away long enough to pull a purple and blue gift-wrapped box from beneath the tree. "I made it myself while you were away."

Riley examined the box, shaking it.

"Careful, it might break." The blue wool sweater, complete with matching hat and scarf would do no such thing, but she enjoyed baiting him.

Riley took his time unwrapping the gift, and it was all Hannah could do not to rush to his side and help him tear away the paper. She watched closely as he lifted the lid. No emotion registered in his eyes as he carefully unfolded the garments one by one and brought them out of the box.

"I hope it fits," Hannah said in a rush, her words blending together.

Riley stood and tried on the sweater, slipping his long arms into the sleeves and then tugging them up past his elbow. He glanced over to her, and appreciation gleamed from his deep blue eyes. "I've never owned anything finer." With a flair that delighted Hannah, he wrapped the scarf several times around his neck and set the hat upon his head. His eyes met hers, and a surge of warm emotion filled her heart. His look penetrated the very core of her being and communicated to her a feeling of love so strong, she wondered why she'd never noticed it before.

Riley did love her, and yet...and yet, he'd barely touched her all night. It seemed he went out of his way to avoid doing so. Hannah strongly suspected he would have stayed on his side of the bed the entire night and made no contact whatsoever if she hadn't moved over to him.

Perhaps having her father so near had intimidated him and he hadn't wanted to consummate their marriage while in his father-in-law's home. But her father's bedroom was downstairs and he slept like a brick. She'd made a point of telling Riley so, although she'd wondered at the time if he was listening.

"Do I get a turn here?" her father asked, effectively cutting off Hannah's train of thought.

"Of course," she answered, pleased he'd chosen the gift she'd made for him. It was a small painting, one of a small loaf of french bread and a chalice of wine set on a rough-hewn wooden table. Although the entire focus of the painting was the bread and wine, she'd worked hard to depict the symbolic nature of the simple elements that had been part of the Last Supper.

"Hannah," her father said, awed as he held up the painting, "this is fabulous. Where did you ever find it?"

She beamed with pride and joy as she told him.

Hannah couldn't remember a Christmas she'd enjoyed more. The meal was excellent, and they ate early in the afternoon. She sat at the old upright piano and played Christmas music for her father and Riley, who seemed to thoroughly enjoy singing the timeless carols. Afterward she took a nap and woke to discover that Riley and her father had done the dishes. While she'd been resting, Riley had loaded the car and seemed anxious to return to the base.

They bade their farewells while it was still light outside. Riley was quiet during the long ride home, but when she asked if there was anything bothering him, he smiled, assuring her there wasn't.

As they approached the base, she realized he was speeding. Riley was a responsible driver, and she couldn't understand why he seemed in such a hurry.

Once they pulled up in front of the house, her husband made an excuse about unloading the trunk and insisted she go inside ahead of him. She offered to help him carry something, but he wouldn't let her.

Not knowing his thoughts, she did as he said, pondering his strange mood. She inserted the key into the front door and pushed it open. Turning on the light switch, she was halfway through the living room before she saw it.

There, against the wall, was a beautiful mahogany piano decorated with a huge red bow.

Chapter Eleven

Hannah stood frozen, unable to speak or move. A piano! A beautiful new piano that Riley had bought just for her. When she could move, she walked across the room and ran her fingers over the polished ivory keyboard. The joyous sound of her music filled the room. She continued playing while she scooted out the bench with her foot and sat down.

She proceeded with every Christmas song she could recall from memory, filling the house with music the way it did her heart and mind. When she finished, she laid her hands in her lap and exhaled a deep sigh.

Turning around, she found Riley leaning his shoulder against the wall, his powerful arms crossed over his chest, studying her.

"How...when?" She couldn't seem to ask a coherent question.

"I take it you're asking about the piano?"

She nodded, knowing she'd only make a mess of it if she were to try to explain. Her heart was full, bubbling over with love and excitement. Not once had she suspected. He'd been so closemouthed about it.

"After hearing you sing and play in church, I decided we needed a piano," Riley explained in that relaxed way of his, as if they were discussing a minor purchase.

"But..."

"There are no buts about it. You're too talented not to have one. You enjoy it. The way I figure, you can sing Sam to sleep."

"Oh, Riley, I can't believe you." She could think of no way to thank him. Nothing she could do or say would ever be enough. She walked over to him and kissed him the way that had been their habit of late, brushing her lips over his. Lightly. Briefly. First on his cheek, then his lips. But the all-too-hasty contact left her feeling empty and wanting. Standing on the tips of her toes, she leaned into him and wrapped her arms around his neck. Kissing him long and hard on the lips, she opened to him, introducing her tongue into his mouth until she created a warm, wet, gentle demand.

Riley held himself stiff against her, then groaned from deep within his throat. He sounded like a man absorbed in pain, and Hannah wondered if she'd done anything to hurt him.

With another groan he wrapped his arms around her waist, lifting her effortlessly from the floor so that her face was level with his own. Their gazes met for an instant before he directed her mouth to his. She'd been the aggressor, but that changed abruptly as he took control.

His tongue circled hers as his lips nibbled at her own. Riley was experienced in the ways of love; Hannah had known that from the first night they'd met. She'd responded to that experience, helpless to refuse him anything. To refuse herself. He seemed to need some kind of response from her, something more, she realized; otherwise he wouldn't be holding himself in check the way he was.

Stroking her fingers through his thick, dark hair, her lips fluttered open, granting him everything she had to give: her mind, her heart, her soul.

Riley's kiss was hungry and demanding, until slowly it began to happen. Her sensations were drowning in warm feelings—feelings she'd experienced so rarely in her life and only with this man. She ached in places she'd never thought to ache. Her breasts throbbed, and she recalled with vivid detail the night on the Seattle waterfront when Riley had taken her nipples in his mouth; and she wanted that again. Anything to ease the heavy swollen feeling that controlled her. The sensation didn't stop there, but sank lower—much lower—to the juncture of her thighs. She felt hot and quivery, hot and excited; needy in ways she barely understood. Suddenly Hannah knew what she wanted. What she needed.

Her husband.

An electric shudder passed through her. Riley must have felt it because he abruptly broke off the kiss.

Hannah sighed. Riley's lungs emptied of air as he slowly released his hold on her waist. His hands reached for hers, which were gripping his neck, and he gently pulled them free.

"I'd better finish unloading the trunk," he said, his voice so low it was a gentle whisper. Following that, he walked away.

Hannah was stunned. He'd wanted her as much as she'd wanted him, and yet he'd pushed her aside and given some flimsy excuse to leave her. She didn't know what was happening, didn't understand the significance of it. What she did feel was alone and lacking. And more needy than she'd ever felt in her life.

Riley stood by the car, letting the cold December wind slam against him. He drew in several breaths, sucking the air deep into his lungs. His head was swimming with the reality of how close he'd come to breaking his self-proclaimed code of honor and making love to Hannah. He opened the car trunk, and his hands shook. Not only his hands, but every part of him—his legs, his belly, his head. It was the kind of shallow-breathing, head-pounding shaking that comes when one realizes what a close brush one has had.

They couldn't have gotten any closer. Another minute, and Riley would have hauled her into the bedroom and damned the consequences. If he were to make love to her now, needing her so desperately, he'd frighten her half to death. Hell, he needed her so damn much it frightened *him*. He was concerned, too, about hurting the baby.

He'd made a promise to himself, one he fully intended to keep. He'd woo Hannah, love her the way a husband loves a wife, but only after she'd delivered the baby. Riley had lain awake most of the night before, sorting through his feelings for Hannah and, more important, what he'd learned about Jerry. He'd never be the husband her fiancé would have been. The way Riley figured it, Jerry, having been the noble man he was, wouldn't have pressured her to make love while she was pregnant, so Riley wouldn't, either.

"Admit it," Riley said aloud. He clenched his hands into tight fists at his sides, resisting slamming them against the trunk lid. It was more than the pregnancy issue. "You're afraid."

The psychologists probably had a fancy name for it. The irrational, inane fear of making love to one's wife. It would take time for him to analyze what was going on inside his head. He didn't doubt his love. Riley was crazy about her, and committed to her, their child and their marriage.

In some ways, as weird as it sounded, Riley felt that he had a responsibility to Jerry Sanders. It fell heavily upon his shoulders. The *Atlantis* would be leaving again in the middle of January, a short three weeks away. All he had to do was keep his pants zipped until then. If he avoided situations such as the one he'd just encountered, everything would work out fine. Once he was back, Sam would be born and he'd face the issue then. But for now, he'd be content to let matters rest as they were.

Hannah didn't know what was different about Riley, but a subtle change had taken place in her husband since Christmas. He was attentive, generous, solicitous. Nevertheless Hannah couldn't shake the feeling he was avoiding her physically. If she had to come up with a word for it she'd say he'd become stingy with his kisses. *What* kisses? she mused, feeling both abused and melancholy.

She was baking cookies, remembering a piece of sage advice from years past. It was said the way to a man's heart passed directly through his stomach. Hannah swore that if chocolate-chip with walnuts didn't do the trick, she was going to do something desperate... like seduce him.

The thought was almost comical. What did she know of seduction? Well, she determined valiantly, she could learn.

Riley walked into the house sometime after five. Hannah had planned it carefully, so the aroma of melting chocolate would have its greatest impact right around then.

"What's cooking?" he asked, eagerly strolling into the kitchen. Absently he gave her a peck on the cheek and reached for a still-warm cookie.

Hannah had left her hair down, brushing it until it shone. She'd once read that men preferred it when women wore their hair loose. She'd dressed in her best pair of navy blue slacks and a pretty lavender top. There was no hiding her pregnancy, and she didn't even try.

"How'd your day go?" he asked conversationally while sorting through the mail, keeping his back to her. He gave no outward indication that he noticed she'd taken extra care with her appearance. Hannah swallowed a sigh of disappointment. Apparently it was going to take more than freshly baked cookies and a different hairstyle. She wasn't worried, however; there was always Plan B.

"My day went great. I got a call from the department store." She paused for effect and lifted the last of the cookies off the baking sheet. "The crib and dresser we ordered are in." She glanced at him out of the corner of her eye. "The man said he could have them delivered tomorrow." She told him the last part, making sure her voice dipped significantly.

"Are you going to be around?"

Hannah nodded. "That isn't the problem."

"Then, what is?"

"Well...it's just that the baby's bedroom is going to be terribly crowded." She raised her eyes meaningfully to Riley, her look heavy with implication. Riley was an intelligent man. It wouldn't take him long to make the obvious connection and suggest she move her things out of her bedroom and into his. The chocolate-chip cookie he was eating stopped halfway to his lips. The bite that was in his mouth seemed to go down his throat whole— a lump moving in such tiny increments that she was certain he would choke on it.

"I was thinking," she continued, "I'd move my things into your room." If he wouldn't suggest it, then she would. "You don't mind, do you?" She smiled over at him, as sweetly as she knew how, and realized he'd gone pale.

"That shouldn't be any problem," he said after a long moment. "I'll move everything for you after dinner."

"Good." Hannah couldn't keep the excitement out of her voice.

Riley mumbled something under his breath, but Hannah didn't hear what it was. She would have asked him to repeat it, but she didn't think what he said was meant for her ears.

Riley walked over to the stove and picked up the lid of the small pot of stroganoff that was simmering on the back burner. He stared into the pot an extra-long time before replacing the top, then turned and walked toward the living room.

"Oh, before I forget, Cheryl phoned," Hannah added. "She invited us over to play cards next Saturday night. Do you have anything planned?"

"No." The word came out sounding far huskier than normal.

"I'll call her tomorrow then and tell her we'll be there. I told her I didn't know how to play pinochle, but she said it was easy to learn and that I'd pick it up in no time."

He nodded, but Hannah had the impression his mind wasn't on Cheryl's invitation or playing pinochle. "Isn't this Friday your poker night?"

He didn't answer her and seemed to be lost in a fog. "Riley?"

His gaze turned upward, meeting hers. The air in the room seemed to go still. Even the radio, which was playing in the corner, seemed to fade. Their gazes locked. Riley's expression was so tender, as though he derived a good deal of joy just looking at her. This night—either by hook or by crook, Hannah decided— she was going to make love with her husband.

From out of nowhere came the memory of the first night they'd slept together. She remembered the way he'd shaped his body around hers, holding her against him cocoon style, his long legs entwined with hers. She recalled, too, how she'd been forced to carefully lift his arm from her waist in order to escape his hold and steal away the following morning. A king-size lump formed in her throat, and it was all she could do not to promise him she'd never run away again.

"Poker?" he repeated after what seemed like a millennium. "I . . . don't remember. Why?"

"No reason. I was just wondering."

He walked out of the kitchen as though he weren't sure where he was headed. He stood in front of the picture window in the living room for several moments, although there was nothing going on outside that she could tell. Hannah had the oddest feeling that if she were to speak to him, he wouldn't hear her. It was at times like these that she felt at such a loss.

True to his word, Riley helped transfer her personal items from one bedroom into the next while she washed the dinner dishes. He cleared a space for her in his closet and then carted her clothes across the hallway several hangers at a time. The chest of drawers took far more time and effort.

They played a game of Scrabble, which she won handily, and watched a little television. By nine-thirty Hannah was ready for bed.

Not so, Riley. He made an excuse of needing to gas up the car. He rejected her offer to go with him and suggested instead that she go bed without him. He promised to join her later. Hannah could only agree, but she was determined to stay awake. He wouldn't thwart her that easily,.

Riley sat in his car in the dark of the night, trying to come up with a logical excuse to find somewhere else to sleep for the next ten nights. It was only ten lousy nights before the *Atlantis* was scheduled to be deployed. Thus far he'd managed to keep his hands off Hannah, but he swore the woman was enough to tempt the saints.

Riley Murdock was no saint.

He didn't even make the pretense of being one. Hannah was home sleeping in his bed, and short of spending the night sitting in the cold, he'd soon be joining her there.

Hannah, all soft and warm with sleep, waiting for him to join her. In their bed. The very thought was enough to drive Riley to his knees.

He hadn't slept worth a damn since Christmas night, when she'd rushed into his arms and they'd come so close to making love. He'd seen the look in her eyes then: bold as could be.

Passion. A desire so strong that it awed him, and had haunted him every night since.

Riley didn't know how he was going to be able to resist her.

He knew his actions since Christmas had confused and flustered Hannah. Hell, he was baffled himself. Questions paraded through his mind each and every night. Plenty of questions and not a single answer.

He was a crazy man not to make love to Hannah when she'd given every indication that she'd welcome his attentions. He was certifiable. A candidate for intensive counseling.

The frightening part of all this was how much he wanted to make love with her. He thought about it constantly, but he couldn't make himself breach the barrier of his fears.

He'd hurt her again. He might injure the baby. He'd been too large for her that first night. She'd been so damned tight and hot.

Quickly Riley banished the memory from his mind, knowing if he didn't find something else to think about, he'd soon fall victim to his own needs.

Slowly, with a good deal of reluctance, he drove back to the house, noting when he walked inside that it was only a little after eleven. Hannah would be asleep by now. At least he wouldn't be left to contend with any of her questions. He wouldn't have any answers for her, either.

He undressed in the dark, showered and as silently as humanly possible, he slipped between the sheets, staying as far away from her as he could. It surprised him how easily he drifted off.

Riley woke sometime in the middle of the night to find Hannah lying facing him. He opened his eyes and breathed in the fresh, clean scent of her. Wildflowers. In full bloom.

A thick strand of hair had fallen across her face, and although he feared he might wake her, he chanced lifting the shiny brown curl from her cheek and gently brushed it aside.

She was wearing the flannel nightgown. Riley never thought he'd appreciate the sexless thing, but he was wrong. He was eternally grateful she hadn't donned one of those sheer nighties. Or something made of silk. Silk was his downfall. The mental image of Hannah wearing a silk gown blossomed in his mind, and he banished the thought before it could take root. He had enough of a problem dealing with the reality of her in his bed without complicating his life by introducing fantasy.

Releasing a deep rush of air, Hannah scooted closer. So close he could almost hear her heart beating.

Closing his eyes, Riley tried to force himself to go back to sleep. Damn, but he could hear her heart beat. It was pulsing like crazy. No, he decided a second later; that was his own heart.

Slowly, against his better judgment, he brought his hand up to the front of her gown—just to determine if it was her pulse that was pounding so violently, he assured himself. If it was, then perhaps there was something medically wrong with her, or with the baby.

His hand slipped past the small pearl buttons, past the lace trim and edging of pink embroidery.

Past the point of no return.

A thin layer of perspiration broke out across Riley's upper lip as he pressed his palm to her chest.

The tips of his fingers felt for her pulse, but the heel of his hand rested against the bulging fullness of her lush breast. Riley's heart seemed to be working just fine, but his breathing came to an abrupt halt. An ache, low in his belly, began to pound like a giant fist.

Only it wasn't his stomach that was throbbing.

A better man than he might be able to resist Hannah. Jerry could resist her, but not Riley. Not for a second longer. His hands shook like a schoolboy's as he captured her breast in his palm. He lifted it, savored its weight and pear shape. She was right; they were fuller, sweetly fuller than he remembered.

Dear God, she felt good. He'd thought to relieve one ache and in the process created another—one that was ten times worse than the first.

He had to touch her, he realized; really touch her, or go mad. The pearl buttons slipped free of the restraining material with little more than a flick of his fingers, her gown spilling open wider and wider, granting him ample room to slip his hand inside.

He sighed out loud as her breast fell into his palm. Her nipple formed a hard bead against him, and unable to restrain himself, he groaned at the small intimacy.

Oh, God, what was he doing? Riley was nearly frantic with the knowledge of how far he'd allowed this little experiment to take him. His breathing was labored and deep. His heart beat high in his throat.

He was about to pull free, thinking he had never sunk lower than he had at that moment, when he noticed Hannah's beautiful gray eyes watching him in the dark.

Then she smiled—the sweetest, most dazzling smile he'd ever seen in his life. It seemed to light up the entire room.

"I remember how you sucked on them," she whispered into the stillness. He remembered, too, and against every dictate of his will he grazed the hard rosy tip with his thumb. He marveled at her quick, ready response.

"Do it again, Riley," she pleaded softly. "Like you did that night."

Riley didn't take the time to think; he couldn't. Instead, he crushed her mouth with his, frightening himself with the powerful need she created in him.

Their kiss was wet and wild. As their mouths ground against each other, Riley cupped her breasts, marveling once more at how incredibly soft her skin felt; softer than anything he'd ever touched. Softer than velvet. Softer than fur or silk.

Consumed in a fire of his own making, Riley slipped his mouth down the ivory perfection of her shoulders and finally to the swell of her breasts. His lips sought the nipple, drawing it forward, feasting on her, suckling until she moaned and arched her hips, seeking the pleasure she'd experienced all too briefly, all those months ago.

Riley longed to show her all the delightfully scandalous things they could do to please each other. But he dared not... not with Hannah. He would shock her, repulse her.

He used his tongue to create a wet, slick trail between her breasts, moistening, laving, sucking. He altered between gentle and not-so-gentle until Hannah raised the entire upper half of her body off the mattress in silent entreaty.

All ten of her fingers dug into his scalp. "Riley," she pleaded, "I need..."

Riley needed her, too. Needed to be released from the desire that was so strong it pained him. So wild it frightened him. So deep it humbled him.

He lifted his head and kissed her, keeping his hands busy molding, kneading, shaping her breasts. God help him, but he couldn't get enough of the feel of her.

Where he found the strength, Riley never knew. Slowly, he drew her head down to his chest and closed his eyes to the agony of physical frustration.

"Riley?"

"Shh... Sleep." He gently stroked her hair, praying, pleading, doing everything he could to force his mind from the beautiful soft woman in his arms.

"Sleep?"

"Sleep," he repeated. "We've both got to work tomorrow."

She was frustrated, too. Unsure. But he wouldn't answer her questions. It took some time before the smooth, even flow of her breathing convinced him she'd drifted off. At least one of them would get some rest that night, but it wouldn't be he.

Hannah chose the soft pink dress Riley had given her for Christmas to wear to Cheryl and Steve's for cards a week later. With a patience she hadn't expected, Riley had spent the better part of two evenings going over the fundamentals of pinochle with her. She'd never played cards much, but she was willing to learn, and Riley was tolerant with her lack of skill.

"You look . . . beautiful," he said, coming out of the bedroom. He stopped as though he couldn't take his eyes off her; but if that was the case, then he shouldn't be able to keep his hands off her, either. That certainly didn't seem to be a problem of late. They might as well not be married for all the good it did them. Riley was scheduled to ship out sometime early the following week, and they'd yet to make love.

Not from lack of trying, at least on Hannah's part.

Sometimes Hannah suspected he was playing a cruel game with her, but if that was the case, he was the one who was suffering.

Not once in the week since she'd moved into his bedroom had they managed to go to bed at the same time. Inevitably Riley came up with some nonsensical excuse to linger several minutes, and oftentimes hours after she was already in bed. Although she tried to wait up for him, she almost always fell asleep.

She found it uncanny that he would know just when she would be sleeping before he'd join her. Only once had he woken her, but when she'd tried to talk to him, he'd pretended to be exhausted, had rolled away from her and gone directly to sleep.

Pretended. Hannah was sure he was as wide-awake as she was.

In every other way, other than the physical aspect of their marriage, he was a model husband. With the exception of the first night she'd moved into his bedroom, they hadn't so much as cuddled, at least not that Hannah was aware.

"I'm going out to start the car," Riley said, turning away from her. He'd taken to doing that lately—making sure it was warm and cozy inside before he came for her, not wanting to chance her catching a chill.

Hannah had been looking forward to this evening with Cheryl and Steve, even if it did involve playing cards. She was grateful for the friendship of the other Navy wives she'd met through Steve's wife.

Riley's hand was on her shoulder as they stood at the front door and rang the Morgans' doorbell.

"They must be making this a round-robin," he murmured.

"Round robin?" Hannah asked.

"That's Lenny's car across the street. And I noticed Floyd's one block over."

The door opened just then and Cheryl stepped forward, grinning from ear to ear. Standing between them, she took Riley's arm and then Hannah's, leading them into the living room.

Pink and blue strands of crepe paper were draped across the ceiling and the table was set with a large lace tablecloth and a pretty bouquet of pink and blue carnations.

"Surprise!" Cheryl cried, laughing and throwing her arms into the air.

Immediately people started popping out from every corner. Four jumped up from behind the davenport. Three came from the kitchen and as many more from the coat closet.

"What's going on here?" Riley asked, clearly perplexed.

"Don't you recognize a baby shower when you see one?" Cheryl chided.

"A baby what?" Riley asked again, scratching his head. He looked to Hannah for an explanation.

"It's a party for the baby," Hannah told him, smiling. She recognized several of the wives and a couple of the husbands.

"Here, 'ol buddy," Steve said, handing Riley a cold can of soda. "Sit down and we'll explain everything." Riley cast a dumbfounded look over his shoulder as Steve led him toward the front of the room and sat him down. Next, Riley's friend escorted Hannah to the second chair and then placed a paper crown from a fast-food restaurant on top of each of their heads.

"I thought only women had parties for babies," Riley muttered under his breath.

"I did, too," she whispered back.

Cheryl dragged out a card table stacked high with gifts.

Hannah couldn't remember a time when she'd had more fun. Jenny Blackwell, Floyd's wife, had baked a cake in the shape of a stork delivering the baby and had done an incredible job. It was almost too beautiful to eat. Riley, however, had no such qualms. He sliced off huge pieces and passed them around to his friends, then wolfed down two slices himself.

When it came time to open the gifts, everyone gathered around. Hannah was self-conscious about being the center of attention as she carefully pried away the paper. Each gift touched her heart. There were so many things, big and small, they needed yet for the baby, and it meant so much to her that Riley's friends would do this for them.

"Is this the gal?" Floyd Blackwell asked, claiming the empty chair beside Riley while the others chatted around them. He had a kind, round face, and a bald spot was beginning to form on the crown of his head.

"Yes," Riley replied stiffly, glancing anxiously toward Hannah.

"I thought it must be." He laughed and took a generous bite of the cake his wife had baked. "I'll tell you right now," he said to Hannah, "you certainly sent Riley on a merry goose chase. He spent the entire month of August looking for you." He turned to Riley, disregarding the deep scowl. "Did that private detective ever turn up anything?"

"Floyd," Riley prompted meaningfully between clenched teeth, "don't I hear Jenny calling you?"

"Jenny. Naw, she's across the room talking to Cheryl. Oh . . . Oh, right. Yes, well, it was nice meeting you, Hannah," he finished, rushing to his feet.

"What was Floyd talking about?" Hannah asked her husband a few minutes later.

"Nothing. He was just blowing some hot air."

Hannah didn't believe that for a moment, and was left to ponder Floyd's words. Had Riley tried to find her after that night? It certainly sounded like it. The knowledge did funny things to her heart. He had cared even then.

It was after eleven by the time they arrived back home. Riley unloaded the gifts from the car while Hannah carried in leftover cake. The night had been such fun, and Hannah had enjoyed every minute of it. Even Riley seemed to be in an extra-good mood.

To Hannah's way of thinking, the time to strike was while the iron was hot, an old cliché she'd often heard her father use.

While she was in changing for bed, Riley sat out in the living room, reading the newspaper.

He didn't look up when she entered the room, and she noticed that he'd brewed himself a cup of coffee as though he intended to stay up a while longer. His hand held a pen as if he planned on working through the crossword puzzle.

She was determined to see that that didn't happen.

"Riley, come to bed."

"I will in a few minutes," he replied, studying the paper, still not glancing toward her.

"Not tonight."

"I beg your pardon." He looked up, and Hannah could have kissed him for the reaction he gave. She'd combed her hair, spreading it across her shoulders like a giant fan. The peach silk gown clung to her, and she reached for its satin tie, releasing the front.

"It's time to come to bed. Now," she said, holding her hand out to him.

Chapter Twelve

Riley's heart sank all the way to the soles of his feet. Never in all his life had he seen a woman more beautiful than Hannah in this silky peach gown, her thick shiny hair as rich looking as velvet.

His heart rebounded just enough for him to breathe. Just enough for the overwhelming physical attraction to bombard his stomach. Nothing seemed real anymore. He felt as though he were sitting in a thick fog, a haze of remorse. Riley had the feeling that if he were to find the strength to stand, he'd crumple to the carpet like a rag doll.

"Hannah," he managed to say, although his voice was little more than a hoarse whisper, "what is this?"

"You mean you don't know?"

The hell if Riley knew how someone so innocent in the ways of seduction could be so damned provocative. She sashayed toward him, swaying her hips with the right amount of allure. A stripteaser couldn't have walked as enticingly; Riley was convinced of that. He couldn't take his eyes off her, feasting on the outline of her swollen breasts and the way the silk seemed to wrap its way around her thighs. His thoughts were in a muddle as he scrambled for some excuse, something to say or do that would help him to gently turn her away.

"It's time for bed," she announced, her smile so sweet it was all he could do not to go into a deep trance just looking at her.

He sat numb, unable to move or think. "I...ah...I'm not quite ready yet. You go on ahead without me."

"Not tonight, Riley." She continued smiling down on him as she removed the pen from his lifeless fingers and tugged the newspaper free from his grasp. Like a man lost in a stupor, he allowed her to do both without offering the least bit of resistance.

She hesitated when he didn't rise from the recliner and mindlessly follow her into the bedroom. It seemed to take her a few seconds to regroup, but she did so with amazing dexterity. She smiled once again and nestled herself into his lap with a childlike eagerness. Only there wasn't anything childish about the look in her eyes, or the captivating way the corners of her mouth tilted upward.

Her gaze continued to hold his as her fingers expertly unfastened the buttons of his shirt. She wasn't satisfied until she had peeled it open and could press her hands fully against his heaving chest. At the feel of her fingers against him, Riley's breath escaped on a ragged sigh. Encouraged by her success, she sighed, too, and her smile deepened.

"Hannah...I don't think..." He didn't finish. His wife bent forward and pressed her soft, sweet mouth against the side of his neck. Her touch—velvet gentle, satin smooth—went through him like a hunting knife. Her breath was as hot as fire. Hotter than a raging inferno. Using the moist tip of her tongue, she seared a trail of moist kisses against his throat.

Riley's head fell back and he closed his eyes.

Despite his pleading, Hannah continued to work her mouth across his face. She paused at his earlobe, taking it into her mouth and sucking lightly, flickering her tongue around the outer edges and gently probing inside. Riley moaned, willing his hands not to touch her, clenching them into tight fists at his sides. The minute he experienced for himself her incredible softness, he'd be lost, and he knew it.

Her splayed fingers slid upward until they'd linked at his nape. Slowly she released his ear, continuing her journey downward, sliding her tongue over the muscular cords of his neck, pausing at the hollow of his throat. Unexpectedly she paused, altering the course of her lips, moving upward, along the underside of his chin and the sharp angles of his jaw, journeying toward his mouth.

"Hannah…oh, God…no." His hands locked around her wrists, his grip viselike. He pushed her away from him and held her there. His eyes burned into hers while his chest heaved with the overwhelming effort of resisting her.

"Yes," she countered softly, apparently not understanding. She was soft and warm and so beautiful. Every part of him throbbed with the need to give her what she was asking for. Come morning, however, he would regret it. Riley knew it as surely as he knew he loved her. He was protecting her, protecting their child.

Turning her away was far more painful for him than it was for her. In time she'd understand he was doing the admirable thing. In time she'd appreciate the sacrifice he was making.

"Not now," he said again, more forcefully this time.

She blinked, stunned. "When?"

"Later," he answered with confidence. "After the baby's born."

Hannah jerked her head back and went pale as if he'd slapped her hard. She was in such a rush to leave him, she nearly fell onto the carpet in the process of climbing off his lap. Her breath came in staggered gasps as she backed away from him, her hands at her throat. Huge, glistening tears brimmed and then spilled like pearl-shaped drops of dew from her eyes. She had the stricken look of someone in great pain.

"Hannah..." Riley thought he'd feel noble and generous, doing the right thing. Instead, he felt like a louse. "I...want you. It's just that—"

"Not now, you don't!" she raged, tears streaming down her face in a flood of emotion. "Not when I'm fat and ugly with your child!" She stumbled as she turned to run from him, nearly colliding with the end of the sofa. She caught herself, then raced toward their bedroom, slamming the door. The sound echoed in the room like a pistol shot.

Hannah's sobs tore into Riley's heart like the edge of a dull, rusty knife. He'd never meant to hurt Hannah. He was only trying to do what was right.

Suddenly he felt weary, more tired than he'd ever been in his life. Tired of being virtuous. Sick and tired of living up to the standards of a dead man. He'd leave nobility for men like Jerry Sanders, who'd been born for such things.

Abruptly he stood, and never feeling more at a loss in dealing with his gently reared wife, he headed for the bedroom. His hand was on the knob when he paused. Sure as hell, he'd hate himself in the morning if he made love to her. The regret would eat at him like battery acid, the way it had the night of Seafair. The guilt of breaking the promise he'd made to himself would consume him, come dawn. It would follow him out to sea and haunt him the long months they'd be apart. If there were any complications when the baby was born, Riley knew he would blame himself for these moments of weakness.

Regrets were a funny thing, Riley mused darkly. He'd lived with them most his life in one form or another. One important rule about remorse, something profound he'd garnered over the years: if he was going to suffer regret, then he made damn sure it was worthwhile.

With that thought in mind, he pushed open the door and walked inside their bedroom.

Hannah was sprawled on top of the mattress, sobbing as though her heart were shattered. Knowing he was the cause of those tears ate at him like the teeth of a piranha. Not knowing exactly what to do to comfort her, he hesitantly walked across the room and sat on the edge of the bed. Poising his hand above her, he hesitated still, then gently began to pat her shoulder.

The instant she felt his touch, Hannah jerked away as though she found him repulsive.

"Leave me alone," she wailed.

"Can we talk?"

"No." She scooted out of his reach, so far away it was a wonder she didn't topple onto the carpet on the other side of the bed.

"I don't find you ugly," Riley said, rushing to ease her mind. "You're so beautiful, I can't keep my eyes off you."

She raised her head and glared at him, her look hot enough to blister paint. It was more than apparent she didn't believe him.

"Come here, Hannah."

"No... If you so much as touch me, I swear... I'll phone the police."

"You'd better start dialing now," he muttered. Standing, he shucked his shirt, balled it up in his hands and tossed it on the floor. His slacks came off next.

"Wh-what are you doing?" she demanded, her voice trembling. She crowded into the corner of the bed, drawing her feet under her, her hands clenched over her breasts.

"What does it look like?" he answered calmly. "I'm getting ready to make love to my wife."

Royalty couldn't have tilted a chin with more finesse. "Don't do me any favors, Riley Murdock."

"The only favors we'll be giving will be to each other," he assured her, pulling back the sheets and climbing inside the bed. She continued to stare at him as though he were a stranger. In many ways he was, even to himself. "I'm going to need some help," he told her, unaccustomed to dealing with the intensity of the feelings she aroused in him. Even though she was on the other side of the bed, her effect upon him was total. His need for her clawed at him. "I don't want this to be like the first time. I don't want to hurt you."

"You didn't," she whispered in a soft, meek voice. "It... was just that I wasn't expecting... you know."

"Yes, I do know. I'm sorry." He held out his arms to her. "We'll start by kissing and go slow and easy. Just promise to tell me if I'm hurting you."

She hesitated as if she weren't sure she could believe him, as though she were frightened even now that he'd reject her.

"Promise me," he repeated, holding his arms out to her.

"I promise." She made the short journey across the bed to his side, slipping her arms around him and pressing her head to his chest. Every place she touched him branded Riley. Closing his eyes, he willed himself to remain coolheaded and in control. They'd go about this slow and easy. With that thought in mind, he directed his mouth to hers.

His intentions were lost, cast into a never-never world where all good intentions eventually landed, the instant their lips touched.

Riley was desperate for Hannah. Desperate and greedy. And she for him. Their kisses were primitive and wild, a raging storm of need, too long repressed.

The desire to woo Hannah, to seduce her gently, to cast aside all fear and pain, was lost; vanished on a tide of need so overwhelming there was no turning back, no time for second thoughts, no time except to feel.

Hannah moaned in welcome, opening her mouth to him. Riley plunged his tongue forward, probing deeply, to mate with hers in a frenzied erotic game. He lowered his head and dragged a gulp of air into his lungs as he blazed fire-hot, love-hot kisses down her throat and neck. Her hands clawed at him, wanting more, demanding more. He tangled his fingers in her hair and rushed his mouth back to hers. Her lips were wet and warm and welcome, so damned welcome.

The sound of her whimper was the purest form of ecstasy he'd ever known. His groan echoed hers as he dragged his hands, almost against his will, down the silky-smooth front of her gown. He was rewarded as the fullness of her breasts filled his palms. Her nipples hardened instantly, and it was all Riley could do not to cry out. Hannah whimpered anew and arched toward him.

Riley's hands continued their downward progression, resting on the swell of her abdomen that was their growing child, reminding him of the rich fruit their lovemaking had planted.

"I'm so big," she moaned between kisses.

"So damned beautiful."

His hands roved around the thickness of her waist and over the sculpted contours of her hips to the perfect roundness of her buttocks. He dragged her closer to him, savoring the feel of her against the heat of his groin. Inch by sweet inch, Riley's fingers worked the silk gown upward until his hands met her bare thighs. Fire, the hottest he'd ever known, singed his fingers as he stroked the warm silk on the insides of her smooth legs.

"Hannah..." He felt he had to warn her of the coming invasion. "I'm going to touch you."

"Yes, oh...please." She parted for him, her eyes bright with passion, locking with his in the muted moonlight. She bit into her lower lip as his finger slipped steadily upward. She groaned softly as he deftly parted the folds of her womanhood. Riley stilled, his heart racing, afraid he was doing something to pain her.

"Don't stop," she pleaded, her long fingers digging into his shoulders. Her hips swayed, urging him to continue. Riley didn't need any encouragement. He wanted this as much as she did. He was ready to explode, had been from their first kiss and he wasn't even inside her yet.

His finger continued its silken journey until he'd sunk as far as he dared go. The heat of her, the moist honey of her readiness produced a groan of heady excitement from Riley.

"Are you ready?" Her body was prepared, but he found it equally important that she be mentally primed for the physical realities of their lovemaking.

His hands trembled as he tugged the gown over her head and discarded it. He longed to talk to her, to ease her fears and any discomfort she might experience when he entered her. But he found himself incapable of muttering a single sound. His fears were rampant. He was afraid he'd be too heavy for her. That he was too large for her. He feared his weight might somehow injure the child.

Hannah must have read the uncertainty in his eyes. "It's all right," she whispered, linking her arms around his neck, bringing him down to her. She kissed him as though that would convince him all was well.

"The baby?"

"Will be fine.... I'm not so sure about me, though, if you keep me waiting much longer."

Riley loved her in that moment, more deeply than he thought it was possible to love another. Taking infinite care, he moved over her, lowering himself between her legs, which she'd willingly parted for him. His gaze burned into hers. Going as slowly as his body would allow, he positioned himself and entered her unhurriedly, watching her closely for any sign of pain or discomfort, giving her ample time to adjust to him, to his body invading hers.

Hannah closed her eyes and dragged in a deep breath. "I'm hurting you?"

"No... not in the least. I... don't remember it feeling this good." Her hands tightened around his neck, and she hooked her feet around the backs of his knees and shifted upward, as though taking in every part of him were of the utmost importance.

When he was as deep as he dared sink, he shuddered, surrounded as he was by the most intense pleasure. Surrounded by joy. And love. He stared down on her, his heart full, and she looked up at him, her gaze as warm as liquid honey.

"You're sure?" He had to ask, had to know.

"Yes... oh, please."

A frenzy of long-denied need overtook him then as his hips pumped against hers. Rhythm was lost to him. So was the proper pacing. He took her swiftly. Then slowly. Then fiercely. Then gently. Their mating was wild and raw and hot. So unbelievably hot that Riley felt consumed by the fire of his need. Of her need. Of them together.

Riley's completion came in minutes, with a flash of pleasure so keen it bordered on pain. It was over. Far too quickly. Much too soon.

He hadn't finished making love to Hannah and already he was worrying about how long it would be before he could have her again.

Holding her against him, his hands in her hair, he savored the closeness they shared. Wrapping his legs around hers, Riley rolled onto his side, taking her with him, maintaining the intimate link between them.

Their eyes met and Hannah released a soft, feminine sigh, then smiled. Tears streaked her face, and Riley reached out and, frowning, brushed them aside. He'd hurt her, only she'd never admit it. His stomach tightened.

Hannah must have read his fears. She captured his hand and brought it to her mouth, kissing his palm. "No...you don't understand. It was so...beautiful. What took you so long, my love? What took you so long?" She draped her arms around his neck and snuggled against him, engulfing him in tenderness and warmth. Her warmth. Her love.

Within minutes she was sound asleep.

Not so, Riley. He lay there, soaking in her nearness, savoring these few precious hours. Drinking in her gentle ways, her generosity and her love. He'd never thought to experience this time with a woman.

If it hadn't been for Hannah, he probably would never have married. He'd rejected the idea years before, not wanting a woman complicating his life. Instead he had brief affairs, so that he could walk away with callous indifference whenever he chose. He preferred it that way, he'd assured himself. He wasn't interested in commitment; he didn't want demanding relationships.

He'd never realized, he'd never known all that he'd been missing until Hannah came into his life. Hunger claimed him—not a physical craving, but an emotional one—for what he'd learned, for what he'd discovered because of the woman asleep in his arms.

Resting his hand on the rounded curve of her stomach, Riley closed his eyes to the wealth of love and emotion he experienced for their child. With everything in him, he regretted he'd be gone when his son or daughter was born. The thought of Hannah in pain, struggling to give life to his child, sent cold chills down his spine.

He knew little of the ways of a woman's body and even less about babies. He had heard the birthing process was often difficult and always painful. It wasn't unheard of for a woman to die while in labor. The mere thought of losing Hannah sent his heart into a panic. From the first visit, Dr. Underwood had assured Riley that Hannah's pregnancy was progressing normally; as far as he could judge. And he'd delivered hundreds of babies. Hannah's delivery would be routine.

Riley fretted about her being alone, but he'd spoken to Cheryl Morgan, who'd faithfully promised him she'd keep in close contact with Hannah.

From a few subtle questions she'd asked and the odd look she'd given him, Riley knew his friend's wife was openly curious about how someone like him had married a sweet innocent like Hannah. It remained a mystery to nearly everyone. Only a handful of people was aware of the story—his commanding officer, the chaplain and a couple of others. For Hannah's sake, Riley strove to keep it that way. The less anyone knew, the better. Not that he felt the need to protect Hannah's reputation. Hannah had more admirers than she knew. His single friends would have welcomed the opportunity to defend her honor, especially Don and Burt.

Riley got a kick out of the way they acted around her. Both were foulmouthed, hard-drinking cusses who welcomed an excuse to fight. Riley found it downright comical the way they stumbled over one another looking for a reason to do things for her.

The baby shower was a prime example. Riley knew Cheryl Morgan had organized it, but he'd never thought he'd see the day Don and Burt would sit around making small talk and eating cake with a bunch of Navy wives. Hell, he'd never thought he'd see the day him-

self. Nor would he ever believe he'd hold up tiny little
sleepers and ooh and ahh over them like a softhearted
woman. But he had, and his burly friends with him.

Riley could feel welcome sleep coaxing him into a
soothing void. Sam would be born with or without him
sometime within the next two months; and God willing, all would go well.

"Riley," Hannah whispered in the early-morning
light. He slept soundly at her side; the even rise and fall
of his chest had mesmerized her for the past several
minutes. She scooted closer and pressed her head
against his chest.

"Hmm."

"I love you." She had to say it, had to let him know
what had been in her heart all these weeks. Tell him or
burst with emotion. "I'm so proud to be your wife."

"After the incredible sex we just shared, I'm proud,
too." His arms cradled her against him, and he wore a
silly, lazy grin. "What time is it?"

"Four."

"What are you doing awake at this hour?" His eyes
were closed, and he seemed far more interested in
sleeping than carrying on a conversation with her.

"Watching you. I have a...question." She was
pleased it was still dark, otherwise he'd know she was
blushing.

"Hmm?"

"That night...in Seattle?"

"Yes?" Slowly, reluctantly, he opened his eyes and
looked at her.

"We...you know...made love twice?"

Riley frowned, as though he weren't sure he understood what she was asking. "Yes."

"Do...men and women often do it twice in one night?" Her finger made lazy circles on his chest, curling the short, kinky hairs around her index finger. Her eyes purposely avoided his.

"Sometimes."

"Oh." She released a long, meaningful sigh.

"Why do you ask?"

"I was curious."

"I'm curious, too," he whispered hoarsely, and tunneling his fingers through her hair, he brought her mouth to his, slipping his tongue inside. While their mouths were joined, he rolled onto his back, taking her with him so that her legs were straddling his torso.

She raised questioning eyes to his, slowly, meaningfully. "There are other ways?"

He grinned, his look almost youthful as he nodded. "Plenty. With you like this there's less likelihood we'll injure the baby."

It was in her mind to assure him they hadn't earlier, but the need for assurances was taken from her as Riley directed her mouth down to his. The only words either murmured after that were sighs, and moans, and whimpers of pleasure and love.

"You've got the doctor's phone number by the bed stand?"

"You know I do," Hannah answered. He'd asked the same question no less than three times in the last ten minutes. She sat on the edge of the mattress, leaning back on her hands, while he finished packing his duffel bag.

"Your bag is packed?"

"Riley," she said with an exasperated sigh, "the baby isn't due for another eight and a half weeks. Worry about your own packing. I'll be doing mine soon enough.''

He stalked to the far side of their bedroom and stuffed what remained of this gear into the thick canvas bag with enough force to punch out the bottom. "I don't want you lifting anything heavier than three pounds, understand?''

"Aye, aye, sir." She gave him a mocking salute behind his back.

"Your job?''

"We agreed when I was hired it would only be for a few months. I won't work past February. I promise.'' Once again she smiled.

"Dammit, Hannah, this isn't a laughing matter.''

"I'm not laughing," she assured him, giving her voice just the right amount of contriteness to convince him she was sincere.

"Then why do I have the feeling you find this all a big joke?'' He straightened and plowed his fingers through his hair. It was so rare to see Riley ruffled that Hannah honestly enjoyed it. Now that he was only a few hours from deployment, the realization he'd be leaving seemed to have hit him like a sledgehammer.

"Honest to God, Hannah," he whispered, "I've never been more terrified in my life and you're handling the whole thing like some . . .''

"Joke," she finished for him. "The baby and I are going to be just fine. There's nothing to indicate we won't be, so stop worrying.''

"I know. But things could go wrong.''

"They won't.''

"I wish I could be here.''

"I do, too. I'm sorry you can't, sorrier than you know. But it isn't the end of the world.'' She did her best to give the appearance of being cool and collected. No one knew better than she how overwrought her husband had become in the last few days before deployment.

"You'll keep in touch?"

Like everything else, he'd explained how the family grams worked a dozen or more times. Half the instructions he'd given her had been repeated so often that Hannah could recite them in her sleep. "I'll send one every available opportunity."

He sighed once more. "You realize the chaplain's office might not be able to contact me right away."

"Yes," she said patiently. "You already explained that, too. If the *Atlantis* is in an 'alert' status, then it could be some time before you're notified of Sam's birth."

"I won't be able to contact you even when I am told."

"I realize that, too," she assured him softly. The teasing banter she'd hidden behind earlier vanished as the reality hit her. She wasn't frightened—not of the actual birth—but everything within her longed for Riley to be able to share the experience with her.

"I couldn't bear it if anything happened to you," he whispered hoarsely.

"Nothing will. I promise." She bravely attempted to console him with a smile.

"Take care of yourself?" His gaze had never been more tender.

"Every minute of every day."

He moved across the bedroom and sank to his knees in front of her. He gripped both her hands and pressed his lips against the tips of her fingers. His shoulders heaved as he exhaled a sharp, anxious sigh. Gently, lovingly, he moved his hands over her abdomen and leaned forward to gently, sweetly kiss her stomach.

"Chinese, again?" Cheryl asked.

Hannah giggled. "I have this incredible urge for pork-fried rice, and before you ask, I wouldn't even think of using soy sauce."

The two were spending a lazy Saturday afternoon in the Kitsap Mall, window-shopping. Hannah's due date was a week away, and she'd never felt more hearty. In the last week she'd accomplished more than in the past several that Riley had been out to sea.

The days had sped past on winged feet, one often blending into the next. She was so busy that despite dreadfully missing Riley, the days piled on top of one another like professional football players.

Her visits to Dr. Underwood were weekly now. Hannah had felt huge at seven months. Months eight and nine were like nature's cruel joke. No longer could she stand upright and view her feet. She'd given up wearing shoes that entailed tying; it would be simpler to wrestle a crocodile. If there was anything to be grateful for, it was that Riley wasn't there to fuss over her. If he'd been solicitous at seven months, she hated to think how he'd behave now.

She was miserable, true; but not overly so. If she had anyone to complain about it was Cheryl, who'd become as much a mother hen as Riley had been. Hannah honestly thought Cheryl had taken lessons from Riley.

Hannah swore her friend would follow her into the bathroom, if she would let her. The only thing she could figure was that Riley had gotten hold of the nurse and made her promise on her mother's grave to take care of Hannah.

For a nurse who dealt daily with the birthing process, Cheryl behaved as though Hannah were the first woman alive to become pregnant.

"Isn't that blue dress a knockout?" Cheryl asked, pausing in front of MaryLou's Dress Shop. "I should try it on, just for the fun of it. Something like that would drive Steve wild. Not that he needs much." She laughed at her own joke. "Hannah?"

"Oh, it's cute, real cute." The dress was that and more, although Hannah had given it only a fleeting glance.

"Something's wrong?"

"No..." Hannah wasn't sure.

Cheryl gripped her arm, dragging her to the thick polished bench in the middle of the mall floor. "Let's sit down."

"I'm all right," Hannah protested. "I'm just feeling a little...strange."

"Strange as in how?"

"Strange as in...oh...oh." Her eyes rounded as she shot her gaze up to her friend. "If I'm not mistaken, that was a...labor pain."

Chapter Thirteen

Riley had been on edge all day. As Hannah's due date approached, the weight of their separation pressed on him unlike anything he'd ever experienced. To love a woman, to care so deeply about her well-being was foreign to him. He was at a loss to know how to deal with his worries.

Others around him slept without a qualm. But the escape of slumber evaded Riley. Rather than fight it, he'd lain back in his berth and stared into the dark. His thoughts were heavy, his anxiety high.

In the last two family grams he'd received, Hannah had claimed all was well with her and Sam. But no matter how many times he'd read the words, analyzed the few sentences she was allowed to transmit, Riley was left with the feeling something wasn't right. His fears were widespread, and once again he silently cursed the necessity of being at sea during these last worrisome months of her pregnancy.

His friends were little help. Steve wasn't a father yet, so he knew little of the . . .

A father. Riley hesitated as the word passed through his mind with the speed of a laser beam. He was about to become a father. Funny, from the time he'd learned of Hannah's pregnancy, he'd never thought of himself in those terms.

A father.

He knew little of such matters, he acknowledged, frowning. He'd never had the opportunity to know the man who'd sired him. From what Riley understood, his own father had been unaware of his birth. The man, who would forever remain a mystery to him, had contributed little to his emotional and physical well-being. The only male influence Riley had received had come from his stepfather, an abusive alcoholic who'd paid him little attention.

Riley experienced an overwhelming surge of gratitude that he'd learned of Hannah's pregnancy. In different circumstances he might never have known of it. He would have gone about his life blithely unaware of Sam's existence, and would have missed so much more than he'd ever thought to experience.

Considering the responsibility that awaited him with his child's birth overwhelmed Riley. He knew so little of the ways of a father, and even less of love. But Hannah had taught him the very meaning of the word, and he was confident Sam would give him all the instruction he'd need to be a father.

A daddy, he amended, grinning.

A sigh quivered through his lungs, and he closed his eyes, content for the first time that day. He could sleep now, entrusting the well-being of his wife and child to a far greater power than his own.

"Lieutenant Commander Kyle would like a word with you."

Riley's heart skipped a beat, then raced with such velocity he went dizzy and weak. There was only one reason the executive officer would want to speak to Riley.

Hannah.

The rush with which he moved through the tight quarters of the nuclear submarine caused more than a few stares. His eyes connected with the other man's, and the lieutenant commander grinned broadly.

"You wanted to see me, sir?"

Lieutenant Commander Kyle was the best kind of officer. Riley had known him several years and liked him immensely. There wasn't a man aboard the *Atlantis* who didn't. Word had it the executive officer had been divorced for nearly two years and then had reunited with his wife. He'd been to hell and back, according to those who knew him best. Whatever the cause of his problems, he'd solved them and took an interest in his men and their lives.

The CO's grin broadened as he held his hand out to Riley. "Congratulations are in order. We received word a few minutes ago that your wife has given birth to a healthy eight-pound three-ounce boy. Mother and son are doing well."

"A...son." The words barely worked their way past a lump in his throat that was so large it made it painful to breathe.

"Hannah?"

"According to the wire, she's fine."

Riley nodded. He'd heard the CO say it once, but he needed to be sure, to calm the doubts and the fears that crowded his heart and mind.

"Eight pounds?"

"Big and healthy." The lieutenant commander slapped him across the back. "You look like you need to sit down, Murdock."

"I feel like I need to."

The commanding officer chuckled. "I understand that well. My second child, Patrick, was born while I was at sea. I wasn't a damn bit of good to the Navy until I knew Carol had had a safe delivery."

A numbness had claimed hold of Riley, starting in his chest and radiating outward, paralyzing his lungs.

"A son," he repeated when he could.

"I take it you wanted a boy."

Riley didn't answer right away. "I suppose I did, but I wouldn't have been disappointed with a daughter."

The other man nodded. "Our first was a girl, and I couldn't have been more pleased, although I'd convinced myself I wanted a son. Somehow, once they arrive, all pink and soft, it doesn't seem to matter."

They spoke for a few minutes more, then Riley returned to the torpedo room. He felt fiercely proud, an emotion so profound it was all he could do not to throw his arms in the air and shout for the sheer joy of it. The crazy part was, the desire to fall to his knees and weep was just as compelling.

He had a son. Samuel Riley Murdock. Moisture blurred his vision, and Riley realized it was tears of jubilation; his heart felt so full of love he couldn't contain it any longer.

He had a son.

* * *

Hannah studied the clock on the wall of her hospital room, which was partially obliterated by two bright-blue helium balloons that were tied to the foot of her bed. Cheryl Morgan was scheduled to go on duty in fifteen minutes and had promised to stop in for a short visit beforehand.

Hannah had been waiting to talk to Cheryl all afternoon. Her mind was on her son, who was sleeping serenely at her side. She'd been overwhelmed by the outpouring of love and attention she'd received after Samuel's birth. She hadn't lacked for visitors. Cards lined her nightstand, and her small locker was filled with gifts.

"So how's it going, little mother?" Cheryl asked, stepping into the room. She was dressed in her uniform and a soft blue sweater.

The minute Hannah saw her, she couldn't help herself—she burst into tears. "I'm fine," she wailed, and reached for a tissue, blowing her nose.

"New-mother blues?" Cheryl asked sympathetically, handing Hannah the entire box of tissues. "Don't worry, it's to be expected. With so many hormones swimming around, your emotions are bound to be in upheaval."

"It's not that," Hannah sobbed, pointing toward the window ledge where a beautiful bouquet of a dozen red and white roses was perched. "Riley had one of his friends on the base send them to me... The card..."

"The card was sweet and sentimental?" Cheryl coaxed.

"No," she wailed. "The next time I see that man I'm going...to...slap him silly. I'm...so angry I could just spit."

"Angry?"

"Read it for yourself. Then you'll know." Hannah picked up the small envelope and handed it to her friend.

Cheryl's gaze narrowed as she slipped out the card and read the few scribbled words. Slowly she raised her gaze to Hannah, her look wide and questioning. "It says, 'I love you.' It's signed, 'Riley.' "

Hannah sobbed once more and in a fit of righteousness tossed the damp tissue to the foot of her bed. "See what I mean?"

"Those are certainly fighting words if I ever heard them," came the sarcastic comment. "Are you going to torture him with the silent treatment once he arrives home?"

"I should." Using the heels of her hands, Hannah rubbed the moisture from her burning cheeks, irked all the more. "He hasn't even got the common decency to tell me to my face," she announced, and swallowed a hiccup.

"Let me see if I understand this," Cheryl said, pulling up a chair and sitting down. "The card claims he loves you, and that makes you angry?"

"Yes," Hannah snapped.

"He's not supposed to love you?"

"Well, of course he is."

"I see," Cheryl replied, frowning.

It was apparent her friend didn't understand anything of what had happened. "You don't see," Hannah argued. "Otherwise you'd be as outraged as I am."

"Maybe you'd better explain it to me." Cheryl crossed her legs and leaned back as though convinced it would take considerable time to explain why Hannah had taken such offense at Riley's card.

Actually, Hannah wasn't eager to rationalize her outrage, but there didn't seem to be any help for it. "It's Riley."

"That much I gathered."

"He...had his friend send the flowers with the card."

"I'm with you so far," Cheryl prompted with one solid nod of her head.

"It's what he said on the card—that he loves me."

"I understand that part, too, only I seem to be missing some key link."

Hannah's eyes filled with fresh tears. "I love him so much and...and he's never told me he loves me. Not even once—and then he has to do it in a stupid card when I can't be there to look in his eyes."

"Ah," Cheryl murmured after a significant pause. "So you doubt he truly loves you?"

"Not really. It's just that he's been too stubborn to realize it. I knew he would in time.... It's just that I wanted to be there when he finally got around to admitting it."

"Ah." The light was dawning in Cheryl's expressive eyes.

"You know what he is? A coward," Hannah answered her own question, without giving Cheryl the opportunity. "Riley Murdock is a living, breathing coward. If word got out what a..."

"Coward," Cheryl supplied.

"Right. If the Navy knew what I do about him, they'd ask for his resignation." She looked to Steve's wife for confirmation and was disappointed.

"I don't agree."

"Come on, Cheryl. You can't join my pity party if you're going to be obstinate about everything."

Her friend's face broke into a wide smile. "Anyone with one good eye would know how Riley feels about you. The man's so bewitched it isn't even funny."

Hannah felt herself go all soft. "Do you really think so?"

"Hannah," Cheryl said, her eyes brightening as she spoke. "If I hadn't seen it for myself, I would never have believed it. The man's crazy about you. He loves you so much it's eating him alive."

"But he's never said so."

"I doubt that he knows how."

"Really?" To Hannah's way of thinking, it would have been a simple matter for him to tell her. She'd told him often enough during the last days before he left for sea duty. Oftentimes she'd been left to wonder. The only time they'd made love was the night of the baby shower. It had been so beautiful, so perfect. Just thinking about the tender way in which her husband had made love to her filled Hannah's eyes with fresh tears.

Her disappointment had been keen when he didn't make love to her again before his departure. She knew he was worried about leaving her, worried about the baby being born while he was at sea. Hannah doubted he'd slept two winks that last night. He'd held on to her tightly until dawn. She'd woken once to find his hand softly rubbing her stomach. Hannah had wanted to assure him that she and Sam would be fine, but in the end he was the one offering promises before coaxing her back to sleep.

"Give Riley time," Cheryl advised softly. "I've seen so many changes in him since you've come into his life, and I'm beginning to think we've only viewed the tip of the iceberg."

Gradually, after listening to her friend, Hannah agreed. Her marriage was in its infancy; the best was yet to come.

"It won't be long now," Hannah whispered to the sleeping infant tucked securely in her arms. Her gaze rested lovingly on her five-week-old son as she held him tightly against her, blocking out the April wind. Within a few minutes, her husband would view his son and see for himself the thick thatch of brown hair and high, smooth brow that was all Riley. The dimple on Samuel's chin wasn't as pronounced now as it had been the first couple of weeks following his birth. Their son was perfect, beautiful. If some doubted Riley was Samuel's father, all they'd need do was to look into her son's deep blue eyes and note the strong, dominant chin to be reassured.

As before, the wharf was crowded with the wives and children of the members of the *Atlantis* crew. Hannah had heard plenty of grumbling among the wives. Cheryl and Hannah had muttered their own fair share. The nuclear submarine was docking nearly two weeks later than the wives had been told to anticipate.

The last sixty minutes felt like sixty years to Hannah. And the days before had merged together—day into day, lonely night into lonely night. If Samuel hadn't demanded nearly every minute of every day, and half of the nights, Hannah swore she would have gone crazy with anticipation.

As before, she'd helped to pass the interminable waiting by preparing every detail of Riley's return— from the candlelight dinner of Riley's favorite meal, chicken enchiladas, to the new pale pink silk gown she intended on wearing to bed that very night. Only this time she didn't need any encouragement from Cheryl to purchase the frothy bit of lingerie. She'd gone down to the Kitsap Mall and bought it all on her own. She might have a long way to go before she could ever be termed a seductress, but Hannah was determined to learn.

The first men disembarked the *Atlantis,* and Hannah heaved a grateful sigh of thanksgiving. "It won't be long now," she whispered into her son's ear. "Daddy's coming."

Cheryl was standing on the tips of her toes. "I see Steve."

"Is Riley close?" Hannah asked, hating the fact she wasn't five inches taller and able to see for herself.

"Not yet... Oh, wait, he's in front of Steve, scooting past everyone, making a nuisance of himself. My goodness, that man is determined to create enemies."

"Cheryl, please, don't tease."

"Who's teasing? One would think he was in a hurry to see his wife and son."

Hannah saw Riley just then, and it was as if the earth came to a sudden, abrupt standstill. The entire world seemed to tip on its axis as though awaiting the outcome of their reunion.

"Riley!" she shouted, raising her hand and waving like a crazy woman. She wasn't the only woman behaving out of character. There was something about these reunions that did that to a Navy wife.

She edged her way past a couple of women and met Riley halfway. He stopped brusquely in front of her, his eyes drinking in the sight of her as his duffel bag slipped from his hands and fell to the pier.

She smiled up at him, but her vision blurred when her eyes filled with tears of profound happiness. After all the trouble she'd gone through with her makeup, she struggled to keep them at bay, not wanting to ruin the effect.

His hand found her face, gently cupping her cheek. His touch rippled through her like an electric shock as his thumb caught the single tear.

"You're more beautiful than I remember."

"Oh, Riley."

Being careful of the baby, Riley wrapped her in his arms and buried his face in the curve of her neck, breathing in deeply as if the scent of her were the only thing in the world that would revive him.

He kissed her then, his mouth desperate but tender. Their lips clung as the tears spilled down Hannah's wind-chapped cheeks.

"Oh, Lord, Hannah," he growled, his arms circling her and dragging her as close as they could with the slumbering child between them. "I love you so damned much. I love you." He chanted the words as if they'd been burning on his lips, in his heart and mind, ready to be shared for far too long.

He searched for her mouth and worshiped her in a kiss that left Hannah trembling and shaken. His tongue sought hers, firing to life a need so strong it burst like fire inside her. "Riley...you make me forget the baby."

He raised his eyes to her as though he'd forgotten for the moment that their son was between them. Slowly he lowered his gaze to Samuel.

All her life Hannah would cherish the look of wonder and love that came into her husband's eyes.

"Riley," she said softly, "meet your son. Samuel, this is your daddy."

Chapter Fourteen

"Hannah?" Riley called to his wife, certain the infant in his arms was about to wake and cry. His heart thundered with dread at the possibility.

"Yes?" She stuck her head out from the kitchen. He didn't know what she was cooking, but he hadn't smelled anything so delicious in months. She'd banished him to the living room, claiming dinner was a surprise. Everything about Hannah was incredible. He'd been struck by her beauty many times, but never more profoundly than now. It took him several minutes to realize the marked difference. In the process of having Sam, she'd made the passage into womanhood. There was a maturity in her beauty, a radiance and freshness that awed him.

She was reed slim, her waist as narrow and trim as the night they'd met. And her hair was longer now, reaching halfway down her back. Watching her as she walked caused his fingers to ache with the need of her. It was too soon after the baby's birth, he realized, to consider making love. Riley was almost relieved. He released a jagged sigh. Many a lonely night, he'd fallen asleep remembering how remarkably good the loving had been between them. A hundred or more times he'd cursed himself for wasting the last precious days they'd spent together. He'd wanted her with a desperation that was with him still. Yet he held back, convinced he was doing the right thing.

"Sam's awake," Riley murmured. After all the torturous days of waiting for this moment to hold his son in his arms, Riley felt terrified. Eight pounds had sounded large for a baby, but the tiny being in his arms seemed incredibly... tiny. Riley was almost afraid to breathe for fear of disrupting him.

"He won't break," Hannah explained softly, walking into the living room, "I promise you. Relax. You're as stiff as cardboard."

A second sigh quivered through Riley's chest. Samuel stared up at him and cooed softly, seeming to enjoy his father's discomfort.

"He's not nearly as frightening as he looks," Hannah teased on her way back into the kitchen.

Riley didn't know how she could be so calm about it. To the best of his knowledge he'd never held a baby in his life. It seemed to him that one should ease into this heavy responsibility. Riley, however, had been given little option. The minute they arrived home, Hannah had donned an apron and thrust Samuel into his arms and suggested the two become acquainted while she put the finishing touches on dinner.

Samuel stirred, wide-awake now. He gazed up at Riley with huge, quizzical eyes that were the precise color of his own, Riley realized, feeling inordinately proud. A warmth took root in his heart unlike anything he'd ever experienced. His heart full, Riley bent down and gently kissed Samuel's brow.

Doing his best to relax, Riley eased his back against the recliner. Only a few months before, he'd lived his life independent of others, free to do as he wished. If he wanted to party away the night and stagger home drunker than a skunk, he'd done so without a qualm. He'd answered only to himself. His life had been his own, free of entanglements.

All that had changed from the minute he'd met Hannah. He'd married her for reasons he had yet to grasp fully. Because of the sins of the past. Because it had been the right thing to do. For her. For his future with the Navy. For his son.

He'd said his vows before the chaplain, never realizing he was bound by far more than a few spoken words. Hannah, and now Samuel, had sunk tender hooks into his heart, and he would never be the same man again.

Gently lifting Samuel in his arms, Riley awkwardly placed his son over his shoulder and patted the impossibly small back.

This was his son. The fruit of his desire for a beautiful woman who had come to him in grief and pain—only Riley had been so absorbed by her beauty and her purity that he hadn't noticed. It came to him that he should plead for Hannah's forgiveness for his lack of insight. By all that was right, he should set her free to marry the kind of man she deserved—someone like Jerry Sanders. While Hannah fussed in the kitchen, Riley tried to imagine what his life would be like without her now. His thoughts grew heavy and dark as his mind froze with dread and fear of an empty life without his wife and son.

He'd found contentment with Hannah. And love. God help him from being weak and greedy, but he needed her.

Hannah returned to the room, paused and smiled lovingly when she viewed them. "Much better. You look almost comfortable."

Riley frowned. "Why do I get the impression you're enjoying this?"

Her smile deepened. "Because I am. Did you count his fingers and toes?"

"No. Should I?" It hadn't entered Riley's mind that there might be an abnormality.

"No." She laughed at his distress. "Honestly, I had no idea you'd be such a fretful father. When they brought Sam to me the first time, I held him in my arms and peeled open the blanket just to be sure. I thought you might feel the same compulsion to check everything about him."

Riley shook his head. "I haven't gotten over the fear of holding him yet. Next time around, I'll think about peeking under the blanket."

"Dinner's almost ready," she told him, taking Samuel out of his arms. She disappeared for a moment and returned with a fresh diaper. Placing Samuel inside the bassinet, she laid open his blanket. The ease with which she changed the infant's diaper astonished Riley. He supposed that in time, he'd work his way up to that, as well.

"I'll feed Sam first," Hannah explained, gently lifting him into her arms, "then put him down to sleep. Hopefully we can have an uninterrupted meal."

She settled in the rocking chair and, mesmerized, Riley watched as she pulled up her blouse, released her bra and pressed her extended nipple into his son's mouth. With an eagerness Riley could appreciate, Sam latched on to the nipple and sucked greedily. Tiny white bubbles appeared at the corners of his mouth.

"Does it hurt...you know?" Riley asked self-consciously. "Nursing?"

Hannah tottered gently in the padded rocker. "It felt strange at first, a little uncomfortable. But gradually we learned to work together. We've gotten to be real handy at this, haven't we, Sam?" Using her index finger, she brushed a wisp of dark hair from their son's brow.

"What about labor?" It was a question that had stayed fixed in his mind for over a month. The thought of Hannah in pain did funny things to Riley's heart. He'd hated not being with her and had often dwelled on what it had cost her to bring Sam into the world. Each time he contemplated her labor, he suffered a multitude of worries. A part of him—a damn small part of him—was grateful he hadn't been with her, fearing he would have been more of a hindrance than a help.

"Labor was the most difficult thing I've ever done," she answered after a few silent moments. "It wouldn't be fair to play it down. I honestly thought I was prepared. Cheryl and I attended every birthing class. I had the breathing down to an art form and faithfully exercised every day, but when the time came it seemed impossible to focus my attention on anything but the pain."

Riley noted that her eyes dulled at the memory; then she looked up and it vanished under the radiance of her smile. Riley wasn't sure he'd ever seen anything like what he saw in Hannah. It was as though the curtain to her soul had been drawn open and he'd been granted a rare privilege. In those few fleeting moments, Riley caught a glimpse of the core of goodness and gentleness of this woman who had so thoroughly captured his heart.

"Then Samuel was born, and Riley...I can't even begin to explain how beautiful the experience was. He was squalling like an angry calf. Then Cheryl started crying and so did I, but not from pain. I felt so incredibly happy. I just couldn't hold it inside me any longer. It was a contest to see which one of us could cry the loudest. I can just imagine what Dr. Underwood thought."

"I wish I'd been with you." It hurt to know his best friend's wife had shared these moments with Hannah instead of him.

The sweetest smile touched her eyes. "I know. Next time we'll try to plan the pregnancy so you can be with me."

Next time. Riley's heart came to a sudden standstill. He stood and walked over to the window, staring blindly at the street in front of their home. That Hannah would be willing to bear him another child, after everything she'd endured, wreaked havoc with his mind and his senses.

Considering her health, considering the pain she'd suffered delivering Sam, Riley found it incredible she'd even consider the possibility. As far as he was concerned, one pregnancy was enough. He didn't know if his heart could withstand another.

Dinner was as delicious as the spicy aroma coming from the kitchen had promised. Riley enjoyed these uninterrupted moments with his wife, answering her questions, asking his own. It would forever remain one of the great mysteries of his life that someone like Hannah could be married to him, Riley mused as he stood an hour later, wanting to help her with the dishes.

He couldn't stop studying Hannah, noting once more the subtle changes he found in her—the fullness of her beauty, the radiance of her goodness, the love for their son that shone so brilliantly in her dove-gray eyes each time she mentioned him.

As hard as he tried to turn his mind to other matters, it was difficult to forget the kisses they'd shared on Delta Pier. Her lips had been soft and sweet and so damn tempting. Even now, hours later, he had to regulate his breathing in order to restrain the mounting desire building within him. He felt the raw, hungry need eating away at him, and repeatedly cursed himself for his weakness.

Hannah set the last of their dishes in the dishwasher, then turned her back to the kitchen counter, her hands braced against the edge. Her elbows weren't the only part of her anatomy that was extended. Riley's stomach pitched unevenly at the way her pear-shaped breasts captured his attention. It was improbable, unlikely, but they seemed to be pouting, demanding his attention It was all he could do to look elsewhere. Yet again and again, he found his eyes drawn back to her front.

"Did you really miss me?" she asked him softly.

"You know I did," he answered gruffly, reaching for the dishrag so he could wipe off the stove. That was his first mistake in a series he was doomed to commit if he didn't do something quick. As he extended his arm, his forearm inadvertently brushed against a hardening nipple. His breath caught in his throat. Riley felt as though he'd scorched his arm. He froze, his mission forgotten.

"You haven't kissed me since we arrived home," she whispered.

"I haven't?" Riley was more aware of it than she knew.

"No. Don't you think we should make up for lost time?"

"Ah . . . sure."

He kissed her, licking his tongue across the seam of her lips, delving into the corners of her sweet mouth. He trembled then, trembled with a need so powerful his knees went weak; trembled with the shock of how painfully good she felt in his arms—in his life.

Hannah wrapped her arms around his neck and moaned in wanton welcome, opening to him. A better man might have been able to resist her, but not Riley. Not now. Not when he was starving for her touch.

"Oh . . . Riley, I've missed you so much," Hannah moaned as if she were feeling everything he was. And more.

They kissed again, too hungry for each other to attempt restraint. Riley felt Hannah's need. It shuddered through her, reaching him, touching him, continuing to transmit into his own body with devastating results.

He twisted his mouth away from hers, inhaled sharply and buried his face in her neck, praying to God for the strength to stop before he went too far. Before he'd reached the point of no return. Before the hungry ache of his need consumed what remained of his will.

"I think we should stop." From where he found the strength to speak would forever remain an enigma to Riley.

"Stop?"

"It's too soon," he argued. He stepped away from her, his chest heaving with the effort. Every part of his body protested the action.

"Riley, love, don't worry. I . . . talked to the doctor." She blushed as she said it, and lowered her gaze. "It's not too soon, I promise you."

"I'd be more comfortable if we waited."

"Waited? Really?" She sounded bitterly disappointed.

Hell, she didn't know the half of it. "Just for a little while," he promised, but he didn't know whom he was speaking to—Hannah or himself.

"If you insist." She bore the disappointment well, Riley decided. In fact she seemed downright cheerful about it, he reflected later that evening.

Humming softly, she gave Sam a bath, dressed him in his sleeper and nursed him once more. The need to be close to her was overpowering. Riley followed her around like a lost lamb, satisfied with tidbits of her attention.

"I think I'll take a bath," she announced a little while later, when she was assured Sam was sleeping peacefully.

Riley nodded, deciding to read the evening paper. He could hear the bathwater running and didn't think much of it until the delicate scent of spring lavender wafted toward him. Lavender and wildflowers.

The fragrance swirled toward him with the seductive appeal of a snake charmer's music. Hannah and wildflowers. The two were inseparable in his mind. During the endless, frustrating nights aboard the *Atlantis*, Riley had often dreamed of Hannah traipsing toward him in a field of blooming flowers, a wicker basket handle draped over her arm. It didn't take much imagination to envision her in the picture she'd painted that hung above the fireplace.

"I'm tired. Let's go to bed," Hannah suggested softly. Riley looked up to discover her standing in the doorway to the kitchen, one arm raised above her head, leaning against the frame in a seductive pose. She wore a pale pink gown that clung to her breasts and hips like a second skin. Gone was Sam's mother and in her stead was Riley's wife: the most beautiful woman he'd ever known.

He swallowed tightly. She didn't help his breathing any when she stepped over to the recliner and took his hand. The power to resist her escaped him, and Riley obediently rose out of the chair and followed her into the bedroom.

"I'm . . . not quite ready for bed yet." He managed somehow to dredge up a token resistance.

"Yes, you are," she returned without a pause. "We both are—if those kisses in the kitchen were any indication."

"Ah...that was a mistake." Riley had rarely felt more tongue-tied in his life.

Hannah's sweet face clouded. "A mistake?"

"It's too soon.... I think we should wait a few more months until you're completely healed." That sounded logical. Sensible, even. The type of thing any loving husband would say to his wife after the birth of a child.

"A few months?" Hannah repeated incredulously.

"At least that long."

The air went still, so still it felt like the distinct calm before the storm. It was. Hannah bolted off the bed as though she'd been burned. Stalking past him with a righteous flair of her hips, she stopped just the other

side of the door, then slammed it hard enough to break
the living-room windows.

He heard another door slam and then another,
flinching with each discordant sound.

Riley closed his eyes, then buried his hands in his
hair, uncertain what he should do. He could follow her
and try to explain, but he didn't know what he would
say. He wasn't rejecting her; he was protecting her.

Hannah was too angry, too hurt to stand by and do
nothing. Slamming doors wasn't helping, and if she
didn't stop soon, she'd wake Sam.

Riley was impossible. Just when she was convinced
he truly loved her, he pulled this stunt. One rejection
was bad enough. Twice was unforgivable. She'd leave
him; that was what she'd do. But she had nowhere to
go. Nowhere she *wanted* to go, she amended reluctantly.

She didn't doubt Riley's love. She'd seen the emotion in his eyes when he'd looked down on Sam for the
first time. Surely she hadn't misread him, and he held
some tender spot in his heart for her, as well.

Quite simply, she decided, he just didn't find her
physically attractive. She might as well own up to the
fact and learn to live with it. This was the second and
last time she'd play the part of a fool. He'd trampled
across her heart and her pride for the last time.

Dragging the bucket from the storage closet, she
sniffled and reached for the mop. It was either vent this
incredible frustration one way or cave into the deep, dry
well of self-pity.

She mopped the kitchen floor with a vengeance, rubbing the mop over the already spotless floor as though it were caked with a thick layer of mud.

"Hannah."

She jerked upright and swung the mop around with her. She held it out in front of her like a knight's swift sword, intending to defend her honor. "Stay away from me, Riley Murdock."

"I think we should talk."

She brandished the mop beneath his nose in a warning gesture. Water drenched the front of his shirt, and a shocked look came into his eyes. "You can forget that. I'm through with...talking." She hated the way her voice cracked. Riley seemed to find it a sign of weakness and advanced toward her. Once again Hannah swung the mop around, determined to deter him. "You've already said everything I care to hear," she informed him primly. "I got your message loud and clear. First thing in the morning, I'll move my things into Sam's bedroom."

"Why would you do that?" he demanded, his temper rising. He attempted to grab hold of the mop, but she experienced a small sense of triumph by eluding his grasp.

"Why?" she repeated with a harsh laugh. "I refuse to sleep with a man who finds me so unattractive." Just admitting as much hurt almost more than she could bear. Tears filled her vision until Riley's image blurred and swam before her.

"It's not you who's lacking," Riley explained. "It's me."

"I don't believe that for a moment," she countered sharply, struggling to hold back the emotion. "I don't 'turn you on.' Isn't that what people say nowadays?"

"Don't turn me on? Are you nuts?"

"Apparently so." She jabbed the mop into the bucket with enough force to slosh the water over the sides. Without bothering to drain off the excess liquid, she slopped it onto the floor. "You must find my attempts to lure you into bed downright hilarious." She gave a short laugh, as if she, too, found them amusing.

"Hannah, for the love of heaven, will you listen to me?"

"No...just leave me alone." She raised the mop threateningly in an effort to persuade him she meant business.

"Put that thing down before you hurt yourself," he demanded with a growl.

"Make me." Hannah couldn't believe she'd said anything so childish. Riley had driven her lower than she'd ever thought she would sink.

Riley shook his head as if he, too, couldn't believe she'd challenge him in such a juvenile manner. When she least expected it, his hand shot out and he jerked the mop free of her grasp and hurled it to the floor.

Hannah was too stunned to react. She backed against the kitchen counter, feeling very much like a small, cornered animal, left defenseless and alone. She'd never felt more isolated in her life. Not even when she'd first realized she was pregnant with Riley's child.

"I'm not good enough for you," he admitted in an emotion-riddled breath. "Don't you understand?"

"No, I don't," she cried.

"Loving you isn't right."

Hannah glared at him with all the frustration pent up in her heart and then hurled the wet dishrag at him, hitting him in the shoulder. The damp cloth stuck there as if glued into place.

"It's a fine time to tell me that!" she shouted. "What am I supposed to tell Sam? That he was a terrible mistake and you rue the day you ever met his mother?"

"Of course not. Hannah, please, try to understand. By everything that's right, you should be married to Jerry Sanders."

"Is that a fact? What would you like me to do about it? Tell God He made a mistake so He can send Jerry back for a wedding?"

"Don't be ridiculous."

"Me?" she countered with a short hysterical laugh. "You're so eager to be rid of me, you're willing to pawn me off on a dead man."

Riley closed his eyes. "I've never known you to be so unreasonable. Think about it for a minute, would you?"

"Think about what? That you don't want me? How will that help matters any? Answer me one thing," she demanded between tears of rage and tears of pain. "Do you regret being married to me?"

An eternity passed before he answered. When he did, she had to strain to hear him. "Yes, but not for the reasons you think."

It would have pained her less had he stabbed her through with a knife. The fight drained out of her, and she dropped her hands lifelessly to her sides. All the weeks and months she'd loved him, cherished each precious moment they were together, treasured the tenderness and the caring. All along, it had been a lie. "I see."

"I'm a bastard!" Riley shouted. "I grew up on the wrong side of the tracks. If I'd looked at a girl like you when I was in high school, I would have been arrested. The fact we're married is a crime. You could have had any man you wanted, and frankly, sweetheart, you could do a hell of a lot better than me." He paused and seemed to wait for his words to sink in. "There are others out there like Jerry. Good, honest men. You should be married to one of them. Not me."

"You seem to be forgetting one minor detail," she said in a voice that was little more than a whisper. "I'm already married to you."

The tortured look Riley wore suggested he didn't need to be reminded. "If I didn't love you so damn much, I would have released you from our vows."

"You want to prove your love for me by abandoning me?" The very idea was too ludicrous to consider.

"Our marriage can't be annulled any longer," he admitted with a pained look. "I ruined any chance of that the night we made love."

"Ruined it . . . You mean you were honestly considering doing such a thing?" Hannah was too furious to think. She glanced around, ready to hurl the first available object she could find directly at her husband. His thinking was so twisted. He left her defenseless and more outraged than she could ever remember being in her life.

Moving quickly, Riley stepped forward and caught her in his arms. The tears he saw in her eyes appeared to distress him, and frowning, he brushed them aside. Closing her eyes, Hannah jerked her face away. She struggled, but Riley wouldn't release her and she soon gave up the effort.

"I love you so damn much," he confessed.

Hannah was about to argue with him when he pulled her mouth to his and kissed her, not bothering to hide the desperation and the pain of his confession.

For the first time, Hannah was able to put aside the rejection of the pain and understand everything Riley had been saying to her. He did love her—more than she dared credit, more than she dared to dream, enough to do what he felt was right and good where she and Sam were concerned.

Her hands found his face, and she slanted her mouth over his, opening to him. Again and again Riley kissed her, and she kissed him until she felt feverish with need.

"Oh, God, Hannah," he whispered, pressing his forehead against hers. "You make me crazy."

"I know," she murmured, raining nibbled kisses along the underside of his jaw. "I've been listening to crazy talk from you for the last several minutes, and I refuse to hear any more."

"Hannah, for the love of God . . ."

She silenced him the most effective way she knew how. "My turn," she said, holding him against her, wondering if any man could ever make her want him as much as she did him.

She led him into the living room and lowered him into the recliner. Once he was seated, she settled on his lap, to be sure she could intercept his arguments before they had time to form.

"You're right. Jerry Sanders was a special man. I loved him—he'll always hold a special place in my heart. But that in no way discounts my love for you."

Riley's eyes widened, and it looked as though he intended to argue with her, but she pressed her mouth on his, teased apart his lips with her tongue and then made a lightning-quick strike before abruptly ending the kiss. Riley was left panting and helpless, just the way Hannah meant to keep him until he listened to reason.

"You're my husband. The love I feel for you and Sam is so powerful it sometimes overwhelms me. I never knew a person could hold so much love inside. It overflows sometimes, and all I can do is sit and weep and thank God for sending you into my life.''

''Hannah—''

''Let me finish,'' she interrupted, pressing her finger to his lips. ''The night ... we met, Reverend Parker at the Mission House and I had a talk. I remember it as clearly as if it were this afternoon. He reminded me that God works in mysterious ways. I didn't believe him at the time—I was hurting too much. Now I understand. God took Jerry from me and then He sent you and Sam into my life. If you want to question God's wisdom that's certainly your right, but I don't. There's a balance to nature. Out of my grief were born the greatest joys of my life—you and Samuel.''

''But—''

''I'm not done yet,'' she chastised gently. ''You can go ahead and try to get rid of me if that's what you really want, but I'm telling you right now, it won't work. I plan on sticking around for a good long time. Ninety years or more.''

Riley went quiet and still. He closed his eyes, blocking her out. He seemed to be battling within himself, fighting her love and everything she was offering him. She knew she'd won when he opened his eyes and studied her, his eyes intensely blue. ''You're sure about this?''

''Very sure. Do you think I might be able to convince you to tag along for the ride?''

The slightest hint of a smile touched Riley's bottomless eyes. ''Are you going to attempt to unman me with any more mops? Or hurl more cold dishrags at me?''

''That depends on whether you refuse to make love to me again,'' she informed him with a prim lift to her voice.

"I don't think that's going to be much of a problem in the future."

Hannah grinned and relaxed. "I'm glad to hear it."

"In fact, I'm thinking we should follow your earlier suggestion and make up for lost time." His hands were at her waist, stroking her hips in a seductive, caressing motion.

"There's lots of time to make up for," she reminded him, linking her arms around his neck.

"It could take all night," he told her, looking so eager it was all Hannah could do not to laugh outright. In one swift motion he rose to his feet, scooping Hannah into his arms as he did so. He carried her through the house toward their bedroom.

"All night?"

"Perhaps days," he said, his eyes shining into hers.

"Days?"

"As long as a month."

Hannah sighed and pressed her mouth against his neck, loving the salty, manly taste of him. "A month?"

"Possibly years."

"Years?" she echoed incredulously.

"What was it you suggested? Ninety years?"

"At the very least," she whispered in reply. "Ninety years and at least three children."

"Three!" Apparently her husband hadn't learned his lesson. He fully intended to argue with her, but Hannah knew the most effective way of all to end contention between them.

*   *   *   *   *

Silhouette Special Edition

COMING NEXT MONTH

#703 SOMEONE TO TALK TO—Marie Ferrarella
Lawyer Brendan Connery was dreading the long-overdue reunion
with his ailing father. But then nurse Shelby Tyree appeared by
Brendan's side, offering to help him heal the wounds of the past....

#704 ABOVE THE CLOUDS—Bevlyn Marshall
Renowned scientist discovers abominable snowman.... Was it genius
or madness? Laura Prescott sought to save her father's reputation;
newspaperman Steve Slater sensed a story. On their Himalayan hunt
for truth, would they find love instead?

#705 THE ICE PRINCESS—Lorraine Carroll
To DeShea Ballard, family meant pain; to Nick Couvillion, it meant a
full house and kisses on both cheeks. An orphaned nephew united
them, but could one man's fire melt an ice princess?

#706 HOME COURT ADVANTAGE—Andrea Edwards
Girls' basketball coach Jenna Lauren dropped her defenses once
boys' coach Rob Fagan came a-courting... again. Familiar hallways
harkened back to high school romance, but this time, love wasn't just
child's play....

#707 REBEL TO THE RESCUE—Kayla Daniels
Investigator Slade Marshall was supposed to discover why
Tory Clayton's French Quarter guest house lay smoldering in ashes.
Instead, he fanned the flames... of her heart.

#708 BABY, IT'S YOU—Celeste Hamilton
Policeman Andy Baskin and accountant Meg Hathaway shirked
tradition. They got married, divorced, then, ten years later, had a
child. But one tradition prevailed—everlasting love—beckoning
them home.

AVAILABLE THIS MONTH:

#697 NAVY BABY
Debbie Macomber

#700 ROMANCING RACHEL
Natalie Bishop

#698 SLOW LARKIN'S REVENGE
Christine Rimmer

#701 THE MAN SHE MARRIED
Tracy Sinclair

#699 TOP OF THE MOUNTAIN
Mary Curtis

#702 CHILD OF THE STORM
Diana Whitney

Take 4 bestselling love stories FREE

Plus get a FREE surprise gift!

SILHOUETTE®
OFFICIAL SWEEPSTAKES
RULES

NO PURCHASE NECESSARY

1. To enter, complete an Official Entry Form or 3" × 5" index card by hand-printing, in plain block letters, your complete name, address, phone number and age, and mailing it to: Silhouette Fashion A Whole New You Sweepstakes, P.O. Box 621, Fort Erie, Ontario L2A 5X3.

   No responsibility is assumed for lost, late or misdirected mail. Entries must be sent separately with first class postage affixed, and be received no later than December 31, 1991 for eligibility.

2. Winners will be selected by D.L. Blair, Inc., an independent judging organization whose decisions are final, in random drawings to be held on January 30, 1992 in Blair, NE at 10:00 a.m. from among all eligible entries received.

3. The prizes to be awarded and their approximate retail values are as follows: Grand Prize — A brand-new Ford Explorer 4×4 plus a trip for two (2) to Hawaii, including round-trip air transportation, six (6) nights hotel accommodation, a $1,400 meal/spending money stipend and $2,000 cash toward a new fashion wardrobe (approximate value: $28,000) or $15,000 cash; two (2) Second Prizes — A trip to Hawaii, including round-trip air transportation, six (6) nights hotel accommodation, a $1,400 meal/spending money stipend and $2,000 cash toward a new fashion wardrobe (approximate value: $11,000) or $5,000 cash; three (3) Third Prizes — $2,000 cash toward a new fashion wardrobe. All prizes are valued in U.S. currency. Travel award air transportation is from the commercial airport nearest winner's home. Travel is subject to space and accommodation availability, and must be completed by June 30, 1993. Sweepstakes offer is open to residents of the U.S. and Canada who are 21 years of age or older as of December 31, 1991, except residents of Puerto Rico, employees and immediate family members of Torstar Corp., its affiliates, subsidiaries, and all agencies, entities and persons connected with the use, marketing, or conduct of this sweepstakes. All federal, state, provincial, municipal and local laws apply. Offer void wherever prohibited by law. Taxes and/or duties, applicable registration and licensing fees, are the sole responsibility of the winners. Any litigation within the province of Quebec respecting the conduct and awarding of a prize may be submitted to the Régie des loteries et courses du Québec. All prizes will be awarded; winners will be notified by mail. No substitution of prizes is permitted.

4. Potential winners must sign and return any required Affidavit of Eligibility/Release of Liability within 30 days of notification. In the event of noncompliance within this time period, the prize may be awarded to an alternate winner. Any prize or prize notification returned as undeliverable may result in the awarding of that prize to an alternate winner. By acceptance of their prize, winners consent to use of their names, photographs or their likenesses for purposes of advertising, trade and promotion on behalf of Torstar Corp. without further compensation. Canadian winners must correctly answer a time-limited arithmetical question in order to be awarded a prize.

5. For a list of winners (available after 3/31/92), send a separate stamped, self-addressed envelope to: Silhouette Fashion A Whole New You Sweepstakes, P.O. Box 4665, Blair, NE 68009.

PREMIUM OFFER TERMS

To receive your gift, complete the Offer Certificate according to directions. Be certain to enclose the required number of "Fashion A Whole New You" proofs of product purchase (which are found on the last page of every specially marked "Fashion A Whole New You" Silhouette or Harlequin romance novel). Requests must be received no later than December 31, 1991. Limit: four (4) gifts per name, family, group, organization or address. Items depicted are for illustrative purposes only and may not be exactly as shown. Please allow 6 to 8 weeks for receipt of order. Offer good while quantities of gifts last. In the event an ordered gift is no longer available, you will receive a free, previously unpublished Silhouette or Harlequin book for every proof of purchase you have submitted with your request, plus a refund of the postage and handling charge you have included. Offer good in the U.S. and Canada only.

SLFC-SWPR

SILHOUETTE® OFFICIAL SWEEPSTAKES ENTRY FORM

4-FCSES-3

Complete and return this Entry Form immediately – the more entries you submit, the better your chances of winning!

- Entries must be received by December 31, 1991.
- A Random draw will take place on **January 30, 1992.**
- No purchase necessary.

Yes, I want to win a FASHION A WHOLE NEW YOU Sensuous and Adventurous prize from Silhouette:

Name _____ Telephone _____ Age _____

Address _____

City _____ Province _____ Postal Code _____

Return Entries to: **Silhouette FASHION A WHOLE NEW YOU,**
P.O. Box 621, Fort Erie, Ontario L2A 5X3   © 1991 Harlequin Enterprises Limited

PREMIUM OFFER

To receive your free gift, send us the required number of proofs-of-purchase from any specially marked FASHION A WHOLE NEW YOU Silhouette or Harlequin Book with the Offer Certificate properly completed, plus a check or money order (do not send cash) to cover postage and handling payable to Silhouette FASHION A WHOLE NEW YOU Offer. We will send you the specified gift.

OFFER CERTIFICATE

Item	A. SENSUAL DESIGNER VANITY BOX COLLECTION (set of 4) (Suggested Retail Price $60.00)	B. ADVENTUROUS TRAVEL COSMETIC CASE SET (set of 3) (Suggested Retail Price $25.00)
# of proofs-of-purchase	18	12
Postage and Handling	$4.00	$3.45
Check one	☐	☐

Name _____

Address _____

City _____ Province _____ Postal Code _____

Mail this certificate, designated number of proofs-of-purchase and check or money order for postage and handling to: Silhouette FASHION A WHOLE NEW YOU Gift Offer, P.O. Box 622, Fort Erie, Ontario L2A 5X3. Requests must be received by December 31, 1991.

ONE PROOF-OF-PURCHASE

4-FWCSE-3

To collect your fabulous free gift you must include the necessary number of proofs-of-purchase with a properly completed Offer Certificate.

© 1991 Harlequin Enterprises Limited

See previous page for details.